the spin

a psychological thriller

faith gardner

MIRROR HOUSE ·PRESS·

THE
SPIN

A PSYCHOLOGICAL THRILLER

FAITH GARDNER

To Faith:
I never met you, but I carry you.

"The only quiet woman is a dead one."
—Sylvia Plath

vitasmile radio ad transcript

Air date: February 1, 1964
(Cheerful music, harp flourish)

ANNOUNCER (female, warm, friendly):
Are you tired, ladies?
Suffering from mood swings?
Do you feel like the sparkle's gone from
your day-to-day life?

Try VitaSmile: the gentle herbal formula
made just for women, with soothing
chamomile and rose hips, plus a dash of
amphetamine sulfate to boost your energy.

VitaSmile helps you greet each day with
your brightest smile!

JINGLE

♪ *Pop a pill? Yes, I think I'll/ pop a pill of VitaSmile!* ♪

ANNOUNCER
VitaSmile: because your family deserves your brightest smile.

june 1964

leo

Sometimes, without moving a muscle, my wife just disappears.

Invisible fingers snap, and that lamp behind her eyes shuts off. Her cheeks slacken; blankness irons out her face. And in this lost, dark moment—ridiculous, I know—I miss her.

I miss her even when she's riding shotgun with me in our station wagon, my palm warm on her stockinged leg, the forest rising cool and tall around us, the Dodgers game bleeding from the staticky radio station, the mountain road a gritty hum beneath us.

"Hey," I say to her, giving her knee a squeeze.

Rose startles, lets out a squeak like a rubber duck, and slaps my hand. When her laughter breaks—a tinkling, golden sound I'll never get sick of—I know I've done it: I've brought her back from the brink of that untouchable darkness.

"What are you sitting there brooding about?" I ask.

"Leo, please, you're going to cause an accident." She tucks a blond curl behind her ear. "Don't tickle me like that."

From the back seat, Melinda chastises in her sharp voice. "Dad, Drive carefully. Mom is *expecting*."

My daughter Melinda is fourteen, but don't let that stop her from thinking she's the boss of the damn car.

"Is she?" I say to the rearview. "I hadn't noticed."

Rose snorts, her hand rubbing the watermelon under her shift dress. She's not due for another month, but she looks ready to pop.

"*Are you tired, ladies?*" the radio says, switching to a commercial. "*Suffering from mood swings? Do you feel like the sparkle's gone from your day-to-day life?*"

"Oh, for the love of god," Rose groans, reaching to switch the radio off.

It's her own voice. When she flirted with the idea of voice-acting last year, Rose recorded a commercial for VitaSmile.

From the back seat, Melinda perks up, taking up where the commercial left off.

"'Try VitaSmile,'" she says loudly and breathlessly, "the gentle herbal formula made just for women, with soothing chamomile and rose hips, plus a dash of amphetamine sulfate to boost your energy—"

"Enough, Melinda," Rose warns sharply.

Melinda obeys but hums the jingle under her breath—a tiny needle of rebellion.

"I hate it every time that commercial comes on," Rose says to me.

"I think it's cute."

"If that's what my voice really sounds like, put me out to pasture."

"No one sounds like themselves on the radio."

"And that stuff made me sick when I took it. When I look in the mirror now, I see a sellout."

"Just because you had an adverse reaction doesn't mean it isn't helpful to other women."

"Do you ever feel like a sellout, Leo? You wrote that awful ad," she says, poking my shoulder playfully.

"Of course!" I laugh. "I'm in advertising, Rose, not writing the next great American novel."

"The greatest novel in American literature is *On the Road* by Jack Kerouac," Melinda pipes up, trying to be part of the conversation. Or trying to bait me into arguing, I can't tell—she knows I hate beatniks, and she knows I disapprove of her reading that book. I'm finding silence is the best way to handle Melinda these days.

"May I remind you," I say to Rose, as if I didn't hear Melinda, "*you* were the one who said you were interested in commercial work—"

"I don't want to talk about it anymore, I just don't want to talk about it," she says in a clipped tone, the lamp going off behind her eyes again.

There she goes. Sometimes keeping her attention is like trying to lasso the moon.

She turns to watch out the window. We're entering the small resort town of Idyllwild, driving by a row of mom and pops advertising everything from ice cream to souvenirs to kayaking gear.

"Can I turn the game back on?" I ask, reaching for the radio.

She doesn't answer. Still as an ice sculpture. Trees blur by the window as we near the end of the road where the turnoff leads to the cabin.

"Rose," I say, louder.

"Mom," Melinda says, "Dad's talking to you."

"Is this real?" Rose whispers.

It's such a strange question, my first reaction is a chuckle.

She's kidding. She must be. But she turns to me, her expression paper-pale, lost.

"Is this a dream?" she asks.

"Of course not." I get a sick squeeze in my stomach at the question. I don't like when she gets nonsensical. It's been happening more often this year—my hope is it's hormones, that once the baby is here, everything will get better.

She seems to recover, swallows. Then she points a pink-painted fingernail at the window. "What I mean is, have we been here before?"

"Rose." I clear my throat, straighten my posture, foot even-keeled on the accelerator. "Darling. Mi amor. We're in Idyllwild. No, we've never been here."

"Maybe it reminds me of somewhere." She puts a hand on her belly, rubbing.

She's chewing something invisible, jaw working. I glance out of the side of my eye.

"Probably just remembering the time we went to Julian," I try. "That looked a little like this."

Must have been at least ten years ago, because Rose's parents were still alive then. They flew in to watch Melinda for a long weekend. Rose and I escaped to the mountains, where we spent three sun-kissed days drinking highballs, barbecuing, and swimming in a private pond like we were teenagers. *We'll do this every year,* we said. But somehow, we never did it again. Her parents died in a car wreck a couple years later. After I moved from writing catalog copy to advertising and Melinda entered private school, our budget shrank. Life piled up too high for Rose and me to pretend we could keep taking little honeymoons. This, here, is the closest one we've had in years.

"Remember Julian?" I ask. "The place with the pond?"

She turns to me, face soft and open as a garden lily, the

lamp back on, her lips turning upward again. "Maybe that's it."

I take a turn. The trees thicken. We head straight into a chilling pool of shadows. I turn up the radio and the pebbles and twigs of a dirt road pop and hiss beneath the car.

I check the address twice before pulling up the cracked driveway and parking in front of the garage. The cabin has a crooked porch, front door blown wide open, staring back at us all like a bad idea.

"Is it haunted?" Melinda asks—not scared, just curious.

"I sure as hell hope not," I say with a half-smile.

And yet, my gut churns.

leo

I rest a hand on the back of Rose's daisy-print dress.

"How long has the door been open like that?" she asks. "What if there's a wild animal inside?"

"Wait here then. Let me go in first and make sure the place is empty."

The front steps moan with every step of my loafers. I pass through the open front doorway and survey the silence inside. Wood-paneled walls, orange carpet, wicker furniture. Could be worse. Upstairs, two bedrooms side by side, austere as monastery cells. Sure, the place isn't how it looked back at the travel agency in Van Nuys. But I rewrite it in my mind. Peeling paint? No sir, that's vintage. Mildew stink in the living room? Rustic charm! I could play this game all day long.

I head back outside. Melinda and Rose are standing big-eyed at the bottom of the stairs, hands clasped in front of them, pretty and patient as a picture.

"Coast is clear," I tell them.

Melinda sprints up the stairs like I just popped the gun for a fifty-yard dash.

I circle to the trunk, open it, and unload suitcases. For a moment, I pause and listen to the wind spill its secrets. I take in the Technicolor of the clear blue sky and the emerald trees.

"I had the most horrible thought," Rose says, still eyeing the house with mistrust.

"What's that?" I ask, *thunk*ing the trunk shut, grabbing the handles of our suitcases.

"That your mother was here," she says, turning her face toward me. She flashes a dimple with her deep-red smile.

This again. "Rose, cut it out. That was *one time*."

"Yeah. Our honeymoon. I'll never get that image out of my head, coming into that hotel room and she's lying on our bed, sobbing."

My mother's always been a sore subject between us. To be fair, Harriet Crawford is a headache in human form, but life is simpler when I don't think too hard about her. Rose could joke at her expense all day long.

I head up the stairs and remind her, "She thought she had cancer. And that was fifteen years ago. Let's appreciate where we are."

Rose's light kitten-heeled footsteps follow me up the stairs.

"It stinks in here," Melinda says, surveying the living room with disdain.

She's got an eagle eye for imperfections. Future editor.

"Open a window," I say. "Air the place out."

I head to the kitchen, inspect the icebox, and am disappointed to see the "ice-cold Coca-Colas" we were promised in the ad are nothing but ghosts. It's fine. There's a market right up the road. We'll get some hot dogs, charcoal, fire up the barbecue, make today count. I open the cupboard for a water glass and squint at what look like mouse droppings on the shelf. I move a plate over them to make them disappear.

"Dad!" Melinda shrieks. "It's a color television!"

"You're kidding me," I say, heading to the living room.

Up close, it's a thing of beauty: a massive Motorola framed in wood. I've never seen a model like this before. There's a knob that says HUE and another that says INTENSITY and in between, an emblem of a blue wheel that says COLOR INDICATOR.

"Must have cost a fortune," I murmur.

Melinda switches it on. A static image of vertical rainbow bars fills the screen, along with an atrocious beeping sound.

"Wow," Melinda says.

"Volume," I remind her.

She ignores me and flips the channel. It's a commercial for a sponge, in full color.

"Easy peasy, sudsy squeezy!" the woman says ecstatically over a bubbly sink.

I swear, the more color creeps in, the lazier the writers get. It's bright. It's cutting edge. It hurts my eyes. Then we return to our regular programming of *Leave It to Beaver* and it's black and white again. Everyone at the agency's obsessed about moving into color TV. It's nothing but a fad. The image quality can't compete.

Rose lights a cigarette in front of the picture window. I come up behind her, circle my arms around her, rub her round belly, kiss her curls.

"You okay?" I say in her ear.

She nods, but I can't help but notice the tremble in her hand as she takes a drag. The way she doesn't turn toward me. How she receives my embrace but doesn't reciprocate with her usual force.

"How about I head over to the market and get us some dinner fixins?" I ask.

"Sure."

"I was thinking hot dogs."

"Oooh la la."

"Fruit and oatmeal for breakfast, maybe. Whiskey, sodas. Want anything else?"

She smooches my cheek. "No, and thanks."

I head to the back porch and check out the barbecue. "Barbecue" is a creative description; it's an ash-ridden tenement for spiders. I'm up for the challenge, though, rolling my shirtsleeves and getting to work with the grill brush. Ten minutes later, I'm sweating, my hands charcoal-stained as a chimney sweep, but we've got ourselves a working barbecue.

Back inside, I wash up in the kitchen and come join them in the living room. Rose is still standing where I left her near the picture window. She's staring into space. Melinda remains infatuated with the television.

"What's going on?" I ask, tapping Rose's shoulder. "I'm about to head to the store. Want to come?"

"I think ..." she says faintly, not even blinking. "Maybe I ought to lie down."

"Yeah? You okay?"

She nods, breaking her gaze with the big nothing out there and giving me a watered-down smile, no dimple this time. "I don't feel well."

"You don't look well." I put a hand on her forehead. Lukewarm. "Coming down with something?"

"Maybe."

"Well, you lie down, and I'll get us some chow, all right?"

She nods and walks up the stairs, so slowly it's more like she floats.

"What about *me*?" Melinda asks with enough drama in her voice to rival Lady MacBeth. "Don't you care if I want to come?"

"Yes, your Highness." I jingle my keys in my pocket. "Please accept my forgiveness."

"You're *rude*," she huffs.

We head outside and I pull the front door shut behind me. I linger for a generous second, my stomach roiling at the sight of the knob. Should I have asked Rose to lock it? Is she okay here by herself? What am I thinking, Judas Priest. Rose is a fully grown woman. She's fine.

Melinda buckles into the passenger seat and I drive away from the house, telling myself the dreadful marble rolling around my belly is nothing but hunger.

leo

As we drive to the market with the windows rolled down—warm summer air and bird music—I can't strike Rose's words from my mind.

Is this real?

My mind flicks here and there, trying to trace the thread of where this all started, trying to find the root so I can pluck it out like a nasty weed from an otherwise perfect life. Sometimes, my wife just disappears. She's always been dreamy, but now that she's going to have a baby, it's much worse. She wasn't like this with Melinda, at least not that I remember. But that was so long ago now. My memory likes to glaze over the bad parts and pick out the happier times instead—like a scrapbook in my head. Give me a few months and I'll be pining for this vacation again.

So I turn up the radio. Some little girl is singing about how excited she is to go get married in the chapel of love. Which stirs a memory I'd forgotten until now, but which stings like a wasp.

Our wedding day, reception at the Elk's Lodge. Rose's

father Earl pulled me aside, drunk and shiny with sweat, carnation wilted in his lapel.

"Take a walk with me, will you, Leo?" he said, clapping my back like I was choking to death.

Earl Hammond, bless his soul, was a chemist half-deaf from an old Navy injury. His half-deafness meant he shouted constantly, assuming no one could hear him. What he lacked in stature—the man was five feet six in elevator shoes—he made up for with his Texas-sized personality. In short (so to speak), he scared the shit out of me. Every time he wanted to chat man-to-man, I braced myself for a lecture. He just had that energy. Standing too close to him could raise my blood pressure.

"Leo, Leo, Leo," Earl said as we walked outside beneath the magnolia trees. "Well, there's no getting around it—my darling Rose belongs to you now."

I lit up a cigarette to give my hands something to do. It seemed a strange way of putting it, when I heard him speak it aloud. Like Rose was not a person, but a thing. A flower to be passed back and forth.

"I need you to take good care of her," he said loudly, bloodshot blue eyes finding mine and holding them hostage. Earl was heavy on the eye contact. Sometimes it felt more like a staring contest, a test I had to pass. "You know she's nervous. High-strung, like her mother. And headstrong—I've never met a more bullheaded young lady."

"Wonder where she gets it from?"

Earl was also allergic to humor. "I really don't know, son. I don't. I've given her everything she ever needed and ... still ..." He raised his eyebrows at me, like I should know what he meant.

I didn't.

"Still what?" I asked.

"This isn't to be repeated." Earl leaned in, though he spoke just as loudly. "She had a touch of melancholia as a teenager."

I'd heard the story. Rose told me it was because her father was philandering with her biology teacher and the rumor mill at school was eating her alive. That "melancholia" of Rose's sounded more like a natural reaction to a humiliating situation that was his damn fault. I didn't offer this tidbit of wisdom to Earl.

"She told me," I said. "Sounds like a tough time."

"It was, Leo. It was. I—I was afraid we'd never get her back." He squeezed my shoulder. "You know she was in a sanitarium?"

Rose had said she'd had a nervous breakdown but hadn't mentioned the sanitarium. I raised an eyebrow. "I didn't."

"We didn't know what else to do. She wouldn't get out of bed. They called it a 'depressive reaction.'"

"How long was she in the sanitarium?"

"Two weeks. Longest two weeks of my life."

"I'll bet."

"Take good care of her, will you? She's a sensitive soul. Moody and dreamy. Don't let her drift away. My greatest fear is one day she'll drift too far and not come back."

"I'll do my best to keep her anchored," I said.

He wiped his pink, sweaty face with a handkerchief. He swayed slightly. The man was bagged. I thanked him, let him clap me on the back again, and didn't think too much of this father-son chat.

Until right now.

I forgot about this supposed "melancholia" over the years. Sure, now and then she's seemed withdrawn, but she's a solitary creature. She can happily while away hours reading a book or painting watercolors or tending to her garden. She's easily bored, sure. She's not one of those housewives who's content dusting the furniture all day and planning dinner parties. I love her for it. She's sharp. No one makes me laugh like she does. No one makes my soul hungry like she does.

All I've ever wanted was for her to be happy. I got her a radio commercial gig through Century, the ad agency where I work. It wasn't a good fit. Next, she flirted with correspondence school before finding out she was with child. Then she decided to participate in a consumer research study but got kicked out for her "neurotic" behavior on day one. Hours into the study, she became agitated. When they restrained her, she tried to bite a doctor.

We try not to dwell on it.

She was a mess when I picked her up. The folks running the study assured me it was fine, but I could practically smell their sympathetic embarrassment as they watched me escort my wife back to the car. And they were right. She was off. Something was strange about her. She took to bed for a week like she had the flu. Boy, was I the laughingstock of the office when my co-workers found out my wife flipped out and tried to bite a doctor. But I told myself it was a one-off, a fluke, maybe a symptom pregnancy. Who knows.

And now here we are, a few months later, with Rose murmuring *is this real?* like a lost little girl.

"Menstruation," Melinda's voice says, cutting through my retrograde hypnosis.

Well, that snaps me back to the present moment. I give her a side-glance as we wait at a stop sign, about to pull onto the main road that leads to the market.

I must have heard her wrong.

"Come again?"

"I menstruate now, Dad."

"Why on earth—"

"Because, *if you care to know,* that is why I wanted to come along." Her tone is so damn haughty. "I need some feminine hygiene products from the market."

I press the gas and try not to react. Melinda's always looking for a reaction. "Fine."

"I was trying to keep it a secret, but then I thought, why? Why should *your* feelings be more important than mine?"

The market's sign gets closer. Melinda's itching for an argument. She picks at me like a scab and I'm not in the mood today.

"Do you know what Betty Friedan calls domesticity? She calls it the *comfortable concentration camp.*"

"Well, thank goodness it's comfortable," I say cheerfully, turning into the parking lot. "Aren't you a little young to be reading Betty Friedan?"

"It was on Mom's bookshelf. Besides, I'm a *woman* now."

"Right. The feminine hygiene products, how could I forget."

Teenagers: now with 70% more uncomfortable conversations! I pull into a parking space and turn off the car, moving as quickly as possible to escape. But Melinda reaches for my arm, stopping me. Looking down at her hand—at its smallness, a peach flower, unwrinkled, unfreckled—I get a sad heart squeeze. Because despite her prickly attitude, somewhere in there, she's still my little girl.

"Is Mom okay?" she asks softly.

The softness, coming from her, is so unusual it's loud.

"How do you mean?"

"You know. The way she's been acting."

Melinda's eyes quiver as she tries to read mine. Hers are the same warm brown as Rose's, a deep amber. She grips my arm, wanting something from me. Always wanting something from me. And me never knowing quite what it is.

I reach out, cup her cheek. "Mel, your mother is fine."

"You swear?"

"Absolutely."

She nods, satisfied, and we head out.

Here's what I don't tell her: the future is, by its very nature, unwritten. We can spin it any way we want.

Which means promises are nothing but hopeful lies.

leo

Melinda and I drive back to our cabin with brown paper bags stuffed with hot dogs, whiskey, and, yes, feminine hygiene products. The sun is sagging in the sky when we turn back onto the road where our cabin awaits. We pull into the driveway. Once again, the front door is wide open.

"What is wrong with that damn door?" I say as we pull up. "I'll bet the doorframe's out of plumb. They should get it fixed."

"It's the spirit of the previous owner who lived here," Melinda says. "Coming back to haunt us."

"Lovely, my little Edgar Allan Poe."

"Do you believe in ghosts?"

"I don't believe in anything I don't see with my own two eyes."

We get out of the car, thump up the creaky stairs. Inside, despite the open door, the house is hot and stuffy.

"We're back," Melinda shouts.

The living room's empty, lights off. Oddly, the television is on—stuck on that color testing screen, the blinding rainbow.

Only now the vertical hold is off and it's rolling like a film strip coming loose. The eerie noise emitting from the speakers, the ringing sound, is like nails on a chalkboard.

I sigh, and turn it off.

Melinda and I work side by side in the kitchen, putting food away. In this quiet, humble moment, the sunshine slanting through the window and lighting up her dark blond hair, I get this glimpse of the adult Melinda is becoming. Of her cooking meals in her own kitchen one day, with little ones pulling on her skirt. I get a swell of something halfway between pride and grief.

"Thanks," I tell her, kissing her head.

"For what?"

"I don't know. Being you."

She gives me a smile. That gap tooth gets me every time.

I pour Rose a whiskey and coke and head upstairs. "Going to check on your mother," I call behind me.

I turn into our room, which is as empty as I left it. Bed made, suitcases still unpacked. I frown and wait, as if Rose is going to pop out and yell *surprise!* Absurdly, I open the closet. It smells like mothballs, and there's no trace of Rose. I pop my head into Melinda's room, thinking she must be lying down in there—but no. Melinda's room is untouched, except for her knapsack on the bed.

"Rose?" I call out.

I wait for a response, the hairs on my neck standing up when nobody answers.

"Rose," I try again, poking my head into the bathroom. I scoot the curtain aside to check the bathtub—nobody there —and head down the stairs.

Melinda has already turned the television back on and parked herself in front of it, lying on the floor, elbows up and chin in hand. She's watching a rerun of *I Love Lucy*. I don't know how Ricky Ricardo puts up with that airhead. I make a loop around the kitchen, dining room, back to the living room.

There's no sign of Rose.

My frown deepens as the noise of a laugh track fills the air. She must have gone for a stroll. That must be what happened. She's been complaining of her ankles being swollen. Sometimes she tries to walk it off. But … something tickles at my throat.

No, this doesn't sit right.

"I think your mother's outside," I say, heading for the door. "Be right back."

Melinda doesn't answer, giggling with the TV.

I step outside, scanning the horizon, which is trees, all trees, a flood of them. In fact, I've maybe never felt smaller than I do right now. I tread down the stairs, slowly.

"Rose?" I call out.

Only the wind answers.

I don't like this.

My loafers crunch pine needles as I circle the house, yelling her name. And then, in the very back, where the porch slopes off into a tangle of brambles, I spot something that stops me cold.

A yellow kitten heel.

There, right there, sticking out of the brush.

I head toward that splash of color, sickly, slow at first, then faster. I pick it up, examining the dirt-covered shoe that I'd know anywhere. My gut pitfalls. I swallow, hard, getting ready to shout for Rose again when my eyes fall to the brush and I spy the second shoe. Her pantyhose, balled on the ground like a giant wad of chewing gum. Beyond, deeper in the brush, I spot something that drains the life from me—the yellow silk scarf that was fixed in Rose's hair.

She wouldn't just wander off in the woods, barefoot and expecting.

What the hell happened since we left for the store?

Did someone take her? Yank her shoes off, throw them in the sticks and dirt?

Is this real? Rose whispers in my mind.

A laugh track bleeds through the open window. A sharp waft of pine wrinkles my nose. I break into a frantic walk toward the woods, scratches on my arms and dirt all over my khakis be damned. A branch hits my face. I slip, almost fall. I stub my loafer on a log. God*damn* it.

"Rose! Hey!" I stop, catching my breath, hearing nothing but the distant shrieks of crows. "Rose?"

I struggle to get enough air in my lungs as I stumble forward, into the shade, where there's no sign of her. None. No paths, even—just trees and brush, poison oak, mossy rocks. Just endless thicket.

Panicking, a thought clangs like a funeral bell, makes me shudder and my eyes water. I hear Earl's voice echoing from the cobwebs of my memory. *My greatest fear is one day she'll drift too far and not come back.*

And it hits me like a truck: somewhere along the line, without my noticing, that became my greatest fear too.

leo

Idyllwild is such a podunk town they don't even have their own police department. When the operator connects me with the sheriff substation, they inform me they have to send someone all the way from Hemet. For the next hour, I pace the property like a madman. Melinda follows me around with a worried expression, kicking the brush with her Mary Janes, scanning the ground for clues.

"I thought you said Mom was fine," she says as I stop to catch my breath.

"She is."

Melinda narrows her eyes. "When I'm a grown up, *I'm* not going to lie to my children."

Her comment is sliced by the sound of tires crackling up the dirt road. *Finally.* It's a squad car, pulling into the driveway behind our station wagon. I check my watch. An hour and five minutes, what service.

"Hello, hello," the deputy says, emerging from the driver's side.

Kid can't be over twenty. He's drowning in his service cap. And he's chewing bubble gum. Already, I'm ticked off.

"Hey," I say, waving him over.

"Got a call that someone's missing?" he says.

"My wife," I tell him.

I give him the essentials: name, description, where I last saw her, et cetera.

"How long has she been gone?" he asks, pulling a pad and pencil from his back pocket.

I check my watch. "About an hour and a half. Maybe two hours. We got settled in the cabin, went to the market for some food, came back, and she was gone."

"Two hours, huh?" He scribbles. "Any chance she went out for a hike?"

"She's in the family way, chief. Due in four weeks. She left her shoes behind. Come look at this."

I pull the kid to the back of the house and show him the kitten heels wedged in the bushes. I point at her scarf, then the pantyhose on the ground.

"Did you see any suspicious people near the property?" he asks.

"I didn't see any people, period. The nearest neighbor's a way up the road, there."

"You two have any arguments or disagreements before she left?" he asks, squatting and investigating the clothes.

A vein ticks on my temple. "No."

"You sure? Anything at all? Women are emotional, you know, especially when they're expecting. Maybe she's just gone to blow off steam."

"That isn't what happened."

"What was her state of mind like, before you left the house?"

For just a blink, I can't respond. The truth is stuck in my

throat. I clear it. "She was tired. Not feeling well. She lay down to take a nap. When I came back, she was gone."

"How about I drive up the road and knock on the neighbors' doors," he says, closing his pad. "Ask if they've seen any sign of her. Why don't you walk around the property again? Search closets, take a peek at the crawlspace? I once found a kid who accidentally locked himself in a shed in his own backyard—everyone thought he'd been abducted."

I nod.

"Ninety-nine times out of a hundred, there's a harmless explanation." He looks at the dirt. "Don't see anything suspicious. No strange footprints, no evidence of an intruder, no blood."

"Her shoes—"

"I'll go knock on a few doors, sir, but if this is all we've got, I think waiting until morning is your best bet."

He drives away in his squad car, up the road. Melinda is still sitting on the porch steps, glum and sullen, chin resting in her hand.

"She's fine, though, right, Dad?" Melinda asks sharply from behind me. "Nothing to worry about."

"Enough, Melinda!"

Shocked, she scrambles up from her position, glares at me, and stalks into the house. She slams the door—which immediately blows back open.

I sigh. My heartbeat drums. I shouldn't have yelled. It's not her I'm mad at. "Rose," I yell, my throat raw.

But her name fades into the trees.

leo

I search the brush around the property until my khakis are dirt-stained, my loafers mud-caked. I haven't felt this scared since I was in the war—that twisted, adrenaline-drunk feeling that you don't know what the hell's going to happen next, ear cocked in the air waiting for the whistle of a bomb. Deputy Pipsqueak checks in with no news, but says he's going to drive to town and ask around down there. That was hours ago.

Back at the cabin, at ten 'til midnight, I sit with my head hung and a tumbler of whiskey at the dining room table. I hear a soft noise: *tap-tap, tap-tap, tap-tap.* A heartbeat outside my body. I stand up, hairs on my neck on end, and follow the sound—it's coming from the porch.

For the first time since this mess started, my dread morphs into something else. Something with teeth. Goosebumps cover my arms. And I realize, with a touch of shame, that I'm terrified of what's behind that door. I'm a little boy with a monster in my closet. I peek out the curtains. There's nothing out there that I can see except the pitchest black.

A new possibility awakens like a beast: What if someone took her? And they're back? Some Norman Bates situation, some psycho with mommy issues hunting innocent people? I hold my breath and talk myself down. *Leo,* I say to myself. *That is not logical. That is a movie.*

"Ridiculous," I say to myself. "Be a man."

I hesitate a moment with my hand on the knob before pushing open the front door.

What I see is somehow both a relief and so much more frightening than anything I just pictured.

It's my Rose, my beautiful Rose. But she's in a state that shocks me so much, I don't know what to say.

She has an electrocuted look: hair wild and tangled and snagged with burrs, eyes so wide you can see the whites around her irises, lipstick faded and makeup smeared black. Her dress is covered with little slits and tears, her fingernails ragged and broken, her hands caked with dirt and shivering at her sides.

"I thought—the lights—I followed—" she stammers.

"Rose," I say, rushing to her, overwhelmed with relief as I engulf her in my arms. I pull back and gently put my hands on her watermelon belly, the warmth there a comfort. "Oh my god, Rosie. Where were you? What happened?"

"My mouth is full of blood," she says, tearing up. "The c-colors ... my eyes."

"Rose," I say, a bit firmer, trying to bring her back to me.

"Bloody, bloody mouth," she whispers.

"Where?" I put my thumb on her lips, parting them to look inside. "Where's the blood? I don't see anything, baby."

I pull her in again and feel her weeping on my shoulder. Her weeping stirs something in me and my own eyes water as I squeeze them shut and hold her against me. My love for her

is suddenly horrifying. A colossus. A tsunami I can't escape.
And as we stand here in the darkness, sharing this nameless
despair, I don't understand how I could feel like I've lost her
and found her at the same time.

almost three years later

session transcript

Dr. Wells' office, Studio City
Date: February 1967
Patient: Rose Crawford
Therapist: Dr. Wells
Session: #13

WELLS: Good afternoon, Rose. That shade of
blue looks charming on you.

ROSE: [softly] Thank you, Dr. Wells.

WELLS: It's been some time since you've
been to my office. I see our last meeting
was [papers shuffling] well over a year
ago, May 1965. Last we spoke, you were
adjusting back to life after your breakdown
and subsequent stay at Woodward Neuropsychiatric Center. How old is your youngest
now?

ROSE: Nearly two and a half. Has it been
that long?

WELLS: Indeed. What brings you back in?

ROSE: Well … [pause, throat-clearing] I
thought I was well again. I really did.
I've been trying so hard. [shifting sounds]
Forgive me for saying so, but you know how
much I dislike being back here, Doctor.
It's not about you—please don't take it
personally. It's just how it looks to
everyone else, seeing a head shrink. [voice
dropping] Leo insisted I come in again.

WELLS: And why is that?

ROSE: Because it scares him, I think. The
things I say sometimes, the way I get. He
doesn't think any of it is real. [pause]
Sometimes it's hard to be a person with a
vivid imagination, you know?

WELLS: Are you referring to your husband,
or yourself?

ROSE: [sharp laugh] Both, I suppose. Though
mine seems more malignant. His makes him a
living, you know, makes him "The King of
the Spin," as they call him at the office.

WELLS: Is he still at the same agency?

ROSE: Yes.

WELLS: How do you feel about that?

ROSE: It's nice to have food on the table.
I try not to think about it, mostly.

WELLS: Are you still carrying shame about
what happened at the study?

ROSE: [softly] Like I said, I try not to
think about it. There's no use thinking
about something you can't explain. May I
smoke?

WELLS: Of course. There's an ashtray on the
end table there.

ROSE: [lighter flicking] Leo and I used to
talk about everything. That was why we fell
in love with each other in the first place,
you know? It wasn't looks, though he is a
tall drink of water. It was words. It was
this … heartfelt connection. We could tell
each other anything and not blink an eye.

I told him things I never told anyone but
Dale. About my father and his mistress, how
I caught them together. About how my piano
teacher used to give me secret kissing
lessons when I was just a child.

Most of all, though, I could tell him all

the silly things that came to mind. The way
that I always see faces in everything—in
electrical sockets, or the fronts of cars.
Or lines I loved and underlined in books I
read. I'd save them just to read them aloud
to him, and it was like anything I thought
was wonderful, he saw it too.

We were one mind. And then on top of all
that, there's this wittiness, this banter
we have … there's no one like him on earth.

WELLS: You love your husband very much.

ROSE: I do. That's what makes it all so
hard. We seem to have drifted apart. He
doesn't want to hear everything I think
anymore.

WELLS: And why is that, do you suppose?

ROSE: It's like I lost his trust, after my
breakdown. After that vacation, where I
wandered off, he treated me with such delicacy, I was practically made of glass. Then
I had Julie, and was sent to Woodward to …
get my brain screwed back in right. He
doesn't trust my head anymore. Maybe I
don't, either.

[sighs] I've missed you. Missed this—just
having a place to say what's on my mind.

WELLS: What's troubling you, Rose?

ROSE: [softly] The nightmares are back. The ones that started before my breakdown.

WELLS: Are they … the same?

ROSE: Yes. Exactly. Like watching a horror film, one I can't turn off.

WELLS: Are you still taking Seconal as needed?

ROSE: Nearly every night.

WELLS: Did anything trigger it? Some kind of … event?

ROSE: I wondered if I might be expecting again, god forbid—but I'm not. If only it were that simple: hormones. It was just a month or so ago, they came back out of nowhere. And this time … [quietly] sometimes it …

WELLS: Rose? Stick with me, Rose, don't float away.

ROSE: Mmm?

WELLS: You were saying something. Sometimes the nightmare … what?

ROSE: Oh. [laughs joylessly] Sometimes it sort of—it's hard to explain. Bleeds into real life. I know that must not make sense to you.

[Sounds of a pen on paper, notes scribbled]

WELLS: Well, my thoughts haven't changed. And though I'm disappointed to see you back here, I must say, I'm not surprised.

ROSE: What are your thoughts?

WELLS: Same as they were our last session. Don't you remember? The reason you walked out of my office in the first place?

ROSE: [faintly] Yes.

WELLS: [gently] I don't think these are nightmares at all, Rose.

melinda

Southern California is all ranch-style dollhouses in the valley, honeyed sunshine and nonstop summer. It's nuclear families and cordial TV dinners. And I could blow it all away like a dandelion.

I used to worry I was mad. When Mom had her first kiss with crazy nearly three years ago, I became convinced I would catch it like a virus. Maybe *that* was why I was tangled in knots down deep. Something was wrong with me. I didn't belong anywhere I went. But then, since I turned seventeen, I had this *revelation* that no, no, no, it isn't me who is mad and it isn't even Mom who is mad. You know who's really mad? Take a deep breath. Look up. Look down. Look left. Look right.

The world. The world's mad, and I'm just trying not to breathe it in.

That's not an exaggeration. There are boys from my neighborhood returning home from Vietnam in body bags. And if you dare pipe up about it, watch out, because the establishment will show up with billy clubs like you're the enemy. I watched it happen with my own eyes. Jim and I snuck out a few months back to check out the Sunset riots. We were high, crouched behind a fence in a parking lot, watching babyfaced LAPD goons beating bearded hippies with batons.

That was the night everything changed. Threshold moment, black-and-white to color. Because not only did I see the world for what it really was (a warzone, a tornado) but it was also the night Dad flipped his lid and grounded me until the end of senior year, which has made 1967 the biggest bummer yet, a real heartsinking letdown. And now the bedroom that used to be my groovy sanctuary has turned into a teenage prison. For two months—*two whole months*—they've put me in solitary confinement. My frown's so fixed on my face these days I might need surgery to get it removed. The only time I smile anymore is after the sun goes down and my plastic family's gone to bed and the house swells with quiet.

When I look up and I see the flutter of movement in my open window, the strangle of honeysuckle on my windowsill, the curtain-flutter.

Jim's here, making his entrance, popping his head in the window with that crooked grin, all bare feet and trouble. Pulling my window closed with a *squeeeeak* and climbing in with his grass-stained bell-bottomed jeans. He's shirtless, hair to his shoulders, and my lips are magnets to his.

"Hey, Lindy," he says, stepping over a pile of records to join me on my bed.

"Jim!" I whisper back.

He dives into me. We lock into an embrace, melting, our mouths one. I pull him to lie on top of me. We rub our jeans together, warmth on warmth. I can taste him: Behind the mint, there's smoke and a sour trace of beer.

"I can't keep living like this. It's driving me wild not

getting to be with you," he whispers in my ear, his lips finding my throat. "All day long at work, I'm aching, thinking about you."

"And only me?"

He laughs. "Why do you always ask that?"

"I guess I'm scared you're going to get impatient."

"Not gonna lie," he says into my ear, electricity buzzing, his hand snaking up my shirt. "It's been hard waiting. You make me hurt."

I give him a minute of fooling around under my shirt, but when his hand starts moving south, I freeze. I swear I hear a bump downstairs. I pause, listening, and remember that my grandma is staying with us tonight. Cripes. I press my palm to his palm and sit up.

"See?" Jim says, putting his hands behind his head as he lies on his back. He shoots me a blue-eyed, puppy-sad look. "I hardly see you anymore and you're pushin' me away."

"I want to get out of here." I stand and stretch. "I can hardly breathe in this house. My grandma's staying over tonight and she's a real drag; I'm scared she'll hear us."

"But I just got comfy. Can't we relax for a minute?"

I roll my eyes and put Jefferson Airplane on the record player, dropping the needle right on "Somebody to Love" with a *hiss-pop-zip*. Then I sit next to Jim, my own personal Greek god, running my hand through his hair.

"How was work?" I ask.

He shakes his head. Jim dropped out last year, his senior year. Since then, he's gone through a laundry list of jobs, trying them on like hats, getting bored, putting them back on the rack. Currently, he's apprenticing at a mechanic shop nearby. So I thought, anyway.

"Not good?" I ask.

"I want to quit."

My brow wrinkles. "How come?"

He props himself up on an elbow. "I'm sick of the rat race."

"But you just started."

"What are you, in cahoots with my mother?" He sighs and anger creeps into his tone, a spider. "Look around. Open your eyes. How am I supposed to think anything's important right now?"

"I'm on your side, geez. Mellow out."

He balls up his fist, studies it, and relaxes it again. He has a little freckle under his left eye, and I don't know why, but it might be my favorite thing in the whole world. "Richie got his notice yesterday."

I gasp. Richie is a real close friend of Jim's. He's a neighborhood kid, went to the same high school. Works at a service station within walking distance to my house.

"What's he going to do?" I ask.

"Says he's gonna ship out in April."

"Fuck," is all I can muster.

The silence between us swells up, despair a cloud that ruins the mood.

"I just know I'm next," Jim says gloomily.

"Don't." I tap my wall, gently, a prayer. "Knock on wood."

"Any day, Lindy."

It turns a screw in my stomach to imagine him out there, dying in some jungle for a bullshit war we didn't even want in the first place. My eyes sting at the thought. All those dead boys, fresh dreams turned to rotting corpses, and for what? I could scream.

"What'll you do?" I ask.

He inhales deeply, thinking hard. "I guess I'd ... I don't know."

"You can't go."

"Like hell I would! But I mean ... I don't want to go to jail, either." He gives me a sorry, crooked half-smile. "I guess I'd take off, lay low, go stay with Jan."

"You would run away to *Frisco?*"

"Nobody calls it Frisco up there."

"You know what I mean."

"Look, this conversation is killing the vibes. Why are we worrying about something that hasn't happened?" He squeezes my hand. "No matter what, we've always got right now." His hand moves up my arm. He pulls me to him, skin to skin, hand to hand, lips to lips. "That's why we've got to make tonight count."

I kiss him, but just once, a spark. Then I pull back away and rest a hand on his cheek. "You bring grass?"

He pulls a joint from behind his ear and wiggles his eyebrows. "Got a light?"

I reach my hand to help him off the bed. "Let's go for a walk and smoke it out there."

I click my record player off, stuff my bed with some clothes so it's vaguely me-shaped. Flick the lights off. Jim and I climb out the window one by one, dropping onto the lawn, *thunk, thunk,* inhaling the honeysuckle in deep, clasping hands, breaking into a run, summer air in our lungs and hair as we stifle our laughter in the darkness.

melinda

The next morning, I wake up to a real bummer. Her name's Mom and she's above my bed, tower-tall and shaking my shoulders.

"Up, up, up," she says.

"Geez," I say, squeezing my eyes shut to try to dive back asleep. But it's no use. She wrecked it.

Her footsteps stomp across my rug. I hear the *snick* of my curtains opening. Tangerine sunshine screams into my room.

"Do we need to glue this window shut?" she asks, fiddling with the lock.

"Why would we need to do that?"

"Come on, Melinda. I wasn't born yesterday. Was Jim up here last night?"

"Of course not," I lie.

She shakes her head. "Your grandma heard everything."

My cheeks want to flush, but I won't let them. "Grandma thinks she hears all sorts of things. Once she told me Jesus transmitted a meat loaf recipe to her in a dream."

Mom's mouth twitches for a second, like she almost thinks it's funny. But lately it's been harder to make her laugh.

"For Pete's sake, let me sleep in." I sit up and throw a pillow at her. "It's Sunday."

The pillow misses her. She doesn't even notice. Mom is in a state. I'm still wiping last night's dreams from my eyeballs, but I can already tell. Dizzy energy, a bottle rocket in slippers, an apron, and hair rollers. VitaSmile mother. Now she's stooped over my floor picking up dirty clothes and tossing them into my hamper.

"Mom," I say louder. I glance at my alarm clock. "It's not even eight o'clock!"

"Oh, are you tired?" She picks up my jacket with the fringe I wore last night and smells the sleeves. "I wonder why?"

A marquee in my head spells out the word in red neon letters: S-H-I-T.

"You've been smoking grass," she says coolly.

I flinch. "What? Of course not."

"You think you're so smart."

She studies me. It's the ice queen act she loves so much, trying to freeze me out with her discontent. She thinks I'll back down, I'll crack, I'll tell her everything.

Mom doesn't know a damn thing about me.

"I *am* smart," I say, cocking my chin. "You've told me so."

We lock into a staring contest. Time seems to stop and it's just her and me. She's either a stranger or a mirror, I can't decide which. But there's something empty in her eyes.

She's the first to look away. That *never* happens.

In the doorway behind her, my baby sister Julie peeks out, puffy pink dress, mop of curls, a cupcake with chubby legs.

"Lin-Lin!" she says, lighting up.

I open my arms. "Come here, Sunshine!"

Julie comes toddling in at full speed toward my bed and dives into my arms. I squeeze her and nuzzle her neck and she giggles from deep in her belly. What a golden soul. I can't get enough. I thought I'd hate being a big sister, but it turns out it's the best thing in the whole world. Sometimes, when I babysit, I pretend she's mine.

"Tickles!" she squeals.

Behind her head, as I press her doughy warmth into me and she rests her curls on my shoulder, Mom stands still. Her mouth is a corkscrew of worry, eyebrows knit tight. She's still holding my jacket as if she's not done with the interrogation. Tunnel vision, and I'm at the end. As if her sole purpose on this sparkling, spinning earth is to nitpick every freaking thing in my life.

"Your dad and I would like to speak with you downstairs," she says.

Great. The old *are you smoking grass?* chitchat. I'd rather go swimming with sharks, but I sigh and nod.

Mom folds the jacket, smoothing the wrinkles out, and sets it on the end of my bed. That faded apron with the apples on it, the red lipstick at eight a.m., the smell of muffins coming through the doorway. Poor woman. Simone de Beauvoir on her bookshelf, but she still cooks every meal and sucks her shape into a girdle and irons Dad's shirts each morning. Betty Crocker with a brain, a damn shame, a cautionary tale. I'll never be Mom, frown-lined and stressed, violet circles under the eyes, doing all the right things but dead inside. "Julie, come to mama."

Julie's too busy squishing my cheeks like Play-Doh to respond.

"Julie Ann Crawford," Mom says sharply.

"Uh-oh, full name," I say to Julie. "You'd better go."

I gently lower her to the floor and set her to her feet.

Mom scoops her up and kisses her cheek, pats her back, even though Mom's eyes are fixed on me. The *oh shit* feeling plummets to a place deep and muddy in me. Mom's hands are shaking. A frosty, aching wind blows through me. Out of nowhere, my memory yanks me to the summer Julie was born when Mom lost it, when Mom wasn't Mom anymore, when she disappeared into herself and I was so scared she'd never come back again that I retched every morning, Cheerios and tears in the toilet bowl.

"Downstairs," she says sharply, snapping me out of it, evaporating my pity. *"Now."*

melinda

There they sit, the Ice King and Queen of the living room, on their red sofa throne. There's a real theater quality to it, what with the stone wall behind them and the oozy mysterious symphony of Henry Mancini filling the air. Dad's in his robe. His hair's uncombed and he's smoking a cigarette. Mom sips a teacup. On the end of the sofa, a knitted blanket and pillow are the only telltale sign that my grandma slept here last night.

"Where's Grandma?" I ask.

"She just took Julie on a walk for a few minutes so we can talk privately," Mom says.

I can tell they're both about to let me have it. But it's strange, the blankness, the lightness I feel about it. Normally I'd be fighting a conniption. These days, though, I've got nothing left to lose. I'm already grounded, already forbidden from seeing Jim. And it strikes me for the first time as I notice not anger, but fear in their eyes, that the power game has shifted. I have the upper hand. They're fighting a war already lost.

"We heard a rumor that you left the house last night, Mel," Dad says, flicking ashes into an ashtray I made him in first grade in the shape of my little hand. "Grandma heard you climbing out the window and saw you on the lawn. She said you were with some ... half-naked *boy*."

Grandma is the world's biggest snitch.

"Don't lie," Mom says. "It's the lying I hate most."

I say nothing and begin counting the stones in the wall behind them.

Dad's voice climbs. "Damn it, we're trying to be reasonable right now."

"I smelled grass on her jacket, Leo," Mom says. "She very well might be high right now."

Dad stubs out his cigarette, closes his eyes, and puts his hands on his face.

"You're throwing your life away." Mom puts her teacup on the coffee table with a clatter. "That stuff will ..." She seems to not know *what* it will do, or maybe she lost her train of thought. Finally, she finds it again. "It'll rot your brain."

"What have we told you?" Dad asks, emerging from his hands again.

I've counted twelve rocks so far, all different colors and shapes.

"We're trying to *protect* you," Mom says.

"Jim's a good guy," I say, finally meeting their eyes. "And I love him. You can lock me in the *basement* if you want. I'm still going to see him."

"I feel like I'm arguing with a brick wall," Mom tells him.

"We worry, Mel, don't you get it?" Dad says, softening his tone. "We're not trying to ruin your life, we're trying to protect you. Wandering around the neighborhood, high on grass, who knows what could happen to you? There are dangerous types out there on the streets."

But there aren't. I remember last night with a sweet pang. That late, under that starless sky, dark silhouettes of palm trees, the houses were shuttered and mum. I don't even remember the headlights of cars, it was so magically quiet, like the whole world fell asleep and now it belonged to only me and Jim.

"Look, nothing happened, all right?" I tell them, coming clean. "Jim and I just walked around for a while, then went to his house and talked. I came back, didn't I?"

Dad shakes his head. Mom stares into outer space.

"His family's bad news and I don't want you hanging out with him, understand?" Dad says.

I roll my eyes. "Give me a break."

"His sister's a dirty hippie who skipped town," Dad says, lighting a smoke, "and his father's a lush who can't even be bothered to mow his own lawn—"

"Who cares?" I burst. "Cripes, you two are always fixated on the wrong things, man."

That's when I see that my grandma's peeking through the front window, spectacles flashing.

"Grandma's spying on us," I say, getting up. I point at the window, where she pulls back and pretends to be analyzing roses. "I'm out of here."

"Ma, are you really?" Dad asks, annoyed, getting up from the couch and striding across the living room to the window. He opens it and whistles at her. "Hey. You. Get over here, don't act like you can't hear me ..."

Meanwhile, Mom's still seated on the couch, but her brain has clearly departed the building. Her eyes are as wide and unblinking as a doll's and fixed on the TV screen, which is off. She's moving her lips as if repeating something to herself.

My heart lurches. Oh god, she's a real-life *Twilight Zone* episode. A mother replica.

Something's not right with her again.

I hurry up the stairs and slam my bedroom door shut. I'm spinning somewhere between disgust, pity, and panic, and I need to be alone. Flopping on my bed, I press my hand to my chest where my heartbeat popcorns.

It's been nearly three years since that vacation when Mom wandered into the woods. Then Julie was born, and Mom went to an institution for a long weekend, and Dad was quiet all the time. But when Mom came back, she returned to her old self again. She sang along with the radio and played checkers and painted furniture. I thought her breakdown was a one-time thing. What if it's not?

At the top of the stairs, I can hear my grandma's Alabama accent, goopy as molasses.

"What this family needs is *church* ..."

I'll bet Mom's still seated there, eyes glazed over, mumbling whispers to nobody. Stuck inside herself, the eye of the hurricane, while everyone around her pretends everything is fine.

harriet

Soon as that word *church* leaves my mouth, Rose shoots from the room like a terrier on the fourth of July. I've never understood what Leo sees in her. Those vacant eyes, always somewhere else, like this patch of earth isn't green enough. She thinks she's Elizabeth Taylor with that crimson lipstick, powdered cheeks, and coiffed hair no matter what time of day. She reads paperback books when I'm sitting right here, as if my conversation's not good enough for her. And I don't care what Leo says, the sin wafts off her like a cheap perfume.

But I shouldn't think such things about the mother of my grandchildren. I do pray for her soul each night. I am a holy woman, after all.

"Ma, I've told you, we just aren't the churchgoing kind," Leo says.

"Every family needs a foundation."

"May I remind you, you never once took me to church when I was growing up?"

"I wasn't saved yet," I say indignantly.

I found the Lord at one of Billy Graham's crusades a few years ago. Leo knows this.

"Well, get your coat and bag and I'll drive you to Bethlehem, all right?" he says.

"You'll go with me?" I ask in surprise.

"I mean I'll *drop you off.*"

I cock my chin. "I do believe I've missed the service."

"You told me they have an eight o'clock and a ten o'clock."

"Oh, the ten o'clock is that awful new pastor, the one with the stutter. Gives me a headache. I can't."

"Ma," Leo says, jiggling his car keys. "Let me take you home?"

I'd just as well stay here today, I don't know what he's so anxious to get rid of me for. I gave them free babysitting last night so they could have a date, and now it's out the door with me. The poor man's stressed because his eldest daughter's a delinquent. Leo's got bags under his eyes and his hair's thinning. The food Rose is feeding him isn't doing his figure any favors. He never had a potbelly when he lived with *me*, I'll just say that.

"Just a minute," I say. "You know how I feel about Irish goodbyes."

I tiptoe to the bedroom and knock softly. When no one answers, I push the door open. The room is cluttered and dusty. A queen-sized bed—the sight of it still steals my breath, the *gall* of it. Back when my Sidney was alive (bless his soul) we slept in separate beds as the Lord intended. Next to Leo's side are a neat stack of books and papers, a cup with ballpoint pens, a crossword puzzle he ripped from the *LA Times* half-finished. Next to Rose's side of the bed are balled-up tissues with red lipstick stains, an overflowing ashtray, a silver hairbrush, a battered copy of *Valley of the Dolls*. Makes my stomach sour.

I sigh, walking over and tidying up her station, since you know *she* won't be doing that anytime soon. I throw away her used tissues (protect me, Lord), return her hairbrush to her overflowing vanity table. Opening the top drawer, I return some of the brushes and tubes to their rightful places.

When I reach the velvet bottom of the drawer I stumble upon her ledger, embossed with a gold rose.

I've seen her writing in it before, scribbling in it by lamplight while the dishes go unwashed. There's an envelope sticking out the top. I pull it out. It's addressed to Rose, stamped by the post office with the date of March 2, only a little over a week ago. The return address is in Pasadena: *D. E. Palmer*. I gasp, recognizing that name.

"Harlot," I whisper.

I open the card tucked into the envelope.

Dear Rose, how can I turn down such a mysterious offer? I'm intrigued. Let's meet in person at Café Bluebird in Altadena on Thursday, March 16 at 10am. Always, Dale

My cheeks flare with rage. The rage settles into a secret triumph. I knew it. "Mysterious offer"; I can guess what kind of offer *that* is. I take the card, slide it into the envelope, and tuck it into my handbag. Then I put the ledger back where it was, hiding in the shadows with the rest of Rose's secrets.

"What are you doing?" Rose asks, appearing in the doorway with Julie on her hip.

"Just tidying up," I say, straightening her perfume bottles.

"We've discussed this. Please don't come into our room uninvited, Harriet."

The nerve of her, talking to me as if I'm a child.

I straighten my posture. "I *came* to say *goodbye*."

"Goodbye," Rose says. "Have a lovely week and we'll see you again soon. Julie, wave goodbye to Grandma."

Julie curls her wee fingers. The cherub! She gives me a special smile, letting me know I'm her favorite in the world.

"You treat that baby good, you hear?" I say.

Rose doesn't answer. I walk to the living room, where Leo waits for me, tapping his foot. He holds my overnight bag in one hand.

"C'mon, let's go," he says. "We've got a company potluck I've got to get ready for."

"Why didn't you tell me, Leo? I could come."

"No, you can't. Time to go home."

That squeeze in my chest turns into a sting in my eyes.

"Ma, don't do this," Leo says, putting his arm around me. "We've talked about this. When it's time to go, it's time."

"I see," I say, wiping my eyes with a handkerchief. "This is what we've come to."

We say nothing, stepping outside in the sunshine. He opens my door for me, and I climb into the passenger's seat. He gets into the driver's side, adjusts the rearview, and puts on the radio. He fixes it on the classical station, for me. And we drive from the Valley to my apartment in Burbank, my heart getting a little more broken mile by mile.

"I like potlucks," I remind him.

"This is a work function. Something I normally wouldn't bother with, but ... I need to make an appearance."

"I don't see why I can't just stay with you through the weekend."

"We've discussed this. There's no room for long stays."

"Three bedrooms?"

"Four people."

"I shared a room when I was a child. Rose is just trying to keep me out."

"Enough. It's not Rose."

"I see how it is."

"Absence makes the heart grow fonder and all that."

My eyes burn as I fix my gaze on the billboards and the palm trees. The traffic. The silver freeways remind me of serpents tangled up in the city skyline. When Leo finally gets to my apartment, he pulls to the curb and helps me out of the car and up the stairs. I unlock my door.

"Stay for a cup of coffee?" I ask him as I push the door open and step inside.

"I told you, potluck."

"At least look at my faucet like you promised."

"I didn't bring my tools."

I swallow. "Well. There's this." I unclasp my pocketbook and pull the card from my bag with a trembling hand. "I found it; I think you should know."

Leo stares at the card in my hand like he doesn't know he's looking at.

"That's right, Leo. A correspondence from Rose's former beau. Are you aware they're in contact?"

"How did you get this?" he asks, turning the envelope over and inspecting it.

"It was—I was tidying up and I ran across it, that's all."

"Uh-huh. Sure."

"Where I found it isn't important. Read the card."

Leo sighs and takes the card, eyes heavy. That expression melts as he reads the note, flickering through confusion, then settling sadly. My poor boy—even if he's losing his hair and getting fat around his middle, I still see that innocent squinty-eyed child with the hangdog face.

"I don't know what this is," Leo mutters, sticking it in his back pocket. He adjusts his hat and stares at me pointedly. "But I know it's not *your* business."

"She's philandering."

"Ma, stop it. Just stop it," he says, irritated. "Always trying to stir up trouble."

I gasp, my hand on my chest. "Me? I—"

"Last night, with the comments about Rose's turkey last Thanksgiving—"

"It was undercooked, Leo! She could have given us all salmonella."

"Then calling us at the Italian restaurant when we're out on a date because you couldn't work the new television? We left you with the kids for an hour—"

"It was stuck on an inappropriate sitcom with an airheaded *genie* woman wearing hardly any clothes—"

"Now this bull." Leo blows a sigh. "You need a hobby."

"How dare you. I have my embroidery."

Leo leans over and kisses my head. "Goodbye, Ma. Call you later this week."

"Fine then." I begin weeping. "Good day."

He leaves, despite the tears. I dry my face as I watch him through the window. He backs out and turns onto the street.

I raised that boy on my own and I'm proud of the man he is, despite his marital strife. I don't want to dwell on Sidney's shortcomings, but I know a thing or two about such things. I've been lied to, cheated on, and shoved around. He moved me out to California when I was in the family way, supposedly to chase screenwriter dreams, but really, he just chased whiskey down the bottle. Even Sidney's death was a disgrace I had to endure. He fell off a rowboat at Lake Arrowhead, drunk as a skunk, with some loose woman. Leo was still in diapers.

I could have spiraled, but I didn't have the option. I went to work instead. And I worked harder than anyone I've ever met. I walked neighborhoods as a door-to-door saleswoman until my heels bled, day in, day out. Leo was the sun my life revolved around. Motherhood's a tale of unrequited love.

That lonely feeling overwhelms me, the silence a whale. But then I hear the clicking of feet above my head—that hussy upstairs. I'd forgotten about my rage for her. The parties. The stomping. The laughter at all hours.

Yes, perhaps that's how I'll spend my afternoon. I'll pen a letter to the landlord.

leo

Rose powders her face in the rearview as I drive up Laurel Canyon Boulevard. We pass palm trees, convertibles, bungalows. There are two hippie kids with their thumbs up leaning against a broken-down van painted with the peace sign. I shudder. Melinda will end up like that if we can't get her to stop shimmying out her window and hanging out with that bum Jim.

"You'll do fine," I tell Rose. "Smile. You don't even have to say anything, just look like you're having a good time. Tell Amanda Bishop how much you love her Jell-O salad."

"What are you, my acting coach?" she quips with a little laugh.

"It's been years since we made an appearance at one of these events. I just want to make the right impression."

Here's what my colleagues know about my wife over the four years I've worked for Century: Rose did a commercial for VitaSmile; later, she signed up for a research study with a group Century works with, where she flipped out, and almost bit a doctor; afterward, she was in an institution for half a week. There was no way I could keep that part from my work, not when I had to take time off. And word got around. So she hasn't exactly made a glowing impression. Today's our chance to remedy that.

She sits in a green polka-dot shift dress, hair in a French twist, a pimento-studded cheese ball on her lap. "Are you worried I'll embarrass you?"

In the silence, I sense hurt feelings. I put my hand on her knee.

"Of course not, my little thorn," I say. It's the joking nickname I gave her when we first started dating, thanks to her endearingly prickly nature.

She doesn't answer, and my nerves dance. Is she's spacing out again? She's been doing it again recently. I'm convinced she's with child—I'm seeing shades of her pregnancy with Julie—but two trips to the doctor have assured us we're in the clear. This isn't the day to dwell on all this, though.

"Rose," I say, to get her attention.

"Maybe you shouldn't have brought me if you're so worried," she says—and now I know she's not spacing out, but brooding. "Bring your mother instead. She'd rather be there, anyway."

Thinking of Ma reminds me of the note she showed me earlier, so-called evidence of Rose's "philandering"—but whatever it is, it's not what she thinks. She'd have a stroke if I told her Dale is a friend of Dorothy.

"No thanks," I tell Rose. "I'd rather bring my partner in sin and better half."

She places her hand on mine. "You're a sap, you know that?"

My colleagues call me the King of the Spin. It's my gift, I guess, that I can take any embarrassing product they hand me and make it sound elegant. Dandruff treatments, constipation remedies, you name it. I'll find an upside, and if there isn't one? I'll invent it.

If I can do all that, can't Rose pretend she enjoys a potluck for one afternoon?

I clutch the wheel harder with my left hand. "Every other family event, I've avoided. I know how you feel about the agency—"

"I don't feel any which way about your job! I don't work with you."

"Other people there, they've got wives who throw regular dinner parties and who show up at every function in furs. Some of the account executives take their wives to schmooze over drinks."

She pulls her hand off mine. "Poor you. And here you are, stuck with me."

I pull my hand from her knee. "Can you just do this once? Act normal, like you're not put out?"

"You said I didn't have to be your accessory," Rose says, her voice tight. "When I told you I wasn't good at this sort of thing. At faking it, small talk. You promised. Remember?"

"Yeah, yeah."

"If I recall correctly, you said, 'That's what I love about you, Rose. How real you are. Not like the other plastic wives out there.'" She snaps her compact closed. "Plastic starting to look better now that you're scrambling up the corporate ladder?"

"Do you want to be able to afford a college education for our kids, or not?" I ask, unable to help my voice climbing. "They specifically told me they're looking for someone who's a *family man* for head copywriter. Someone tapped into the *nuclear family*. You know why they said that."

"Look, if I have to hear once more about how I've humili-ated you in the eyes of your coworkers so long ago ..."

I sigh, parking behind a turquoise Cadillac and turning the wheels toward the curb. "Just act natural."

"Act natural." Rose turns to me, fixing her cat-eyed sunglasses on her face. "Ever contemplate that phrase deeply?"

I reach and brush aside a stray curl, then kiss her fore-head. "Maybe you contemplate everything too deeply. Maybe that's your problem."

A wry smile dances on her red lips. "Or *yours*."

I clasp her hands. She freezes in my grip. "Rose. I mean it, I do."

Her smile melts. She's like an animal sometimes, trying to wriggle away from me the tighter I hold her.

"I won't embarrass you this time," she says quietly.

I let go of her, give her a grateful wink. We step into the sunshine, arm in arm, and stride toward the most ostentatious house on the block: a cubist barnacle growing from the hill-side, flat-roofed and glass-walled. The front yard is all cactuses and desert rocks, the front door painted bright orange. This place must have set Victor back fifty grand.

"Hey-o!" Victor says, swinging the front door open, a brown drink with some ice cubes in hand. He's like a blond bulldog in a Hawaiian shirt. "I spotted you pulling up here in that land yacht. You still driving that thing?"

"Still waiting for that jackpot call from *Queen for a Day*," I tell him, stepping inside.

We shake hands, his grasp tight enough to shatter bones.

"Is that really you, Rose?" Victor says, nodding at her. "I was starting to think you'd run off and joined the circus, it's been so long. Since ..." He snaps his fingers, eyes sparkling.

"Since that study for expecting mothers." His smile falters. "Hope it's all smooth sailing these days?"

"Right as rain," Rose says, voice dripping with saccharine.

"You're looking much improved." Victor bows to Rose. "And you got your figure back, too."

"Where shall I put my cheese ball?" she asks.

"I'll take your cheese ball," he says, taking the plate. "Never played much cheese ball myself. More of a football man."

Rose checks her watch. I force a chuckle at his "joke."

I clap Victor's back, maybe a little too hard. "What's it take for me to get a drink around here?"

"Go ask the gal over there mixing cocktails, Natalie, the new one from the front office. I just saw Gleason sneaking in through the back and I need to tap him about the Fresca pitch." Victor squeezes my arm and disappears through the living room across a red sea of carpet.

"He makes my skin crawl," Rose whispers in my ear.

"He also puts food on our table," I whisper back. "Heads more accounts than anyone else at the agency. His lips are in Alfred's ear."

Near the console wafting with the sugar-voiced Supremes, Natalie is glowing over the drink cart with her bright smile, bouffant like a chocolate ice cream cone.

"I'm playing bartender!" she giggles. "I don't know a thing about mixing drinks. I can make a martini, and I can make a highball, and that's it. Hi, Leo. This your wife?"

"Yes. Natalie, Rose. Rose, Natalie. She works front desk now."

"Nice to meet you," Rose says. "I'll have a martini."

"Make that two," I say.

"You got it. Hey, Rose," she says over the cocktail shaker. "Is it true you used to do commercials at Century?"

"Just one," Rose says over the cacophony of ice clinking.

"Back when VitaSmile was radio ads," I say. "Before they switched to TV spots."

"With that face? You should have been on TV!" Natalie pours the drinks into two tall glasses, ice clinking.

Rose and I take our drinks through the sunken living room, past a couple of account executives locked in a riveting debate about how to make creamed corn a conversation piece. Speaking of which, the dining room is crowded with appetizers: paper plates with Vienna sausages and cheese cubes stabbed with toothpicks, lumps of tuna noodle casserole, seven-layer salad. We go outside, descend the spiral back stairs to the yard: neon-blue pool, neon-green lawn.

"This isn't a martini," Rose murmurs in my ear.

"Yeah, what's with the ice?"

"And the tequila?"

We giggle, and for just a second, it's summer between us again. It's our Mexican honeymoon. It's bike rides at Venice Beach. Malibu Canyon picnics and a hundred small adventures we've shared. The sun hits her hair in this way that makes it glow gold, and even the freckles on her shoulders make me crazy.

The junior copywriters congregate near the bougainvillea, staring out at the skyline and smoking tea. The media buyers known as the two Bobbies float in flamingo and swan inflatables, bickering like a vaudeville show no one asked for.

"It's called high-frequency repetition."

"Call it whatever you want, we both know it's just pumping jingles into housewife heads..."

I shove my hands in my pockets and admire the view. It's a weird time at the agency. I've been here four years, so I'm not new. But I'm also not a partner, a senior anything, or a bigwig account executive like Victor which, judging from where I'm standing, is clearly a few steps up. The Hollywood sign and the staggering vista of LA glitter in front of me, a mansion behind. For a split second, the envy eats me alive. But it fades with a breath or two. This is just a reminder of what's possible if I'm hungry enough.

"Seems like Victor's doing well for himself," Rose says.

"You think?" I sip the drink, which really is awful. Medicine, I tell myself.

"And he's still not married?"

"Don't know if he's the type to settle down." I squeeze her arm. "You interested?"

She snorts. "I'd rather screw Godzilla."

"Rose," I say. "Not so loud."

"No one can hear me." She looks at her watch. Despite the drink tasting like antiseptic, she's downed most of it already. She appears cool and collected, but the rate she's drinking betrays her nerves. "How long are you thinking we'll stay?"

"I don't know." I do a three-sixty to take in a cannonball off a diving board, a game of croquet on the green, clouds of smoke and peals of laughter, glasses cheersing. "It's a party."

She lights a cigarette. "Sometimes these things feel more like performances."

Heat rises in me. I grip the glass a little harder. "Look around you. Everyone's having a ball."

"You're right." She smiles. "It's wonderful."

I wrinkle my brow, debating if that was sarcasm or not.

She starts to walk away, blowing me a kiss. "You start schmoozing, I'll keep boozing, it'll be grand."

In a snap, she turns on the charm like a faucet. She waves at a group of women seated around a glass table, under a striped umbrella. They beckon her over and she joins them.

All those women in their sundresses, sandals, and sunglasses are a real picture.

"Is that you, Amanda Bishop?" Rose coos. "I thought I was staring at Audrey Hepburn. That hat is to *die* for!"

She sounds unlike herself, a B-movie actress, but the women stand up and greet her with squeals. You'd never know, looking at Rose. You'd never guess that she's not like them at all.

leo

I met Rose the year after I came home from the Pacific Theater, a year when I felt lucky to be alive and Los Angeles sparkled like a diamond mine. Democracy had won, the war was nothing but nightmares, and I was home on dry land. I pulled into a drive-in burger joint one afternoon. Ordered my usual. When Rose glided out on her roller skates in her waitress uniform, her blond pin curls bobbing above her shoulders and that dimple unbuttoning me, I was done for.

"Here you go, sir," she chirped, delivering my tray to the driver's window.

"Hey. Can I get some extra napkins?"

She glanced down at the two napkins already on the tray. "You planning on writing the great American novel?"

"Well, I do feel inspired," I said, flashing her a smile.

She rolled her eyes and then skated away. A minute later, she was back with an entire paper bag full of napkins, which she halfway threw at me through the window.

"There," she said with a playful smile. "Now you can detail your car when you're done too."

"You're a smart aleck, you know that?" I asked, leaning my arm out the window.

"Takes one to know one."

She smoothed her pleated skirt and began to skate away. The desperation to keep her attention flapped in my ribcage like a bird trapped in a house.

"Hey! I need one more thing," I said.

Rose turned, hand on hip, one eyebrow raised. Her curled hair was a marvel, a silhouette that deserved a painted picture. Behind her, cars were honking and pulling in and out of parking spaces. Here she was, prettier than Veronica Lake, skating around a drive-thru for minimum wage.

"Let me take you out to dinner," I said.

She stared back like I'd spoken gibberish.

"Come on, I'll read you the novel I write." I waved a few napkins at her, the way a queen might wave her handkerchief from a parade float.

Then her lips perked up and she laughed—the sound of a green light.

"Tonight?" I said.

"My shift's done at seven." She started skating away, then thought the better of it and came back around my way, circling elegantly as a figure skater until she was at my window again. "It better be someplace classy. If I have to smell another French fry, I'll combust."

"No French fries," I promised.

She started to turn again, but I whistled and got her attention.

"What?" she asked.

"Shouldn't we know each other's names?"

"Oh, sure," she said, as if she didn't care either way. She pointed to her uniform. "Rose."

"*Leo.*" Victor claps me on the back, interrupting my story. We're in his living room, eating cocktail weenies, tipsy. Lording over his picture window and staring down at his yard as twilight seeps in. The party mills around us: laughter, "Strangers in the Night" on the stereo, and ice clinking in so many glasses. "No wonder I hear you're such a pain in the neck to edit."

"What? You asked me how I met my wife—"

"And you're narrating a novel." Victor might be handsome as a dime store Tab Hunter, but he chews with his mouth open and spits when he talks if he's had one too many gin and tonics. "I'm not paying you by the word, you know."

You're not paying me at all, I'd like to quip back, but this guy's the equivalent of teacher's pet at the agency.

"Ever think you're in the wrong business?" Victor asks, pointing a sausage-finger in my face.

I wrinkle my brow, lean in. "How so?"

"You know. You and your purple prose. Maybe you missed your calling as a poet." He leans in and I get a rotten whiff of juniper. "I laugh every time I think about you saying color television's a fad."

"Everything's a fad," I tell him. "Don't you know? Our job's selling it." I put my empty drink glass down. "Excuse me, I'm going to go find my wife."

I haven't seen her in a couple hours, since I left her outside with the ladies. In the meantime I've downed two drinks and made my way around the room. She might be getting restless. I go out on the back deck. The breeze has a bite to it now that the sunset has passed. A few faint stars struggle to blink in the twilit sky. Below, the pool is empty except for an inflatable flamingo. The music is muffled out here, the quiet a relief.

Then I hear Rose's voice drifting from below. She must still be down there, parked at the same table. It's encouraging that she's making friends, bonding with the other wives here, and I start thinking that maybe this is the beginning of a new era for us. One where she's proudly at my side at company events instead of hiding back at home. But then I hear what she's saying. And how slurry her voice is.

"... it was some kind of test," she mumbles. "And I *failed*."

"But darling, why would they want to test you?"

"They did something to me, rearranged my brain."

"Maybe you need a cup of coffee," one woman suggests.

"You going to slip me something?"

They laugh uncomfortably. A woman says, "Well, this conversation has taken a strange turn."

Rose's voice drops. "You know what I'm thinking? Those weren't scientists. They were *Satanists*."

The other women respond with a gasp and a groan.

"Rose, have you been smoking grass? Honestly!" one of the women is saying.

Oh, good Lord. I take a step toward the edge of the deck and look below. Rose is still there at the glass table where I left her well over an hour ago, with three other women. They're all seated on one side with their arms crossed, clearly trying to distance themselves from her. And I can see why. Rose is slumped and belligerent.

I bound down the spiral steps to the patio.

"There are demons working at Century," Rose is telling everyone.

Demons?

"What's going on down here?" I say loudly, coming up

behind her, putting my hands on her shoulders. "Rose, what do you say we pack it in?"

Amanda is one of the women at the table. She twists her gold cross, disgust in her eyes. Seeing me, all three ladies get up in a hurry, as if they've been held captive by Rose and are finally free.

"Rose, look! It's your husband," one of them says, too cheerfully.

The three of them hurry up the stairs, as if they can't leave the scene fast enough.

Rose spins on her chair and gazes up at me. There are three empty glasses in front of her and an ashtray full of cigarette butts. The sun's gone, but she's still wearing her sunglasses. It's as if she's turned to stone.

"Ready to go?" I ask.

She doesn't answer. My throat is tight. Above us, at the railing, Amanda's pointing at us and talking to Victor.

"What did I tell you?" Rose says, as if she's having a conversation with an invisible person at the table. "He's here to shut me up."

I help Rose to her feet. She's unsteady. She's drunk, that's all this is. This isn't a breakdown, this isn't wandering off in the woods and speaking nonsensically. I don't look up at the people watching us. I ignore my gut sinking like a rock in the Pacific; I pull the both of us toward the gate at the side yard.

"Need help?" Victor calls from above.

"Nope, everything's fine." I say without looking up. "Tell Natalie it's her martinis' fault."

I smile and wave on my way out. Give it the old Leo spin. The gate swings behind us. We pass trash cans and a driveway full of cars.

"You never want me to mention it, Leo," Rose says as we

head to the car. Her voice is wet with tears now. "You want me to pretend it never happened."

I open her car door and push her into the passenger seat. "I don't know what you're talking about."

But I'm lying.

I know *exactly* what she's talking about.

And I don't want to talk about it ever again.

leo

The whole ride home, the silence is deafening. No music. No words. She opens her window, the freeway air a static scream. Soon I pull into the driveway, quivering with rage, and something even worse: disgust. I can't bear to look at her. I switch off the car, pull the keys, and head toward the house without going around to her side of the car to let her out. By the time I reach the front door, that seems too much of a jerk move. So I double back and let her out—but don't acknowledge her as I hold the door open.

"Appearances," she mumbles to herself.

"Let's get you to bed," I say through my teeth.

I help her inside the house, where Melinda and Julie are watching a rerun of *Gilligan's Island* in the dim living room. Two kids on the couch, two TV trays, three TV dinners, four big wide eyes lit up blue by the TV glare.

"Your mother's drunk," I tell them as I help her into our bedroom.

"*Mom!*" Melinda chides, not even looking up from the screen.

Rose shrugs me off like she doesn't need my help, pushing past. In our bedroom, she plops on the stool at her vanity and violently undresses herself. She pitches her high heels at the wall and tears off her pantyhose.

I'm not in the mood. I go into the closet and undress in there, grateful for the dark. As I unknot my tie and unbutton my shirt, it all catches up with me. I close my eyes. The anger turns to hurt. I change into my robe and come out of the closet, where Rose is in her slip, sobbing at the vanity.

"Wash your face, Rose," I say, standing behind her and looking at her reflection. "And go to bed."

"Who are you?" she asks with a bitter edge to her voice.

Is she talking to me or the mirror? I'd rather not know.

"What is it with you and Century?" I ask her, unable to help myself. "Are you purposefully trying to sabotage me?"

"You, you, you."

"You knew how important this was. And then you go around and—*demons*? Really, Rose?"

"Recording me."

"*Demons.*"

"Something like that," she says vaguely.

A violent impulse flashes through me, as if I might shake her until her skull rattles and bring her home to herself again. I wouldn't, of course. It's just a thought.

I pick up my jacket off the bed. An envelope falls out of the pocket and a fresh wave of rage rises. I almost put it away, but no, the flame's too high—I flick the envelope her way. It lands on her vanity top next to a powder puff.

It's the envelope Ma gave me earlier, trying to stir up trouble.

"What's this?" Rose asks, picking it up, her expression a touch more sober.

"What's it look like?"

"How'd you—?"

"Didn't realize you were still writing love letters to old Dale."

She drops it on the tabletop. "Oh, stop. He's the only one who'll listen to me. Him and my head shrink."

My expression hardens, a mask. The idea that this is more than a momentary lapse of sanity—that this is beyond one-too-many-cocktails behavior and a recurring streak of paranoia about my job—hits like a hammer.

"Stop going around telling people this nonsense," I say softly but firmly.

"They believe me."

Great. Now I've got a headache coming on. Exhausted, I try to explain in the simplest terms that I can. "They do not believe you, Rose. Dale's blowing smoke. Dr. Wells is paid to nod and smile. You're seeing things. There is no conspiracy at Century."

Since the study gone wrong, this has become a fixation of Rose's. There's no logic behind it.

"I work at an ad agency," I go on. "There are no demons there; furthermore, there are no such things as demons."

"You're one, too," she says, meeting my eyes in the mirror.

It breaks my heart. She's not there. The Rose I know—she's not there. She's spun out.

I feed her a Seconal and tuck her into bed.

Before leaving the room, I pluck that envelope off her vanity and pocket it again.

Melinda is on the phone in the kitchen, twirling the cord on her fingertip and murmuring into it.

"Grounded means no phone, Mel," I remind her.

"Apparently I'm responsible enough to babysit but not to use the telephone," she says pointedly into the receiver while glaring at me. "Ciao for now."

She hangs up with a sigh.

"You'd better not be talking to that shirtless derelict," I mutter.

"He has a name, Dad," Melinda says, crossing her arms. "Jim. And I wasn't talking to him."

I take a bottle out of the cupboard, pour a finger of Scotch. On second thought, make it two.

"Who were you talking to, then?" I raise a brow. Is Melinda stoned? Or crying? "And why are your eyes red?"

Julie runs around the corner with no pants on for some reason, hands in the air. "Uncle Jim watch *Gilligan!*"

"Uncle Jim?" I repeat.

In the beat that passes, I now understand why Melinda was so friendly when I came home, why the back door was ajar, why there was an extra TV dinner on the tray. Melinda invited that loser over when we were out today and snuck him out the back as soon as we got home.

"Was he—" I close my eyes, a boiler about to pop. I stop, hold it in, deep breath. "Put your sister to bed, put yourself to bed, and we'll talk about it in the morning."

Melinda keeps her chin raised, but she takes Julie's hand and goes upstairs. I sit at the kitchen table and pull out the note again, rereading it.

Dear Rose, how can I turn down such a mysterious offer? I'm intrigued. Let's meet in person...

I pull out the phone book, find Dale Palmer's number, and make a call.

"Hello?" Dale's nasally voice answers on the fourth ring, mid-laughter, conversation and music in the background.

"Dale. Leo Crawford."

"Leo! What's good, love?"

"Sounds like a party over there."

"Jazz records, bridge, and fine company. You should come on over."

Dale has this flirtatious quality to him that crawls under my skin. What Dale does behind closed doors is his business, but does he have to flaunt it?

"Thanks for the offer," I say dryly. "I'm calling about Rose."

"How's our darling girl?"

I'm not about to fill this clown in on specifics, especially considering he's got the loosest lips of anyone I've ever met —a columnist at a weekly paper, pure society gossip. But Dale has known Rose since they dated in high school. He has insight I don't. And I need to know why she was reaching out to him for the first time in months, maybe years.

"Well—she's sick in bed at the moment." I clear my throat. "But I know she was planning to meet up with you. Found a note about some meeting at the Café Bluebird on the sixteenth. What's this about?"

He laughs. "Why don't you just ask her about it?"

Because I can't believe a word she says. "Because she didn't want to tell me."

"And I do?"

"No, but you're more likely to give it to me straight."

"There's another bottle in the kitchen cupboard," Dale yells to someone, then returns to the conversation. "You're smarter than this. You know why she's reaching out to me. She has a story."

"She has *delusions*, Dale, and you're feeding into them by entertaining them as if they're true."

"What's wrong with listening to her?"

"Because it's *lies* and the more you listen to her, the more she believes them."

"Look." He sighs. "At Rose's behest, I've done some research into the program she was involved in, and there are some ... strange inconsistencies—"

"Dale. It was through my agency. Stop looking for the second gunman. It was advertising research for bored housewives."

He laughs. "Have you looked into Harold Lumer? His former institutes have more red flags than a Spanish bullfight."

"Who the hell is Harold Lumer?"

"The researcher who led the program. Look—Leo. I've got a bridge game to get back to here. You want to meet up sometime, get a drink?"

"C'mon. Man to man. Stop talking to Rose about this. You're making her paranoid."

He sighs. "All right, old man."

"Enjoy the game."

"Oh, I will."

I hang up with a clink, read the note one more time, rip it into pieces, and scatter them in the garbage can like snow.

leo

On our first date, I took Rose to the Brown Derby, a historic restaurant on Hollywood Boulevard shaped like a giant brown derby hat. It was old Hollywood charm—dark wood paneling, wine-red vinyl booths, a haze of cigarette smoke and vibrant conversations. Considering all she'd told me was "no French fries," I thought this place was pretty impressive. Clark Gable was eating a Cobb salad a few tables away from us, for Pete's sake.

"I've been here before," she said, drinking a martini with extra olives. "With my best friend Dale. He's so into celebrities he's like a paparazzi with no camera."

"Your best friend's a man?"

"Yes. He's the man in my life who's loved me best, and he prefers the company of men." She laughed at herself, a little self-consciously. "So that should tell you a lot about me."

She was so different, so confident and funny. I couldn't stop staring at the way her brown eyes sparkled in the light of the table lamp.

"What?" she said, a little sharply. "Have I put you off already?"

"No, I just can't stop staring at you."

"Oh." She smiled, softening, and popped an olive in her mouth. "I get a little defensive, I guess, because other guys I've gone out with aren't exactly fond of me being best friends with a man."

"It's unusual, I'll give you that."

"Well, you should probably know there's more where that came from." She drank another gulp and I realized, for the first time, that she was nervous. Beneath her charm, she was afraid of being judged, and that flicker of vulnerability made her even more interesting. "I'm unusual in many ways."

"Do tell."

"I'm double-jointed," she said, showing me how she could bend her elbow so far it almost looked like it was going the wrong way. She made sure to assure me, "It doesn't hurt."

I didn't flinch, just shrugged. "I've got a cousin who can do that."

"I sleepwalk."

"I sleep*talk*."

She smiled at me. This was fun. She peered down at her menu.

"Sometimes I wish I could live a thousand different lives," she said, from nowhere, as she tried to decide what to order.

Right then, I knew if I only had one life, and it was with her, it would be enough.

"That's why I read so much," she says, closing the menu. She giggled at herself. "And why I love sleeping."

"You and I have so much in common," I said. "We both love sleeping. And eating."

"And breathing ..."

We laughed. There wasn't a pause that entire night—it was jokes and stories and breathless banter from the time we walked into the restaurant, through drinks and three courses, and all the way to her apartment—where we had to climb up the fire escape and through her open window, because she'd locked her keys inside. She was chaos and I loved her for it.

But now, all these years later in this quiet house in the suburbs, it's hard to believe that was us.

I get the kids upstairs, pour a low-ball glass of Scotch, light a cigarette next to the open living room window, and sit in my recliner and rationalize. I spin my wheels, edit the party scene, recut it into a funny story. One of our account executives vomited on the Heartwell Foods president during a pitch meeting last year, and he still works at Century—and Heartwell's still our flagship account. So my wife had a couple too many. To Amanda Bishop, everything's a scandal.

But there's this ugly thrum underneath the stillness here. A buzz beneath the wallpaper, the lamp light sour, smoke tickling my throat. I think of Victor interrupting me today, chiding me about my *war stories and purple prose*. Fight a war in another continent, defend democracy, now I'm a joke. Victor belongs to that new crop of men who skipped the unpleasant parts of history and still manage to collect all the rewards. Then there's Rose.

It's like you do every damn thing right and life shrugs.

I stub my cigarette out, lock the last window, and head upstairs. Crawl into bed next to Rose. She's so cold, so unmoving, I panic and put a finger under her nose. But I feel her breath. I match it with a sigh of my own.

"Sleep it off, Rosie," I whisper, and turn the other way.

I ride the easy waves of Scotch to sleep. A thick forgetful sleep—until it isn't.

Disoriented, my eyes snap open. Darkness. Whispers.

I twist in the sheets and reach out for Rose, but my fingertips meet empty space, messy blankets. Sitting up, I scan the room. Shadows and stillness. Moonlight on wrinkled sheets.

"Rose?"

I can hear her voice, buried beneath a hum. Quiet, but pleading. Whispering but desperate. As if she's a buzz trapped in the walls.

Pushing myself up and out of bed with a groan, I follow the noise.

"Rose, what is it?" I say, poking my head out into the hall.

The light coming from the living room is bright and flickering. I squint and follow it, heading downstairs. It's the glow of the television. Rose must be having insomnia. As I reach the bottom of the steps, I see her there, in the dark, seated on the floor in front of the blinking screen like a child.

But there's no show on TV.

Just those vertical rainbow bars blaring along with a beeping sound, flickering in a way that hurts to look at too long.

"Rose," I say.

She doesn't move. I circle a few steps so I can look at her face.

Rose is hypnotized, eyes locked on the screen. Those rainbow bars quiver in her unblinking eyes. Her expression is deadpan except for tracks of tears on her cheeks. I swallow a lump of fear.

"What are you doing?" I ask.

Her rigid posture—her stillness, her messy teased hair—I want to tell her to get it together.

But then a voice rises from her throat. Guttural, animal, deep, and unwomanly.

"Bite down," she growls, her eyes fixed on the screen. *"Sit still. This won't hurt."*

It's like someone knocked the wind out of me. I don't know what to say. I shudder and fight the urge to run—from my own wife, as if she's a wolf.

"You're sleepwalking, Rose," I say, as steady as I can.

She turns, breaking her gaze with the screen, and I'm relieved to recognize her somewhere in there. She points to the bars on the screen with a quivering finger. "This is where they live."

"Who?"

Rose drops her voice, as if they might hear. "The d-demons."

I sink about ten stories. It's been hours now. The alcohol should have faded. She's still talking about demons. A surge in my throat makes me want to scream or weep, I don't know which. But I hold my mouth in a hard line.

"Goodnight, Rose," I say, reaching to help her up.

She pushes me away instead, and says, in that horrid guttural voice, *"Goodnight, Rose."*

Not knowing what to do, I reach for the knob and turn until it clicks. The television turns off. I lean down and pull her to her feet.

"Bloody mouth," she hisses.

That phrase spins my stomach.

I pull her toward the stairs. "Come to bed—"

"Are you tired, ladies?" Rose chirps suddenly. "Suffering from mood swings? Do you feel like the sparkle's gone from your day-to-day life?"

It occurs to me that, for the first time in longer than I can remember, I don't know what to do. I don't have an answer. I don't know how to talk to her. I don't know who to call. I don't know if I should give her another pill or call the doctor.

I don't know if a drink or a chat or a good night's sleep will make this go away.

Home safe—yet never more lost.

melinda

Monday mornings, I iron my hair to get it perfectly straight. I lay my head on the ironing board, put wax paper over the length of my hair, and iron it carefully while checking myself in my bedroom mirror so I don't singe an ear off. While I'm doing this today, though, male voices vibrate through the house's bones, up the ironing board legs, buzzing my eardrum. And I think, *who's the mystery man Dad is talking to?*

I put the iron down, admire my hair in the mirror, and follow my curiosity to my bedroom door. Cracking it, I cock my ear to listen.

"...didn't even sound like herself," Dad is murmuring.

Then a voice I don't recognize. "You mean the things she was saying, or—"

"The things she was saying, but also her voice. She sounded ... unfeminine."

"What was it she consumed last night?"

"Couple cocktails, a Seconal, that's it as far as I know. I tried calling her psychoanalyst this morning, but apparently he's on vacation this week ..."

The curiosity is a wildfire, burning me from the inside out. I step out into the hall. Dad and, to my surprise, Dr. Anders are standing there. Our family doctor who doles out polio shots and lollipops.

"What on earth?" I ask, hands on hips.

"Good morning, Melinda," Dr. Anders says amiably. He looks so out of place in his sweater and khakis, no white coat on, standing next to my fourth-grade school picture on the wall.

"Get back into your room, Melinda," Dad says, his face pale and uncertain, his shirt untucked.

"Geez, I have to get ready for school, remember?"

Julie's crying behind her bedroom door. Chaos. The two men exchange a look. My stomach cartwheels, because nothing about this scene feels right. The stink of the unsaid is too much to bear.

"What's *happening?*" I ask.

"Your mom is unwell," Dad says. "We're trying to help her."

I get a flicker of something deep, dark, and sick. A remembering I've pushed down. I slump.

"Unwell how?" I ask. "Like before?"

"Melinda, this isn't your business."

"I live here, don't I? Where is Mom?"

"She's lying down. For Pete's sake, stop making everything harder!" Dad barks.

I retreat into my bedroom, seething, slam the door. Sometimes I swear I could burn it all down. Nothing adults do makes a shred of sense. If I get up late, I'm in trouble for sleeping in because I might miss the bus to school. I get ready on time, and I'm sent back to my room. Does Dad even hear himself sometimes? Meanwhile, the baby is crying, ignored.

I can't hear what's going on anymore. Some kind of pandemonium, shuffling, footsteps on the staircase. Then the slam of the front door. I scramble to my window. Crossing the green lawn, Dr. Anders leads Mom on his arm, taking her to the passenger side of his Buick parked at the curb. She's in her herringbone coat and sunglasses. I can't read her face from here. But I get a lurch in my belly—as if I might never see her again.

Dad comes into my room, holding Julie, her face wet and cherry red.

"Your mom had to go to a doctor's appointment," Dad tells me. "It was unexpected. I'm going to need you to watch your sister—"

"I have school. Remember? The importance of my education?"

"Save the lip today, Melinda, I'm not in the mood."

He puts Julie on the floor. She comes running to me, hugging my leg, putting a thumb in her mouth.

"I'm going to go pick up Ma because I need her to watch Julie." Dad fixes his hat. "I'll be back in less than an hour, then I'll take you to school."

This is too wild for words. Something so fishy is going on and he won't tell me what it is, but clearly Mom's in trouble. Trouble worse than ever before. The way Dad won't meet my eyes—the invisible smoke of shame clouding the air—what does it all mean?

I think of the stubborn, unreachable expression I glimpsed in her recently. I think of the night she went missing in the woods. The flashback to Not Mom. And I'm too scared to press for more details.

"Please," Dad says, finally meeting my eyes. His gaze is brown, beat down, and I wonder when it was that hope died in him. I vow to never let it die in me. "I need your help this morning."

I nod, and he heads downstairs. Julie looks to me, touching her tiny sticky hand to mine.

"Okay, Lin Lin?" she asks.

I crouch and cup her dear cherub face in my palm. I will not do to her what others have done to me all my life. I will not be a liar who grows up and raises more liars.

"Nope, Jules. Nothing's okay. Not today. But you and me, we'll make it out all right."

I scoop her up, kiss her cheek, and hug her the way I wish someone would hug me.

melinda

Sometimes life is nothing but a movie. My high school is flat as a set, concrete and palm trees. My teachers and classmates might as well be actors. It's like when Jim got me high the first time behind the bleachers last year, I saw through it all and now I can't un-see it for what it is: fake. A prison. An institution that's trying to cookie cutter us all into oblivion. In my desk, notebook open, pen moving, I doodle the words *Jim and Melinda Carroll* and *Mrs. James Carroll* and daisies and stars. My secret rebellion. They can make me sit in here eight hours a day, but they can't know my heart.

"Miss Crawford?" my teacher Mrs. Paganini asks. "What is a *bildungsroman?*"

I stop doodling and snap to attention. Everyone's gaping at me, whispering and giggling. My cheeks flush.

"Um," I say, floundering. "A ... Roman building?"

The entire class erupts with laughter. Mrs. Paganini shakes her head, razor lips a slash of red. Her heels click along the floor as she approaches my desk. "Writing notes in class again?"

I cover my margin doodles, splaying my fingers on the page. Mrs. Paganini takes her liver-spotted hand and moves my palm to read what I've been writing.

"Mrs. James Carroll. Jim and Melinda Carroll," she pronounces to the class with flourish. "I do hope we're all invited to the wedding?"

Everyone laughs out loud. She gloats, the mean cow.

I don't look her, or anyone, in the eyes. I stare at my paper and will myself to remain absolutely still. Mrs. Paganini proceeds to click her ugly heels up and down the aisles of desks, *smack-smack-smack*, lecturing us all on the importance of paying attention, but I don't hear a word. I tune her out like a radio station, my ears picking up on one thing only, a girl's voice saying quietly but still aloud:

"Her mother's in the looney bin."

My head snaps up, breath stuck. The hurt cramps my chest and for a second, I'm sure I imagined it—but then I see my next-door neighbor Alison Fenmore whispering to that know-it-all Gladys Nevins and I realize, with horror, that they know. It's only been three days since Mom went away to the institution. Soon everyone will know.

With a twist of despair, all I want in this world is Jim. This school is soulless without him here this year. My eyes flood. I grab my books, my knapsack, and race out the door, even though Mrs. Paganini is yelling my name.

I snag a ride on the chugging slug of a city bus to the garage where Jim works in Van Nuys. When I show up, greasy-haired buffoons in blue coveralls stop snickering and straighten up, and one in glasses rolls out from under a Chevy.

"Hey, it's the schoolgirl," he says.

"Don't tell me you're looking for that bum of a boyfriend," another chimes in.

"Is he working?" I ask uneasily, scanning the dark garage for Jim's sandy hair.

"I fired his ass a week ago," booms a man, walking out of an office with an oily cloth on his shoulder. "After the umpteenth time he didn't show up to work. When you find him, why don't you tell him to bring back my crescent wrench. That way I don't have to call the cops."

It's as if I've been kicked, an invisible boot to the gut. I saw Jim just nights ago. He never said a word about being fired.

The men laugh, showing off their crooked teeth. Are they joking? I catch a glimpse of myself in a hubcap: a warped girl in a plaid skirt and bobby socks. I wish I could burn my school uniform.

Outside, my heart races. I'm a lost little lamb, ditching class, what am I doing out here? I suppress a sob, suddenly longing for Mom. But Mom's in a hospital somewhere *resting*. That's how Dad put it, she's *resting,* as if she's off enjoying a cat nap. He won't tell me the real story, no matter how many times I ask, so I have to piece it together myself like a puzzle, one that I never have all the pieces to. It's maddening.

I get back on the bumpy bus, stop after stop after stop, until we finally get to Canoga Park. I hop off a block from my house but head the other way, toward Jim's instead: the corner lot with the overgrown lawn and the red picket fence with peeling paint. Their garbage cans are still out by the curb even though pickup day was Monday. Mom has pointed it out to me every time we drive by, as if it's a mark on their family's character.

Knock-knock-knock. I can hear shouting behind the door—typical. His parents are always home, ever shouting, his dad in chronic pain from an injury that ended his carpentry career, his mother in a perpetual mood, both of them each with a bottle. Jim and his sister Jan never even flinch at it, as if their ears learned how to tune out the noise long ago. But it will never feel normal to me. Then again, who am I to judge about normal?

Her mother's in the looney bin.

The door opens. It's Jim's mother in a house dress and curlers, cigarette dangling from her lip, lowball glass of brown liquid with clinking ice.

"Hello darlin'," she says to me. "He's not here."

"How are you, Mrs. Carroll?"

"You don't want to know."

"Who is it now?" Jim's dad calls. He lumbers out, hunched, and when he sees me, he grimaces. "Oh, you. He stormed outta here days ago."

"You threw him out," Mrs. Carroll says, annoyed.

"You have no idea where he is?" I ask.

"Prob'ly bumming around Sunset for spare change," his dad barks.

I'm surprised they don't know more. Then again, Jim is Jim. I thank them and leave, stepping over unopened newspapers scattered on their porch.

At the end of the driveway, I peer over my shoulder and note the mailbox, open, mail spilling out. An envelope has fallen on the ground. It has dirt on it, as if it has been stepped on. I pick it up. Plain, white, with Jim's name typed on it. The return address makes my heart skip a beat, my stomach drop.

LOCAL SELECTIVE SERVICE BOARD.

I shove the envelope in my knapsack and walk back to the bus stop, the world blurring as my eyes water. It's too much.

I'm being crushed from all sides. Like the poem Mrs. Paganini made us memorize, *the center will not hold.*

Down the block, there's my house, my pretty blush-pink house with its lawn flamingos and shut curtains and empty driveway. For a blink, I imagine it isn't my house.

I turn the other way and take the bus to Sunset.

melinda

The letter is a bomb ticking in my knapsack.

The whole excruciatingly long bus ride from Canoga Park to Sunset, all I can think about is ripping it open to learn Jim's fate. But somehow, on this ghostly city tour through blinding sunshine, I already know what it's going to say. They only send letters like that for one reason.

He's going to Vietnam.

I blink away tears. Outside the window, movie posters with perfect painted women snap by, liquor store signs with neon promises, advertisements for cigarettes and hairspray. Glamorous lies, all of it, a lure created by men like Dad, while boys like Jim are shipped to jungles half a world away to die.

While the bus idles at an intersection, I spot a man up on a ladder beneath a billboard, painting it black. I get a shiver as if I've stepped in a shadow when I see the ad he's covering, instantly recognizing the cursive word *VitaSmile*. The woman grinning on the billboard isn't Mom, but she's Mom-shaped. He paints over her eyes with a paintbrush. She's still smiling blindly as he works his roller over her face.

I hop off at Sunset and Vine. In the late afternoon, there's a sleepy sparkle to the boulevard's energy. Music clubs are just opening their doors but no bands play yet, bars dark and half-empty, and the double-decker tourist buses whizz up and down the road with some bozo shouting in a megaphone about movie stars. Buskers strum guitars and hippies wander around barefoot and the lazy electricity turns my lips into a smile as I walk up the street toward a string of clubs in a row plastered with psychedelic posters for The Doors, Buffalo Springfield, The Byrds.

I let out a sigh of relief when I spot Jim's shaggy hair and that familiar maroon suede jacket. He's in front of a dive called the Lion's Roar, chatting with two girls with long, stringy hair and bandannas. Leaning on the doorway with his sunglasses on, whispering in one of their ears and making them giggle, hand full of fliers for whatever show's happening here tonight.

"Jim," I say, his name coming out of my throat like a bird chirp.

The three of them turn toward me.

"Lindy," he says with surprise, pushing his sunglasses up and revealing bloodshot blue eyes. "Shouldn't you be in school?"

"Is this your kid sister?" asks one of the girls.

I prickle at the question, but Jim scoffs. "Nah, my girl-friend." Jim slings an arm around me and kisses my temple. I beam at the way the girls look at him—like they wish they were me. The same way my classmates looked at me when Jim and I started going steady last spring. "You all right?"

I shake my head. I haven't seen Jim since I snuck him out of our back door the other night when I was babysitting Jules, the night everything fell apart and Mom went away the next morning. I have so much to tell him, and the letter in my bag—but he doesn't seem to notice, nodding toward the girls.

"This is Leslie and Susie Q." He grins at the girls. "Would you believe they're twins? They've been pestering me all day long."

The girls giggle.

He winks at me. "They're waiting around for Stephen Stills."

"We hitched all the way from Nashua," one of them says.

"Blew off midterms," the other says with a laugh.

"They're trying to stay out here," Jim says. He has a cigarette dangling, unlit, on his lip, and teases, "Couple of college dropouts."

"Jim," I say to him, urgently, in his ear. "Can we talk?"

He fixes his sunglasses back on. "What's up?"

"I mean—somewhere else?"

The girls are a two-person audience, watching us with curious amber eyes. One lights up two cigarettes, then gives one to her sister.

"I'm workin'," he laughs.

I bite my tongue, dying to ask him about what happened with the mechanic job, about not coming home for days, but now's not the time. And I can tell he's high as a kite anyhow, the way he can't stop smiling and won't take his sunglasses off. So I pull the envelope out of my bag and thrust it toward him. My hand is shaking.

"It was at your house," I tell him.

He peers closer to read the return address. "The draft board."

"Shit," one of the girls says.

Jim blows out a sigh but doesn't react otherwise. In fact, he keeps smiling as he snatches it. "Well. It was just a matter of time."

We watch, unmoving, as he rips it open. A tension thickens, a solemn moment in the sunshine despite the bustle of the city street. I swallow a lump, wishing these girls weren't here, witness to this fateful moment that should be ours, just ours, just his and mine.

His face doesn't change. He stares at the letter through his sunglasses, that cigarette hanging from his mouth unlit.

"What's it say?" I whisper, stepping aside to peek over his shoulder. But he pulls out a Zippo lighter, flicks the flame to life, and lights the paper on fire. Then he leans in with a grin, lights his cigarette off it, and lets the blazing page fall to the ground.

The girls gasp, radiant with surprise, jumping up and down. My mouth is agape as the paper burns to ash on the sidewalk—the consequences of this rushing through my mind in a hurried, anxious whisper. I glance left and right, imagining if a cop were around, but there aren't any.

"Piece of paper doesn't get to tell me how to live and die," he says.

"*Jim*," I say.

"What are my options, Lindy?" he asks, laughing, incredulous. "I'd rather sit in a jail cell than be sent half a world away to shoot women and children."

The draft notice is nothing but ash on the ground. There's no way to undo what he just did. He must see the tears welling in my eyes, because he leans over and nuzzles my cheek.

"Don't worry. I got a place to crash. Jan, remember?" He kisses me. "Frisco ain't so bad."

No one-way tickets. Jim is my past, present, and future. I can't let us get split apart.

"What about college?" I try. "You could sign up for classes—"

He scoffs. "It's almost April, way too late."

I wrack my brain, squeezing his arm. "Something medical? An injury or asthma—"

"Hey, you said Frisco?" one of the girls interrupts. "We're thinking of heading there next."

"Our cousin went out there for the Human Be-In," says the other. "She said it's far out."

I'm suddenly so irritated by these groupie girls I could spit. Can't they see he's busy?

"It's where everything seems to be happening, man," Jim says to them. "My sister's been there for months ..."

Their voices turn into nothing but background noise. All I can think is, I'm going to lose Jim. Whether it's Vietnam, jail, or him fleeing this city—he's not here for long.

But I can't let that happen.

melinda

It's been one week since I last saw Mom, six days since she went away to *rest*.

Six days of me comforting Jules and singing her lullabies at night.

Six days of waking myself up and fixing breakfast each morning.

Six days of mail piling up with MRS. LEO CRAWFORD on the envelopes.

Six days of no radio, no singing, no banter, no laughter.

Six days of Grandma sleeping in the living room and overwhelming our house with her constant complaining, her overpowering talcum powder and violet perfume, her cursive notes she leaves all over the house as if she thinks she's suddenly become queen and makes the rules. *No snacks after supper, it makes you stout* on the refrigerator. *Waste not want not* inexplicably taped above the toilet paper. *Vanity is a sin!* taped to my bathroom mirror.

Six days of Dad walking around in a frowny daze with his

shirt misbuttoned, muttering, "I don't know," every time I ask a simple question.

It's not that I can't handle being on my own without Mom. It's just been the longest week of my life.

Since it's Sunday morning, though, I get a little peek of sunshine through the clouds when Dad takes Jules and Grandma to church and I'm left alone. It's all the way in Burbank, and she pesters the pastor with dozens of questions afterward every week, and they're stopping for lunch afterward—so I have a few hours to sneak off with Jim.

Jim drives us around the city in his dad's beat-up Bel Air. The radio's busted and it smells like stale cigars, but we don't care. We zip up our jackets, crank the windows down, and let our fingers ride the wind. We sing "California Dreamin," making sure to get the harmony just right as we drive into Topanga Canyon. Then when the fog thins, the air turning from silver to gold, he pulls over and we devour each other like two starving people. I straddle him, kissing and moaning, his hands all over me. I only stop him when he reaches to unzip my jeans.

"Not here," I say.

He bites his lip in frustration, squeezing his eyes shut as if it hurts. "Not anywhere, Lindy. I've waited so long."

"We're pulled off on the side of the road in the middle of the day," I remind him, catching my breath. I point to the landscape surrounding us outside the open window: the chaparral and sage bush, the distant violet glint of the city through the haze. I can feel him against me, hard and pulsing. I ache with it too.

"You know you're the only thing keeping me here, right?" he asks me, stroking my face.

I nod. I hate it when he says that, but I know it's true. Ever since Jim burned his draft letter a few days ago, he promised he wouldn't make any life-changing decisions without me. But every day he talks about San Francisco like it's Eden.

"I'm scared that if we ... you know, go all the way," I say, not looking him in the eyes, playing with one of the buttons on his open shirt. "You won't have anything to wait around for anymore."

He leans his head back, his Adam's apple bobbing as he sighs. "You know that's not why I'm with you."

"I just want it to be special." I take his collar and pull him closer, meeting his eyes with mine, then his lips with mine. "So wait for me."

We press our foreheads together. I lose myself for a moment, trying to decide the right name for the exact color of his eyes. They're so twinkly bright, yet darkly striking. Cerulean? Indigo?

"Of course I'll wait," he says, but he doesn't smile.

"I'm graduating in less than three months," I remind him. "Then we can do whatever we want. Just—hang with me until then?"

"If the FBI doesn't come knocking on my door first," he mumbles, buttoning his shirt. "Come on. I should take you home before your dad finds out your deadbeat boyfriend snuck you out of the house."

"I should have never told you he called you that," I sigh, climbing back into my seat and adjusting my shirt.

"Probably not," he agrees, turning the ignition.

No "California Dreamin'" harmonies on the way back to Canoga Park, just silence. Jim seems distracted as he drops me off at my house and even when he assures me everything is fine, it doesn't settle the butterflies in my stomach. I watch him drive away, feeling like a little girl.

Inside the house, there's static silence. I've never liked

being home alone. There's something uncanny about hearing every tick-tock of the cat clock on the kitchen wall, every drip-drop of the leaky downstairs faucet. I see myself in the television screen, which is off, but reflecting the scene back to me in gray. I'm distorted and tall, an Alice in Wonderland version of myself.

I get the urge to smash it.

Silly, I know, but part of me blames that television for Mom's *issues* (as Dad has begun calling them, as if they are frivolous as glossy magazines). I can't help it. It was the television that seemed to set her off in the cabin years ago when she first spun out, and then last week it was the television that set her off again. No one has turned it on since, as if we all secretly think it's cursed, and Grandma has now put a note on it that just says PASTOR WHITAKER!

I start to head upstairs, then pause instead in my parents' bedroom doorway. It's deathly silent, dust in the air, the bed neat and made. A backward homesickness pours over me—but how could that be when I'm already home? I step inside, swallowing as I approach Mom's vanity table. I touch the powder puff I've watched her put to her face a hundred times and the perfume bottles she spritzes on the insides of her wrists. Pulling the drawer open, I take out her favorite tube of lipstick, bright red, and tuck it in my pocket like a greedy little thief. I imagine her coming back and finding it gone, shouting at me; I wish she would in a backward kind of way.

There's a notebook with a gold rose, the ledger I've seen her making entries in late at night in the dark kitchen lately. Keeping track of our expenses. Always looking for a bargain, clipping coupons, priding herself on cutting costs. I flip it open.

Then, I stare in shock.

I don't know what I was expecting. Numbers, notes, equations, shopping lists, prices. But no. The entire page is black ink penned from margin to margin, tiny perfect penmanship covering every square inch. I squint to read it.

I'm so engrossed in this horrific microscopic diary masked as a ledger that I don't hear anyone come into the house, I don't hear footsteps or conversation, and I don't hear anyone behind me until Dad says, indignantly, from the doorway, "What on earth are you doing?"

I jump, flipping the ledger shut and closing the drawer.

"So this is what happens when we let you stay home from church," he says dryly, loosening his tie. "I catch you snooping around our bedroom."

Grandma stands behind him in the doorway in her ridiculous Kentucky Derby hat she wears to church every Sunday. "Shame on you, going through other people's personal items." She tut-tuts. "How unbecoming."

I can't wait until that old bag goes home again. She's got this squinched expression all the time like she's sucking a lemon.

"When is Mom coming back?" I ask, unable to help the quiver in my voice.

Just the mention of her seems to darken the room.

"I'm supposed to get a report sometime next week," he says in a clipped tone. "Everything'll be fine."

I cross my arms. "Would you even tell me if it wasn't?"

Back up in my bedroom, I lie on my bed, dizzy from the day, brain full of spiderwebs. So much sticking in my mind I can't separate it all. My whirlwind date with Jim, and then that awful ledger. Those couldn't have been Mom's thoughts, could they? She sounded mad, much madder than I assumed she was—the kind of mad you don't come back from.

And for the first time since she left, I cry.

harriet

The good Lord intended Sundays to be a day of rest, yet here I am—sweeping up other people's messes, ankles swollen, and sweating like a summertime hog. Maybe if Rose had ever properly cleaned before she decided to abandon her family, I could rest as the Lord intended. As I make my way toward Leo's study, chasing dust bunnies with the broom, I stop to straighten some photographs on the wall, noting there are twelve photos and only one of them includes me. The treatment I get!

I hear Leo behind the door on the telephone, speaking in a low voice: "She's in the hospital."

Then silence. *Who's he telling our business to?*

"Nothing like that. It's—something to do with her head."

Silence.

"No. Nerves."

The curiosity is positively burning me alive. I'm tempted to open the door, but I restrain myself, looking at the ceiling. *Give me strength.*

"Gee, sorry you weren't the first person on my list to call, Dale."

I gasp. *Dale? Her high school beau?*

"That's a pretty rotten thing to say. You know I'd do anything in the world for her."

This is too much; I can't withstand it any longer. Leo needs me right now, but how can I help him if I don't understand? I take my broom into the kitchen, set it aside, and pick up the other phone quietly to listen.

It's Dale's voice, dandy and haughty. "...ever since that time she wandered off in the woods, and every time she said something to you, you ignored her—"

"Because it's insane!"

A static silence. I hold my breath.

Leo sighs. "Dale. What is this? What is it you want?"

"I want you to admit that there could be something to what she's said."

"Oh yeah? Then how come, in high school, she had a similar breakdown?"

"I *knew* her in high school—"

From behind me, a voice cuts in. "Grandma?"

Startled, I gasp and hang the phone up, swirling around.

It's Melinda, greasy straw-colored hair desperately in need of brushing, wearing *pants*. I still can't imagine letting your daughter dress this way. What is this world coming to? My angel Julie sucks her thumb and holds onto her sister's pant leg.

I swallow. "I was ..."

"Oh, I know what you were doing," Melinda says, raising her eyebrows and smiling wickedly at me. She's always had such a wicked smile, with that crooked eyetooth—same as her mother. "Eavesdropping." She tut-tuts at me. "How unbecoming."

My cheeks burn with rage. In my youth, I'd have been slapped for such smart remarks.

"We're going to watch cartoons," she says.

"Not on the Lord's day you're not."

"Isn't every day the Lord's day?"

Melinda turns around as if I haven't said a word to her, holding her sister's hand. My mouth drops as she heads over to the television set. I follow, nearly killing myself on the edge of a side table.

"No, you can't!" I shout. "Not until Pastor Whitaker has laid hands upon it!"

Melinda turns around, confused, looking far too petulant for her own good. "You want your *pastor* to bless our television?"

"Cover her ears," I snap, pointing to Julie.

Melinda does so, her face still looking pinched as a raisin.

"Your dear *mother* saw *demons* in that television," I whisper loudly. "*Demons.*"

"And you think they're real?" Melinda squints at me. "So you don't think Mom was seeing things? You think it's the television that is the problem?"

Now she's got my words all mixed up. I'm tongue-tied.

"So you think Mom should come home, then?" she asks. "You think that nothing is wrong with her nerves?"

"All I know is, when it comes to demons, you don't play."

Melinda just blinks at me with a stare as blank as a peeled potato. Then she reaches for the television, turns it on, and starts flipping channels. She might as well have stabbed me in the belly; I'm so shocked I can't even speak. Then, to dig the knife even deeper, she settles on a loud, violent, obnoxious cartoon with that rude rabbit.

Leo walks into the room then, perfect timing. I turn around.

"Leo," I say. "Your daughter is being so cruel."

"Which one?" he asks, walking over, his gaze caught by the television.

"Melinda, of course."

"She wanted the pastor to come pray over the television," Melinda says as Julie crawls onto her lap. Lord, that little one needs better role models. "But we want to watch cartoons."

"Ma, you asked him at church. How many times do you have to hear the word 'no' before it sticks?"

"I was a saleswoman," I remind him. "I know how to turn a no into a yes."

Leo sighs, passing me and stepping to the sofa. I think he's about to lecture his obnoxious daughter, but instead he moves to take a seat next to Melinda and Julie. Choosing them over me, breaking my heart again for the thousandth time. The pain of motherhood never ends! Before sitting down, he picks up a flier from the couch and hands it to me.

"Here," he says. "This came this morning. Why don't you go to the Concerned Neighbors Meeting? It's happening four houses up right now. I know how much you love vigilante justice."

I squint at the flier. I saw it earlier but didn't think much of it.

CONCERNED NEIGHBORS MEETING

Let's come together to keep our neighborhood safe!
Sunday 2pm at the home of Gerald and Marnie Baskins, 348 Palo Verde Drive. Refreshments will be served.

"I do love justice," I murmur.

"Well, better polish your pitchfork and head over there," Leo says. "It's 2:12."

I put my favorite hat back on and hurry out the door. The community needs me. At least someone does.

harriet

The Baskins appear to be good people. They have fresh sod on their front lawn, not that ugly gravel landscaping like the house next door, and I count five crucifixes in their living room alone. I take a seat in a folding chair near the back. Women in their Sunday best and sensible shoes. Clean-shaved men with crew cuts. The holy book whispers through me: *your people shall be my people*. I breathe a sigh of relief—it's an oasis of sanity in a neighborhood full of unbuttoned shirts and sideburns.

"... parked his vehicle in front of my driveway for *sixteen minutes*," a woman in a floral dress says, wringing her hands. "Next day, I saw him do the same thing in front of Marty's house. Idling his truck and walking the bottles from door to door rather than just driving them there."

"He's a milkman, Ida," an exasperated man says from beside her. "And it was a *porcelain poodle*. I don't think a milkman is breaking into houses, stealing knickknacks."

"Perhaps it was misplaced?" a voice asks.

The woman in the floral dress shakes her head. "There's a

prowler in the neighborhood, I just know it. I heard a sound out my window that same night my trinket went missing."

A few exasperated sighs tell me just how seriously this crowd is taking this poor woman.

"But the milkman works in the morning," someone says.

She shakes her head. "It's the perfect cover. He cases the houses, then, you know, he comes back in the middle of the night."

"She's been watching too much *Dragnet*," the man says.

Everyone laughs.

"I'm sure the milkman is up to no good, but it's not how you're thinking," he says with a wink to the other men in the room. He has a Yankee accent—Brooklyn, maybe.

To my horror, the room erupts in laughter again. That man is disgusting. I detest comedians, clowns with no makeup. That poor woman in the floral dress stares at her lap in shame.

I raise my hand and begin speaking. "If I may? I believe her. These streets are running rampant with hoodlums." Everyone's heads turn. I stand up, to make sure everyone can get a good look. "Hello, my name is Harriet Crawford. I'm Leo Crawford's mother."

Folks whisper to one another when I say this. They're probably gossiping about Rose, but to keep my cheeks from flushing, I imagine they're admiring my hat and wondering where I got it. I smile, allowing them a moment before continuing my speech.

"I was a door-to-door saleswoman for many years, and I have an eagle eye for shady characters. I'd be happy to be on the lookout for you."

"Thank you," the woman in the floral print dress says, smiling at me.

We share a look of understanding. I've seen her before,

across the street, watering her peonies. She had a Barry Gold-water sign on her lawn during the last election. She's good stock. I don't mind helping her, that's the kind of person I am. And anyway, I'm not afraid of thugs.

Why should I be? I carry a pistol in my purse.

a letter from the doctor

March 20, 1967

Dear Mr. Crawford,

Thank you for numerous messages inquiring about your wife's condition. I have enclosed an abbreviated report of her current status. We appreciate your patience as we help her get stabilized so she can receive visitors and will reach out via telephone soon.

Sincerely,
Dr. Wallace Monroe, MD

WOODWARD NEUROPSYCHIATRIC CENTER

Patient: Rose Crawford
Age: 39
Marital Status: Married
Date of Admission: March 13, 1967

Attending Physician: Dr. Wallace Monroe, MD

REASON FOR ADMISSION: Patient was admitted
following reports of severe emotional
distress and a paranoic complex, including
hallucinations.

DIAGNOSIS: Schizophrenic with paranoic
tendencies, psychosis.

TREATMENT TO DATE: Medication with partial
response. Given the persistence of symptoms, continued inpatient treatment is
strongly recommended.

NOTE: Patient arrived fixated on "demons"
and a "study" where she claims her brain
was "scrambled." The patient was hospitalized in the fall of 1964 with similar delusions. Discussion of the patient's
delusions is not recommended and may serve
to reinforce maladaptive beliefs.

leo

In June 1944, I was wounded in the Battle of the Philippine Sea as a Navy shipman aboard an aircraft carrier. I caught some shrapnel in the abdomen. The burn scar I have now is the size of a golf ball and superficial. It was hardly anything compared to the injuries I witnessed on that ship during the War, but they gave me the Purple Heart anyhow.

I always thought the body had the mercy to forget. We can remember painful things happened, but we can't feel them in the same way again. It's kept in some secret box somewhere inside. Our own pain can't hurt us.

But that secret box flew open last week.

I woke up in a half-empty bed in the dead-choked night, belly twisted, tears leaking. That burn in my abdomen remembered how to hurt. All I could think about was Rose somewhere behind locked doors in that private hospital. The times I told her to put on a happy face and dismissed her. My missteps, even if I don't understand them. That study she's fixated on was some harmless consumer research program for pregnant women, but it was through a research group

Century works with. Maybe if she'd never gone, this switch would have never been flipped.

Then again, the switch flipped with her going to Idyllwild three years ago for no reason at all. It flipped again the other night after the potluck. It flipped for her back in high school, too. If only I could make it make sense, but madness is random by nature. I'm haunted by the medical mumbo jumbo in the hospital's report that came in the post this week—words like *paranoic tendencies* and *psychosis*. Last night, I lay awake until the sun showed his smug mug in the window. Then I got up to start the day, spin the old carousel one more time again.

The throbbing in my belly is a steady drum through breakfast, Ma and Melinda bickering like a couple of pissy hens, Julie banging her spoon on the table for attention. It intensifies as I get in the station wagon and drive the few miles to Century, the clean roads and palm trees bleeding to car dealerships and industrial buildings. I pull into the parking lot, turn off the car, but sit a minute with my hands on the wheel.

Century! screams a glittery gold-painted sign on the flat, beige building that constitutes our office. It's a far cry from Madison Avenue. Stucco, surrounded by crooked cacti and chain link. A trailer out back generously referred to as *Century Studios*.

"Well, this isn't exactly Hollywood," Rose said the first time she saw it—the day she came and recorded the VitaSmile ad. Her disappointment screamed louder than her red lipstick as she stared at the building.

"And you're not exactly Grace Kelly," I told her jokingly.

The memory's interrupted by a loud clacking sound. I look up and see it's Victor outside, knocking on my window.

"Hey, old man. You forget where you are?" he chides.

I force myself to smile, grab my briefcase, and join him outside.

"Respect your elders," I tell him, even though there can't be more than five years separating us. "Barely caught a wink last night. Almost fell asleep at the wheel this morning."

"You've looked pretty spent this past week."

"Well, got my mother sleeping on my couch, teenage daughter with a temper, and another squirt still in diapers. Wait until it's your turn, young man."

"What about Rose?"

Victor's question whizzes through the air and wakes me up like a bullet.

"How do you mean?" I ask.

"You mentioned your mother sleeping on your couch and your daughters. What about Rose?" Victor's gaze is piercing, probing, like he knows something he shouldn't. The pain in my gut intensifies. Does everyone in the office know? I told my supervisor Del, creative director, and I asked for discretion—but discretion has never been this industry's strong suit.

"Rose is in the hospital," I tell him.

"Geez. Sorry to hear."

"She'll be out soon."

"Of course she will."

I can't tell if he's being smart or not. He offers me a piece of gum, but I shake my head.

"Is this like the last time?" Victor asks, leaning in. "With Rose. Woodward again?"

"What do you know—" I start to ask. But then I pause, and say, "Yes, exactly."

Because how could I forget? Victor handles every pharmaceutical and medical account we have—including Woodward itself. Including the study she dropped out of in 1964. Of course, after her confinement that year, he heard things. No wonder Rose didn't want to face Victor at that party. He thinks she's a lunatic, that's all he knows of her. Maybe he's right.

"Well, Woodward's at the forefront of research when it comes to women with paranoic tendencies. I'm sure they'll zap Rose back into shape," he says, his palm snapping my shoulder.

"You know, I meant to ask—I can't remember the name of the study Rose was in. You know where I'd find that?"

"Study? The one she—well, she didn't complete it, right?" Victor peeks at his watch, gold winking in the sunshine, and scuttles toward the entrance. "I have a meeting with the Berner Specs team at ten. You'd better start brainstorming how you're going to make bifocals sexy. Give it the ol' Leo spin!"

"Do you know how I could find out the name?" I call after him.

But he doesn't respond.

Inside the building, I mutter hello to everyone and no one. I hang up my hat on the hatrack, cross the carpet, through the sing-song trills of typewriters and conversation. I duck into my office. Get a glass of water, Alka Seltzer, *szzzz* in the glass. I gaze through the picture windows that peer into the office's heart, over the secretaries' bouffants and beehives, and into Victor's corner office on the other side. It's spacious. On one far wall inside, he has an enormous mural with Century's slogan painted like a rainbow: *We Sell Dreams.*

And as if my brain's got a one-minute delay, I think—*hold on.*

Paranoic tendencies. How did Victor know that exact phrase?

leo

Woodward Neuropsychiatry Center is unassuming, a gray concrete block of a building with a simple sign hanging above the front entrance that says INPATIENT. The robust iron fencing hugging the perimeter is overgrown with ivy and gives the place an air of privacy. I park in the visitor's lot and emerge from the car, unable to help the shiver the horrible quiet gives. The rolling green grass, soulless concrete, ghostly faces pressed to the barred windows—a cemetery for the living.

"We've got to get you right again, Rose," I murmur as I climb the front steps, manila folder in my hand.

I would have visited sooner, but her psychiatrist advised waiting for her to get stabilized. This is my first visit since Woodward admitted Rose over two weeks ago, but I've been here before. The memory hits like her last confinement was yesterday instead of over two years ago: the lemon antiseptic stink. The empty waiting room with its brick-red vinyl chairs and brown carpeting. Toothless jazz oozing from a radio, a woman behind the counter smoking a cigarette.

"Your name, patient's, doctor's," she says, pointing to the paperwork. "Sign here. When the doc's ready, I'll buzz you in."

I give her my autograph.

"You might want to take off your tie," she tells me. "Could be a hazard."

I touch my striped tie dangling around my neck in disbelief. "For what?"

"You don't want to know, sir." She stubs out her cigarette and puts her palm out, face up. "But I can keep it here behind the counter."

She's right. I don't want to know. I loosen the businessman's noose and hand it to her, then sit and await my fate. On the wall is a framed poster I recognize right away. Century designed it. It's a photograph of a man's hand holding a woman's hand, both of their wedding bands visible. *Woodward Neuropsychiatric Center,* it says. *You're In Good Hands.*

A buzzing noise scares the daylights out of me. The nurse says, across the waiting room, "Dr. Monroe's ready for you."

I get up, immediately trying to adjust the tie that's no longer there. Deep breath. The double doors click, as if she's unlocked them from behind her desk. I push them open and step through, into the buttery light of the hall, that endless river of linoleum. A man in a white coat waits at the end. He's so far away he looks tiny at first, growing larger as I approach him, until we stand face to face. He's short, with a pencil mustache and a clipped badge that says DOCTOR WALLACE MONROE.

"Mr. Crawford," he says. "Right this way."

I follow him down a corner, and another, dizzied by the labyrinthine nature of this place already. The flickering lights. The closed doors, all with doctors' names emblazoned, tombstones on hinges.

Last time, I was just picking her up and didn't have to step beyond the double doors that led into the hospital. I wasn't sure what it was like back here, but I didn't expect it to be so cavernous and chilly. The brochures I've worked on show well-lit rooms, comfy beds, and good-looking nurses. This looks more like a morgue.

"Where's Rose?" I ask.

"Patient rooms are upstairs. This is the administrative floor. Let's have a quick chat before your visit," Dr. Monroe says.

He leads me into his office. It's full of dust, books, and leather furniture. On the wall, a painted picture of a golden retriever offers the only surprise in the room.

"That's my pup, Misty," he says, sitting behind his desk. "If I believed in soul mates, she would be mine."

Is it possible to have a soul mate that can't talk back, I wonder. I take a seat across from him, placing the manila envelope on the table. "I brought a copy of the report you mailed—"

"No need. I have everything we need right here." He opens a folder in front of him. "Mr. Crawford, I'm not going to sugarcoat it. Rose has been a challenge."

"How so?"

"Hysterical symptoms. Screaming, crying. She bit a nurse."

"Oh, god." I try to imagine my wife's jaws around someone's forearm. "I thought her condition was supposed to improve when we brought her here."

"Two and a half years ago, she was here on a seventy-two-hour hold. That was different. I'm afraid this is much more serious."

My heartbeat's knocking with urgency. I tell it to stop. Whatever he says, whatever this is, it has a solution. There's always a way out. You can't drown in dry air.

"As you probably read in the report," he continues, "we're recommending extending her confinement. She's been resisting treatment, has persistent delusions, and is in no condition to be caring for children."

"What are her delusions now?"

"She has a persecution complex. She's convinced that demons implanted something in her brain and that they're trying to communicate with her through the television."

He must see the blood drain from my face, because his twitches with a moment of kindness. He folds his hands on the table.

"Mr. Crawford, there's nothing that you could have done. Your wife has schizophrenia. These things happen in the most stable of homes."

Schizophrenia. I pause and let the word echo. It sounds like a country where vampires live. Foreign and sinister, a place of exile. And so *final.* How do they decide these things? How do they look at a grown woman at her worst and decide who she is for the rest of her life? It makes no sense.

"But—why now?" I ask. "I've been married to Rose for eighteen years."

"Sometimes there's no reason for what triggers a psychotic episode."

"I feel like it started after that study she was booted from. You have records of that, right?"

"Mr. Crawford, you've got it backward." He makes a note on the paper. "She was removed from the study *because she had a psychotic break*. But she exhibited symptoms of schizophrenia before that. Many people have their first break with reality as a teenager. I see she was hospitalized at the age of sixteen."

"Well, yes."

"I see here in notes they say she is 'intellectually restless' and 'prefers reading over socializing.' She refuses to come to group sessions."

The way he describes her prickles in my ears. Because he's right, I've just never seen it as a problem. But line the colors up and they start to paint a picture. "She's a bit of a lone wolf."

"She has a flat affect. She withdraws. She's depressive. Is it true she's been seeing a psychoanalyst for years since her last confinement?"

"On and off."

It's the oddest sensation, as if I'm floating above my own body. As if I'm a fly on the wall of my own life.

"I'd like to connect with him, if you don't mind," the doctor suggests.

"Sure." It's a suckerpunch to realize I don't even remember the guy's name. I just signed the checks, grateful she had someone to talk to about her worries because I don't have the capacity for them. "I'll have to look him up at home and phone you with his contact information."

He nods and closes the file folder. "Frankly, I worry he might be part of the problem. Apparently, he agrees with her delusions. He's been encouraging her to explore this ... idea of demons controlling her through the television. Do you know about this?"

My mouth goes dry. "I don't know anything."

"Well, if there's any merit to what she says—which, who knows—you might have a malpractice suit on your hands." He pulls papers from his desk. "Quick signature to continue treatment until her condition stabilizes, and then we can go see her."

The print swims in front of my eyes. I see the words *consent for recommended treatment* and *continued confinement*. My pen hovers above the page.

"This is how your wife gets better," he says gently.

I sign my name. I don't know what else to do. Woodward has the best reputation out of anywhere around. They know far more about any of this than me.

We stand up and leave the room, entering the chilly hallway again and walking up a dark flight of stairs.

"Now, a few things before you see Rose," he says, huffing up the stairs. "First, don't be alarmed at her physical state. Poor hygiene is a symptom of schizophrenia. If she tries to discuss her delusions, simply don't acknowledge them. Change the subject. Avoid stimulating topics or anything emotionally charged. Please don't discuss her treatment. And we need to keep visits short for the time being to avoid overwhelming her."

He pats my back as we make it to the landing in front of a door that says STAFF ONLY. Distantly, I hear a panicked scream.

"Are you ready to see your wife?" he asks.

And even though the answer is no, I nod.

leo

There's something chronologically uncanny about the sight of Rose here in front of me on her bed. Like she's somehow an old lady or a little girl, but not the woman in between. She wears a hospital gown, hands folded on her lap, slippered feet dangling off the bed. Her hair is flat on one side and explosively curly on the other. Her lips are chapped, skin wan, and her eyes wild. She jumps up when she sees me and yells my name, her bony arms wrap around me, squeezing me. Her hair doesn't smell like her hair. She stinks of chlorine and sweat.

"Leo," she whispers. "Leo, take me out of here. Get me out of here, Leo."

"It's okay," I say into her temple. I savor her warmth, closing my eyes, feeling like I've rescued her from drowning at sea. I don't let her go for a long time. "We're going to figure it all out."

"It's been so awful," she says, crying into my shoulder. "I feel like I'm in prison. I'm being punished."

"Nobody's punishing you, baby, we want to help you."

"They've been trying to drug me. I swear, they want to kill

me. They want me to overdose. They're trying to make it look like an accident."

Behind her, I can see the doctor watching this whole thing in the doorway. He offers a single sad nod, then moves on to give us some semblance of privacy.

"And the doctors?" she says in a shaky voice in my ear. "They're demons. They're *demons*—"

"Rose," I say, pulling back and cupping her face between my hands. "Calm down."

"No, you don't understand," she whispers. "This is real. They want to fry my brain and shut me up. You have to take me home."

"You're in no condition to go home."

"You can't leave me here," she begs, squeezing my hands, brown eyes glistening. "You know I don't deserve this."

I pull her to sit next to me on the bed, at a loss. It's not even like my heart is breaking, it's worse. My heart is dead inside of me and my body's somehow still living and breathing without it.

"You're right," I tell her. "You don't deserve this. That's why we've got to just—roll along with the treatment plan. You've had a breakdown, that's all. So let's do what the doctors ask and then you can come home."

"They're trying to poison me with pharmaceuticals," she whispers. "But I spit the pills down the drain when they leave the room."

I sigh. Well, no wonder she's acting this way. She's not even taking the pills they're trying to give her to help her.

Should I tell her? Have they told her the diagnosis, or is it up to me?

"You have schizophrenia," I tell her, slowly, with emphasis. "You need medicine."

These words seem to confuse her so much she can't talk

for a second, her lips moving as if she's speaking silently to herself.

"Schizophrenia?" she says out loud. "No."

I nod.

"That's what they're saying?" she asks. "What about—what about the study? This started with the *study*."

"Can we please stop with all that?" I beg her, just wishing I could end this all, wishing I could walk out of my own life like a bad movie. "The more you keep saying that, the longer they're going to keep you. These are doctors, Rose. They know what they're doing."

"Anyone can put on a coat and call themselves a doctor."

I lace my fingers with hers. Her nail polish is chipped and her hands are shaking. "If you don't get with the program, Rose, they're going to keep you here longer and longer."

Her face falls. Her grip on my hand goes limp.

"The more you resist, the worse it'll get," I tell her. "Can't you see we're all on the same side?"

"No," she whispers, pulling her hand away like I'm suddenly a hot stove. "Not you too, Leo."

"Rose—"

"Get out of here," she says, pushing me with sudden violence. "Get out. I mean it."

Shocked, I stand up.

"You're not my husband," she shouts. "You're not the Leo I know. Get out."

It's the terrified look in her eyes that gets me—like I'm some creep who's cornered her in a dark alley. It's the same look in her eyes I saw that night at the cabin. That vacation from hell.

"What's going on here?" Dr. Monroe says, stepping in from the hall.

Rose has backed herself into a corner of the room and turns away from both of us.

"I think I should let her rest," I tell the doctor.

"I agree."

I wait for her to turn around, for her to say something—for just a glimpse of the woman I've loved for two decades. But she crouches there like a scared child.

Joining the doctor in the hall, I remind myself to breathe. My walk is the walk of a dead man. Distantly, someone is screaming. We walk silently down the stairwell, through the hallway, and to the double doors that lead back to civilization. The doctor says nothing but looks back at me with sorrow.

"I've never seen her like that," I tell him. "It's ... not easy."

"No. Of course not."

I blink, wiping my eyes before the tears can burn out of them. "She didn't even ask about the children."

"As I noted earlier, she's in no place to be caregiving."

"Right, I ... I don't know what I expected. Not that."

Now the burn in my eyes spreads past my nose, deep into my throat, and for a second, I can't speak. The doctor offers me a handkerchief, but I hold my hand up and shake my head. I exhale a long sigh. The burn fades.

"Be straight with me. Is she going to make it out of this okay?" I ask.

"If she follows treatment, we have one of the best recovery rates in the state."

"She's stubborn. I don't know what to do."

"You've got to do what you can to convince her. The more we can all work together on this, the better outcome we'll have."

"Well," I say, a little reluctantly. "She told me in there she's been spitting her medication in the sink. You know about that?"

He raises an eyebrow. "No, but thank you for telling me."

"Maybe if we could get her to actually take it, she'd improve."

"I agree." He shakes my hand. "See? The more we work together."

"Keep me updated?"

"Absolutely. And please forward me the name of her psychoanalyst so we can compare notes."

"Right. Will do."

I must look pretty pathetic, because he says, "You're a good husband." Then he claps my back and leaves.

As I head through the waiting room in a daze, the secretary waves and reminds me, "Sir! Your tie!"

"Right," I say, taking it from her.

The gorgeous sunset outside is wasted on me. I walk to my car, tie hanging from my hand like an empty leash.

leo

I come home to a scene even more chaotic than the one I just left at the asylum. Three females in various states of unrest, all accosting me the second I walk through the door.

"She's a juvenile delinquent!" my mother is yelling, pointing at Melinda with a spatula.

"She's an old fascist witch," Melinda says, her dirty feet propped up on the dinner table.

"I don't like a eat shepherd!" Julie says tearfully from her highchair.

"Enough," I shout, hanging up my hat and coat. "I just walked through the door." I sniff the air, noticing the smoke. "What's that smell?"

"Your daughter burned the shepherd's pie," my mother says, lip trembling. "I stepped out for *one hour*. All she had to do was take it out of the oven. Instead, she went on a joyride with her boyfriend. And she took the baby!"

"Uncle Jim!" Julie yells.

Within me, a war between exhaustion and rage ensues. I don't know which will win.

"Melinda," I say, shaking my head. "Are you kidding me?"

"I wish the whole house had burned down instead," Melinda answers, slapping the table. She leaps to her bare feet and bounds up the stairs with the energy of an orangutan. Then the door slams and the music starts.

"I can't live like this, Leo, I can't," Ma says, her hands over her face.

Julie imitates her, putting her tiny hands over her own face and doing an exaggerated whimper. The smear on her plate is an unsavory brown flecked with burned bits. *Honestly, I don't want to eat shepherd, either, kid.*

"All I do for these girls, day in and day out. I'm worn thin," my mother weeps. "I get no respect. No privacy. No peace and quiet."

"Tell you what," I say, wiping Julie's face with a napkin and picking her up out of her chair. "I'll take the girls out for burgers and bring you back something."

"Oh, my supper isn't good enough?"

"I am *trying* to give you the peace and quiet you just *asked* for," I say, my voice rising.

"You need to talk to her about the way she speaks to me, Leo." Ma wipes her eyes. "It's unacceptable. If I'd spoken to my elders that way, I would have gotten the belt."

The belt. That old foe. I shiver just remembering the sting of it. "Well, in this house, belts are for keeping your pants up." I give her a kiss on the silver fluff atop her head. "Enjoy the quiet house, will you?"

"I'll try," she says. "I'm going to go check in on poor Ida across the street. She thinks a prowler has been breaking into her house and stealing knickknacks. First, it was a ceramic poodle. Now she discovered she's missing a candlestick, too."

"Did she ask Colonel Mustard about it? I hear he was in the conservatory at the time."

She stares at me blankly. "I don't know anyone named Mustard."

"Enjoy yourself, Ma," I tell her, and head upstairs to retrieve my oldest and orneriest daughter.

"She stinks like vinegar and baby powder." Melinda pops a fry in her mouth, continuing her litany of complaints about my mother. "She puts notes all over everything. This morning I found one note taped to my Rolling Stones record that just said 'They are going to Hell' on it."

I can't help it. I start laughing.

"She's snooping around my things!" Melinda says.

"I know, it's just she used to do that on my old swing records." I pull the pepper away from Julie's reach. "It only made me like them more."

Melinda is unamused. "She tells me I'm ugly."

"When did she say that?" I ask through a mouth full of burger. "Come on."

"Just this morning. She said, 'Why do you insist on making yourself so ugly?'"

I chew and swallow and sprinkle another few fries on Julie's plate. "Break that sentence down. She's implying that ugly is a fashion choice, not that you're intrinsically ugly."

"Sometimes, Dad, I think your optimism is your downfall."

"Heh." I force a smile and look around the restaurant. Families. Couples. Three cops on dinner break. I'm the only single father in here and I feel the empty space where Rose would usually be sitting beside me, probably busting my chops in a way Melinda would appreciate. "Well, if you've got to have a downfall ..."

"You don't think I'm ugly, do you?"

"No." I sip my soda. "But I do think you need to stop seeing Jim already."

Melinda says nothing, dipping a fry in ketchup and drawing a heart on her plate.

"I'm serious. You know I don't think he's a bad guy, but he's not the right guy for you."

"Did your parents get to choose who you went steady with?"

Cripes. I shudder at the thought. Ma would have set me up with a nun.

"No, but if my mother had forbidden me from seeing someone, I would have accepted that she knows best."

"Does she?" Melinda asks this not in a provocative way— but with her brow knit, as if she's really trying to understand. "How do you know?"

"Melinda," I say, untucking the napkin from my neck and putting it on my plate. I'm suddenly stuffed. "It's time to give the guy some space. Concentrate on what matters."

Melinda doesn't answer. She's staring hard at something. I look at the end of the table to see what it is: Just a little menu card that says BEER ON DRAFT. Then her eyes meet mine, shiny and full of spirit and sadness. "He's supposed to go to Vietnam."

Even though I'm not the president of the Jim Carroll Fan Club, my stomach drops. "Oh, honey. I'm sorry."

"Are you?" she asks bitterly, tears brimming. "Or are you happy to finally have him and me half a world away from each other?"

"Lin-Lin, why you sad?" Julie asks from her highchair.

I give her a straw to play with and turn back to Melinda. "Mel, of course not. I don't wish Vietnam on anyone."

"Well, good." Melinda sits up straighter, wiping her

freckled face. She meets my eyes. "Because he burned his card."

I push my plate away. "Oh, for Pete's sake."

"He wants to run."

"Great. So he's a dodger now? Now I *really* don't want you seeing him."

I've always been able to see the wheels turning behind Melinda's face, but I've never been able to understand where they're going.

"I thought you said you don't wish it on anyone," she says.

"Doesn't make what he did right."

Melinda leans in, trying to read my face. "Well, what's he supposed to do?"

"Obey the law. Go sit in a prison cell and protest the draft if he wants. Don't run like a coward. Face your fate like a man."

"Follow orders, you mean."

"It's part of the Constitution. If you went to class these days, maybe you'd understand how it all works."

She rolls her eyes, and that really gets me. The disrespect. This child sitting here, acting as if she knows a thing about war. The faces of men whose names she'll never know flash through my mind—men who never got to see the peace they fought for. I can't stand how entitled this generation is.

"We didn't get to choose," I tell her.

She juts her chin. "Well, we do."

Something has come over me—a heat rising under my skin. All at once, I understand my mother's frustration. Melinda is a brick wall.

"Let's get one thing straight," I tell her. "If you want to live under my roof, you're going to stop seeing Jim. And that's that. I've let this go on long enough."

Her eyes glaze over. She picks up a spoon and stares at herself in its reflection. "If you say so, Dad."

I flag the server, gesturing for the check. "You know I saw your mom today," I tell Melinda, trying to lure her back to me. Trying to melt the ice. "She's doing much better. She should be home soon." The words ache in my throat. "She misses you."

"Does she?" Melinda asks, putting the spoon down.

"Mama," says Julie, looking at her hands.

"She does. She says she loves you both very much."

We sit, the fan whirling overhead and reflecting on the Formica tabletop. I stare at it like a patient, hypnotized, wondering when it was that I accidentally got so good at lying to the people I love.

leo

I'm brainstorming copy for Berner Specs when a knock at my office door startles me. I drop my pen on a piece of paper that's more like a battlefield of scribbles.

"Come in, come in, whoever you are," I say, swiveling on my chair to see who it is.

Laughter spills in as soon as the door opens. It's Victor, smiling like a bingo winner. He's standing with two of the partners, Russell and Hogarth. I can see they've been celebrating something by their pink cheeks and glassy eyes.

"King of the Spin!" says Russell by way of greeting.

"To what do I owe the pleasure?" I ask.

"We'll let you two talk," says Hogarth, clapping Victor on the back.

He and Russell continue walking, leaving Victor in the doorway. Victor steps in and closes the door behind him. I brace myself, because usually when account executives show up unannounced it's to deliver bad news: that a client decided last minute to ditch a campaign I've been working on, to shift directions, or that they dropped us entirely. Instead, he plops on my easy chair in the corner and props his loafers up on the coffee table.

"Busy?" he asks. "I can never tell with you creatives. Your work looks like people just staring into space half the time."

"That's because our work actually requires thinking," I tell him.

"Well, what do you think about this? We just had a meeting with Meridian Pharmaceuticals. Since VitaSmile just got recalled, they've been pivoting to a new direction."

"I'd have thought they'd be filing for bankruptcy."

"On the contrary. They're rebranding and launching a new line of sleep aids. They want to go with us again."

"Sleep aids. Do these ones contain morphine?"

"This is serious, Leo." Victor drops his usual grin. "No jokes like that."

The VitaSmile craze was boom and bust—the drug hit the happy housewife market in 1964. Rose tried the pill just once, after her commercial taped in 1963, and warned me it was poison.

"This stuff shouldn't be sold in supermarkets," she said after staying up all night. She was pale and shaking. "Mark my words. I can't believe I recorded that ad."

"It's one adverse reaction," I told her at the time.

Turns out, though, Rose was right. After too many happy housewives got hooked on the stuff, regulators pulled it from shelves last year. Meridian stopped advertising campaigns with Century and switched to damage control with some PR firm. But now, apparently, they're back.

"Sorry," I tell Victor, even though I'm not. "Okay. So they're pivoting."

"Because of the whole... *stimulant* fiasco with VitaSmile, they're shifting to supplements. Natural ingredients, *all* natural, a hundred percent safe."

I don't remind him that hemlock is also natural.

"And I want you to lead creative," he says.

This comment is tossed in so casually, it takes a second to grow wings and fly in my brain. I've never been asked to lead creative on a campaign before, and Meridian is big. After the humiliating company potluck, I figured my chances of scrabbling up the ladder were zero.

"Well ... that's great," I say as my shock subsides. "I'm honored."

"It's about time. You're the best writer this company has."

"I don't even know what to say. Thank you for giving me a shot."

"I vouched for you in there, you know. I told Russell and Hogarth you were the right man for the job."

"Why not Patrick?" I ask.

"Because Patrick's got enough on his plate, and besides, we want someone with a different perspective for this. We want a family man."

The word *family* reminds my stomach to ache again.

"Russell and Hogarth agree that we'll need to hire out for this," he continues. "You can work with Natalie on it. I'm thinking three, four freelancers."

"Sure," I say, sitting up straighter.

"Great. It's settled then." Victor gets up, dusts off his jacket sleeves. "Can I tell Meridian you'll meet with them next week?"

"Of course."

He crosses over to me and I stand up. We shake hands.

"I appreciate the opportunity," I tell him. "I've needed a shot of good news."

Victor smiles at me, but there's something sad in it. "How's Rose?"

"She's ..." An image of her, wide-eyed and hysterical in her hospital gown, flashes through my mind with an electric pain. "She's on the road to recovery."

"I'm sure they'll have her back to you in no time. How are the kids?"

"They're fine. My mother's staying with us."

"How wholesome." He flashes a grin. "She a nice old lady?"

"She's rude to everyone except me, her pastor, and door-to-door salesmen."

Confusion crosses Victor's face.

"She was a door-to-door saleswoman growing up. She sold ties. She forced me to go along with her and model them."

"You're a real character, you know that?"

He starts toward the door, but a question it still burning in me. "Hey, Victor, real quick. Can I ask you something?"

Victor cocks his head, hand on the doorknob.

"What was the name of the study that Rose was in? She's got this ... fixation with it. She even reached out to her old friend, who's a reporter."

Victor's eyebrows shoot up.

"I'm not—saying I agree with her," I tell him. "Just trying to understand."

"I can't remember off the top of my head," Victor says. "That was ages ago now."

"Is there a record somewhere?"

Victor's posture slackens. He sighs and turns, hands on hips. "Look, Leo, I'm going to be straight with you. This, right here—" He points between us. "This is worrying me. Think about optics."

His reaction is so strange, I feel like we're having two different conversations.

"It was a question," I say.

"We can't have you leading this campaign if you're also going around asking bizarre questions like this."

My throat tightens.

"It was a bit of a battle for me to get you across the finish line considering everything … you know … with Rose," Victor says. "This is a huge opportunity. I'd hate to see you get in your own way."

"I apologize." I clear my throat. "It won't happen again."

He considers this, chewing the inside of his cheek. "A reporter. From where?"

"Old friend of hers, a gossip columnist—it doesn't matter. It's all in her head."

Those last five words land with a delicacy that softens Victor's beady eyes. I can tell the man truly pities me. I'm fine with pity for others, but I hate how it looks on me.

"Keep it together, Leo," he says. "And congratulations."

He leaves. I sit down at my desk, eyeing the phone, wishing I could call Rose and tell her the news about leading the Meridian account. Wishing she were sane enough to care.

I ignore the sting.

I pick up my pen.

I go back to work.

leo

Without Rose snoring gently beside me, sleep is lonely. I spin my wheels in bed far past midnight and get up with the sun. Maybe it's me chasing the only peace I can in these golden, silent hours—the only time no one is yelling, crying, or begging me for something. This morning, I tiptoe into my study and start outlining some ideas for NightEase, Meridian's sleep formula.

Let mother nature lull you to sleep.

All natural. All night.

Slip into something more comfortable ...

It's all garbage. I cross them out. The clock on the wall says it's seven already. Ma is bumping around the kitchen on the other side of the wall, murmuring to herself while making breakfast. The phone rings and I pick it up.

"Crawford residence," I say.

"Mr. Crawford, I hope it's not too early," a male voice says. I can't place him. He sounds older, gentle, a little hoarse.

"Not at all," I tell him.

"This is Allan Wells," he says. "Rose's psychoanalyst."

"Oh, yes, hello." I push my work away. I can hear Julie crying and Ma going upstairs to get her. "What can I do for you?"

"Well, this week, Woodward Neuropsychiatric Center reached out to me for Rose's records."

"Right. I gave them your information. Is that a problem?"

"I do have ... concerns I wanted to discuss."

"Let's hear them."

The static silence goes on so long I think the call dropped. But then he clears his throat. "How much has Rose spoken to you about the Human Response Study?"

Ding-ding-ding. There it is, the name I was trying to get out of Victor. The study Rose dropped out of in 1964. I write it down on my legal pad in front of me.

"It's been hard for us to talk about, if I'm being honest," I say. "First off, her memories of it are hazy. She flipped out and she left early."

"Do you know why?"

"She didn't want to be restrained, she tried to bite a doctor, that's all I know." I swallow, forcing myself to go on. "When I picked her up, they had sedated her. She was confused. I try not to think about it, it was all so embarrassing."

"Right. You work at Century Advertising, and your company had something to do with the study—is that correct?"

"Not exactly. My company works with a third party for focus groups, things like that, and this was through them."

"The Pacific Institute of Human Research."

I tap my pen on the page, scribbling the name in a corner. "Could be. All those market research programs sound the same."

"What do you know about the Pacific Institute? Do you still work with them?"

It's like the tables have turned, here, and I'm the one getting interviewed. "I'm sorry, I'm just an ad copy guy. Really not my wheelhouse. Why does this matter?"

"Because after hearing Rose's concerning experiences in the program, I tried to track down the institute. I couldn't find any record of it."

"You do realize my wife is delusional? They say she's got schizophrenia."

"Is that what you think?"

Upstairs, Julie's crying. Someone's banging on a wall or a door. I put a finger over the ear that isn't covered by the phone and close my eyes so I can concentrate on this conversation. "That's what Woodward thinks."

"She was hospitalized at Woodward in 1964 after the Human Response Study, correct?"

"Yes. Months later, though. After her breakdown that summer, right around when the baby was born."

"And, out of curiosity, why did you bring her back to Woodward again this time?"

"I don't know." My forehead prickles. "Should I not have?"

"Between us, I don't always agree with Woodward's approach. They move fast and intensely to contain behavior, often at the expense of understanding it."

"I don't know what that means."

"I've seen a lot of patients go through their programs. They come out quieter. They don't necessarily come out *better*."

"Are you telling me I should move her out of Woodward, or ...?"

"Have you looked at other options?" he asks. "I could give you—"

"Leo!" my mother is wailing behind the door. "Leo!"

"Ma, I'm on the phone," I yell to her, then turn my attention back to the phone call. "I apologize, it's a zoo over here. What can I do for you?"

"Woodward is asking me to transfer all notes to them from Rose's file, including reels I've recorded of sessions, and full notes. Copies will not suffice. It's an unusual request and I'm not comfortable handing everything over without your consent."

"Is it that unusual a request?"

"Frankly, yes. Usually, a written summary or carbon copies would suffice. But it's up to you."

"Whatever you think," I say. "You're the expert."

"I'll hold onto them, then. And Mr. Crawford—"

"Leo!" Ma says, bursting into the room in her bathrobe, hair still in curlers. "It's an emergency. It's Melinda."

"I am so sorry," I tell the doctor. "Can I call you back? I'm getting interrupted left and right."

"That was all I needed for now," Dr. Wells says. "Tell Rose I say hello and I wish her a quick recovery."

"Thanks, Dr. Wells."

I hang up. I can't be certain if it's rage at being interrupted, or panic at the thought of something happening to Melinda, but I'm suddenly short of breath.

"What?" I ask. "*What?* Can I have a moment, just one single moment to deal with one crisis at a goddamn time?"

My mother balks, touching her face as if I slapped her.

"Sorry," I mutter instantly.

She doesn't respond, her lip quivering, her blue eyes watering.

"Ma, I'm *sorry*. Just spit it out. You interrupted my phone call. What?"

"Melinda is gone."

melinda

I'm lost and I've never been happier.

My bloodshot eyes blink at the scene. Jim and I spent the whole night hitching our way here, a starry whirlwind snoring in the backseat of bumpy cars, and it still feels like I'm dreaming as I survey Haight Street for the first time. It's not even lunchtime, but the scene is buzzing. Girls in granny dresses carry baskets of flowers, boys in turtlenecks distribute manifestos, and newfound friends panhandle on street-corners. The sky is silvery and foggy. Even the smell is different, incense mixed with cigarette smoke, and the soundtrack is nothing I've heard before: jangling tambourines, laughter overlapping, and guitar riffs drifting from open windows. Except for the cops walking around in beetle helmets, fingers curled around billy clubs, everyone is free and smiling.

San Francisco. The name sings—a promise, not a place. I have arrived.

"What do you think, Lindy?" Jim asks.

"Far out," I murmur.

"Hey, you know where the stew's at?" a guy in a beret and

Mexican poncho asks. He's leaning against the wall of a record shop. Like Jim, he's got a guitar slung over one shoulder and a backpack over the other. He can't be much older than Jim.

"Diggers are supposed to be servin' somewhere," the guy in the beret says.

Jim and I don't answer because neither of us understand what he's talking about.

"We just got here, man," Jim says. "I don't know a thing."

"Hey, I just got here last night myself," the guy says with a nod. "Rode a Greyhound for five days, all the way from Charlotte. Name's Boone, what's yours?"

"Jim, and this is my girl, Melinda."

"Y'all got a crash pad? I know a place."

Jim looks the guy over—his grin with one tooth chipped in front, wild brown eyes, his hairline that's already receding despite his youthful face.

"Uh ... I don't think so," Jim says. "We're trying to find my sister."

"Where's she at?"

"Some place on Waller? I don't know, exactly."

An unkempt bearded man appears from thin air, joining our conversation. "The hour of reckoning is upon us. The oppression will come to an end." Then he moves on, swept up in the sidewalk traffic.

A shirtless guy yells from the back of a pickup truck driving by: "Free food at four!"

Boone grins at me and Jim. "Four? My belly's grumblin and it ain't even noon." There's a goofy, lopsided look about him that endears him to me. He pushes off the wall and beckons us to head up the sidewalk with him. "Let's go smoke a joint. I'll show you around."

For someone who arrived last night, Boone knows a lot:

the cafes that stay open latest, which direction Golden Gate Park is, and the locations of the public restrooms. He says "hello, sweet angel" to the girl in the knit hat selling incense from a stand on the corner. He calls out "got some good shots?" to the guy in Buddy Holly glasses photographing the scene. He points out a narrow house and claims it's where the Grateful Dead live. And then he turns a corner and shows us Waller Street, which runs parallel to Haight one block up.

"So your sis is up here somewhere, huh?" Boone says. "You know the address?"

Jim scratches his head, squinting up and down at the endless rows of unfamiliar houses. "I haven't talked to her in weeks."

Boone sparks up a joint and passes it to Jim. "I'm sure we'll find her if we ask around."

We sit on a stoop, getting high, and Jim and Boone talk about the draft. Apparently, Boone's a dodger, too. *A peaceful anarchist* is how he describes himself. As the boys talk, I become invisible and marvel at the trees. I should be in school right now. I should be sitting in my English class, listening to that old witch of a teacher drone on about some dusty book no one cares about. I pity my sorry classmates: sardined in their desks, rows of paper dolls with no idea that there's this whole magical world out here.

Even worse, I remember my mom stuck in a hospital room somewhere, and my knees weaken. But I can't dwell on it. I came here to forget all that.

This is my life. *Mine.* No one else's.

"What do you think, Lindy?" Jim is asking me.

I snap to attention. The two boys are laughing now, arms slung around each other's backs.

"About what?" I ask.

"She's so cute when she's stoned," Jim tells Boone.

"Ain't we all," Boone says, and they burst out laughing again.

"Pancakes. She invited us." Jim nods his head to a barefoot girl in pigtails who waves at us from the porch of the stairs we've been sitting on. "Free breakfast."

"She just ... invited us?" I ask, confused. "Do you know her?"

"Everyone's a friend here, little girl," Boone tells me.

He must be right, because we head into a stranger's house for pancakes. We're escorted to a long table in the dining room, which is nothing like my dining room at home. First off, the table has sawed-off legs and we sit on beanbags instead of chairs. There's a mural of a naked woman in a field of flowers on the wall. It feels like a hundred people live here, so many people drift around. The woman feeds us pancakes and tells us about how Jimi Hendrix crashed here once.

"He passed out right over there," she says, pointing to a mattress on the living room floor.

"These are the fluffiest pancakes I've ever had," I tell her.

I'm not kidding. I'm practically eating clouds.

"You want the recipe?" she asks.

"Sure," I say, opening my knapsack.

I take out the pen and notebook, both stolen from the kitchen drawer back at home. Mom keeps extra school supplies there. It's supposed to be brand new, so I'm shocked when I see her neat handwriting on the first page.

January 1

Ho hum, another New Year with another hopeful heap of New Year's resolutions. Weight Watchers and journaling. Will it last longer than my exercise vow last year, when I did calisthenics thrice before calling it quits? Only time will tell...

I turn to the front cover. *1964,* in tiny handwriting. I hadn't noticed that before; I grabbed it last night without thinking, assuming it was empty. But this is an old journal of my mom's. It feels like some strange, divine sign I can't interpret, that her voice has found me here.

"Ready?" the hippie woman is asking. "One cup of flour, one cup of milk—"

"Wait," I say, flipping past Mom's entries—only a few in the beginning, the rest of it blank. I swallow a lump and smooth a fresh page. "Okay, go ahead."

melinda

Four dreamy hours later, the fog has evaporated and the sun is smiling on us. After pancakes, the three of us have wandered the neighborhood, and I'm so high I'm a loose balloon. We started asking around about Jan but then forgot our mission and got swept up in the beautiful fever. We stopped to listen to a busker named Portland Dave and then Jim and Boone ended up jamming with him for a few songs. We gaped at cosmic blown glass in head shop windows and gazed at the mod-clad mannequins in boutiques. Then we joined in some chanting in a street corner protest.

"Hey, hey, LBJ, how many kids did you kill today?"

"Stop the war machine!"

And when the cops shark by in their cruisers, we scream, "No more fascist pigs!"

The crowd positively hums. There's kissing, grinning, fists raised. I get this stir inside me I haven't felt since Jim and I watched the Sunset riots, like the world is tipping, it's at the edge of something, and I'm not just a witness. I'm in the writhing, beating heart of it.

"Jim," I whisper in his ear, over the sounds of honking and chanting. "I want to live here."

"Boone says right now, around the corner!" he yells back.

I scrunch my brow. I don't think he heard me. "What?"

"Let's check it out!" Jim says, arm around me, leading me away from the throng to follow.

Boone dances up the sidewalk in front of us. No matter how much dope he smokes, he has an endless fountain of energy. It's mesmerizing. He leads us through a side street for a couple blocks, whistling, the far-off drone of electric guitar mounting louder, louder, until we hit a long, narrow strip of park.

There's a band set up on the grass, the long-haired drummer banging a beat as two barefoot men strum guitars. Couples twirl. Girls dance with scarves. We find a shady spot and sit, cross-legged, joining the audience. The music is fresh and new—skull-buzzing, psychedelic, screaming. I imagine Dad's voice barking, *You call this music?* and laugh. Then Mom comes to mind, saying, *Jim's family is bad news* and suddenly it seems backward and upside down and sad, just downright *sad* that she of all people said that and now she's—

I sit up straighter, hand to my chest, the thought of my mother a knife.

"You okay, Lindy?" Jim murmurs in my ear.

"Yeah. My heart's beating fast."

"We're out of weed. Boone was saying there's a guy right around the corner selling lids for ten bucks. You mind if we go real quick?"

Boone is swaying his arms in the air, lost in the music.

"But we just got here," I say. "Don't you want to watch the band?"

"You wanna stay?" Jim kisses me with a half-smile. "We'll be right back."

I hesitate for a split second.

"It's a skip and a hop away, Boone said."

For the first time since we met him this morning, I gaze up at Boone's crooked goofy grin and wonder how long he's going to tag along with us. But I shouldn't think that. He's been nothing but generous, showing us around, introducing us to every new friend he meets.

I smile. "Okay."

Jim and Boone disappear up the street together back the way we came, practically skipping. I use my backpack as a pillow, lie back, and watch the gnarled oaks while the music is a river that drifts me away.

When I startle awake, the sky has brightened to a deep orange. Sunset is nearing. The band isn't playing anymore. The crowd has dispersed. I wipe my eyes and ground myself in my surroundings again—the park, the Victorians across the street.

I don't even know what this park is, what street I'm on.

I don't know what time it is or how long Jim and Boone have been gone.

I stand up and scan the scene for Jim or Boone, but they're nowhere in sight. I'm not panicking though, because Jim does this kind of thing. He loses track of time. And the Haight isn't that long—we've wandered it back and forth all day long and some faces have started to become familiar. It seems like the kind of place where you can't really get lost.

So as night settles in, I wander it again, alone this time, stopping to ask people if they've seen a guy with a maroon fringed jacket carrying a guitar. I smoke a joint with a random girl in front of a record shop, who also hitched here from LA after dropping out of Hollywood High. When I ask her name, she says, "I used to be Judy, but I go by Caterpillar now."

That joint is so strong I sit in front of a closed deli and

relax. Which is probably the best way to find Jim anyway. Like Mom always told me, *when you're lost, staying put where you are is the best way to be found.* So I watch the night parade go by for a while. The neon signs light up outside of bars, the streetlamps flicker, shopfronts go dark. Police sirens *womp-womp* and live music bleeds out of a club. There's a wicked smile about it all, people walking faster, clutching their coats, laughing louder. Across the street, the girl from LA I met waves at me. She's unfurling a sleeping bag.

I frown for maybe the first time today.

"What time is it?" I ask someone walking by.

"Half past nine," they answer.

This is a sobering slap. *Nine* o'clock? It's been hours.

Where the hell is Jim?

The air gets colder. The fog is back, veiling the street scene, and I wonder, with a gulp, if I'm going to have to spend the night here on the stoop of a deli. Knocking against the side of the building, about ten feet away, there's a plastic bucket hanging on a string. People walking by peer at it and drop coins with a *ping*. It's such a weird sight, I get up and investigate the bucket hanging there next to the deli window. It has a piece of paper taped to the top like a little sign that says KEEP THE FREAKS FED! My eyes follow the string up to the open window of the upstairs apartment, where three giggling young women hold it like they're fishing.

"Atta boy!" one of them shouts when someone throws a nickel in.

"Keep it coming!" booms another.

Another one whoops like she's at a football game. There's something oddly familiar about the sound of it, something that tickles my memory. I raise my hand to block the light and get a better view of them. Immediately, I recognize the matted, wild blond hair and seashell necklaces.

I smile, doubts scuttling away. "Jan?" I shout up to the window.

"Who is that?" she asks, squinting down at me in the darkness. Then she gasps. "You're kidding me. Is that Little Lindy Crawford I see?"

"Yeah," I say.

She screams excitedly, then disappears from sight. Twenty seconds later, she bursts out of a door downstairs and comes running to hug me, nearly knocking me down. She smells strongly of body odor and patchouli and squeals in my ear.

"Unreal!" she says, pulling back to look at me. "Can you believe this?"

"Have you seen Jim?" I ask.

She blinks, her eyes a deep blue with lashes so blond they're nearly invisible. "What do you mean?"

"He and I came up here together. We were trying to find you. But then there was this show in the park, and he left and didn't come back."

"Nah, I haven't seen him, but you know how Jim is. He'll turn up!" She tousles my hair. "How cool is this, man? I just moved in! Come on, come upstairs. You need a place to sleep?"

She leads me through the door next to the deli and I follow her up a dark, carpeted staircase that smells like cigarette smoke. There are four apartments at the top of the stairs. She pulls door number two, smoke spilling out of it as soon as it opens.

"Hey gals, look! You'll never believe it, but this is Lindy. She's my little brother's girlfriend. She needs a place to crash. And Lindy, these are my roomies, Deb and Sue."

Within an hour, they've fed me a peanut butter and banana sandwich, let me shower, and spun me their favorite records. They tell me they usually make enough money *fund-*

fishing, as they call it, to pay for food and fun, and make rent by selling handmade jewelry on Haight. Their apartment is covered in tapestries, strung with fairy lights, beaded curtains instead of doors. I can't keep my eyes from flicking to the clock every now and then, calculating how long it's been since I saw Jim. I keep drifting to the open window to scan the street for a flash of him, but the later it gets, the quieter it gets out there, too.

"I love how you've decorated," I yawn, sitting on the floral couch in the living room.

"All found furniture!" Jan says, drinking wine from the bottle as she goes through her record collection. "You see the Free Store?"

I shake my head.

"It's exactly what it sounds like. A store where you don't need money. You just, like, walk in, and you see something you want ... and it's free."

I wrinkle my brow. "How's that possible?"

"Because we donate to it, too. It's a cycle, man. This isn't your mom and pop's world anymore. We're building some-thing new out here. For kids like you and me, it's everything, you know?"

"Like you and me?" I ask, flattered that she thinks we're the same. Jan, a senior when I was a freshman. Jan, Jim's rebellious older sister, always untouchable. The fact she thinks we're in the same category warms me.

"Yeah. We make our *own* families."

Jan's eyes are bright despite how many times she hit the bong tonight. Her words almost make me tear up. Like she can see how much I've been hurting and pretending to not hurt. Like she can see how much I needed this, how far away my blood family has become.

I can feel the ghost of the girl I was yesterday leaching

from my bones—a girl who would have been scared to not know where Jim is, stranded in San Francisco.

But I'm not that girl anymore. I'm not a kid living under my parents' roof. Jim's not my daddy.

The gals set me up with a pillow and blanket on the couch, say "night night!" and head into their rooms. I lie here with the window open, watching the shadows skitter across the ceiling, reflections from passing cars. I beam a thought to Jim: *Wherever you are, I'm your lighthouse. Come find me.*

I remind myself that he always has. He disappears often, but never for long.

When doubt knocks again, that secret ticking clock, I reach deep into my backpack until my fingers meet the cool kiss of porcelain. I pull out a trinket I brought with me from Canoga Park: a little porcelain poodle. I lie back on the couch and admire it in the moonlight. One night a few weeks ago, Jim and I snuck out together. He swiped a few knickknacks out of someone's open living room window and gave them to me. The others I left behind, but this one I took with me.

The figurine reminds me of him, and of home, all at once.

harriet

I sip my hot lemon water at the kitchen table, peering down at the pamphlet our neighbor Ida put in our mailbox this morning. How thoughtful of her to think of me when she was at the police station. I convinced her it was worth filing a report about the petty thief who stole her knickknacks, even if it happened weeks ago. Let the police earn their salaries.

Ida pinned a note to the pamphlet that says, *Some ideas for today's Concerned Neighbors meeting.* CRIME PREVENTION AND YOU, the pamphlet says in block letters. I inhale sharply at the advice inside: Lock your doors! Fasten your windows tight! Keep valuables in the trunk! What a state we're living in, where we have to worry about crooks invading our homes.

"Protect us," I whisper, staring at the ceiling.

At that moment, the phone rings. The Lord is listening! I get up to answer the call.

"Crawford residence, Mrs. Harriet Crawford speaking," I say into the receiver.

The sound bleeding through the earpiece is jarring, loud

with honking and unintelligible noise. To call from such an environment is irritating and reeks of bad manners. Whoever it is doesn't say a word.

"Who *is* this?" I demand. "Speak now or forever hold your peace."

"Grandma, it's me," Melinda says.

I gasp and put a hand to my chest. "Melinda Grace Crawford," I scold. "Where on earth *are* you?"

"Is Dad home?"

"You will answer my question this instant."

"I need to speak to Dad."

Her voice is clipped, snotty and rude. She didn't get that from my side of the family—I was raised to respect my elders.

"Well, I'm not putting him on until you tell me where you are and what you're doing. You do realize that he's been out looking for you all week, sick to death?"

"I left two days ago, how could he have been looking for me 'all week?'"

"He's out *right now* talking to your school principal—"

"So he's not home," she says flatly.

"Where *are* you?"

"I'm fine. Just tell him I'm fine and I'll call him back soon."

"I absolutely will *not* tell him that, I—"

A click sounds in my ear. It might as well be a bullet in my brain. I can hardly breathe. The nerve! To hang up on me like that. I slam the phone on the receiver.

"Take me, Lord!" I whisper to the ceiling.

Right then, Julie begins crying upstairs, roused from her nap. I could weep, too. Will I ever get a moment's rest? With a deep breath, thinking of Job and how much we have in common, I head toward the stairs. But I stop in the doorway of Leo's room, glaring at the bedside table set up like a shrine for Rose. A water glass still sits there as if she'll be back to drink from it soon. Then there's that trashy *Valley of the Dolls* book.

With a fit of rage, I reach for the book and tear a page out of it.

Then I tear more pages, roaring like an animal. I rip them to pieces, and the pieces to pieces, wishing I could rid the world of such filth. The pieces fall to the floor, cream-colored confetti.

All at once I realize what I've done. I stand still, recovering my breath, and return the disgusting book to the table. I stoop down and pick the pieces up and put them in my apron pocket.

Then I head upstairs to the screaming baby.

harriet

Leo has been quiet as a sinner in Sunday school since Melinda ran away nearly a week ago. At breakfast this morning, I'm tempted to snap my fingers in front of his eyeballs. He's dressed for work. The paper sits next to him unopened. The headline reads: NATION DIVIDED AS WAR ESCA-LATES. I serve him breakfast, grapefruit sprinkled with saccharin. Do I get a thank you? A smile? No. He stares at it as if he's never seen fruit in his life.

"Where's my bacon and eggs?" he asks.

"You're going on a diet," I tell him. "We can't have you dropping dead of a heart attack. Your girls need you."

He tucks the napkin into his collar. "Well, one of them does."

"I do hope the police pick Melinda up in that detestable city, Leo." I sit at the table. "A night behind bars might cure her of this nonsense."

Leo sighs.

"What *are* you going to do about her?" I ask as I spoon-feed Cream of Wheat to Julie.

"What can I do? At least she called to tell me she's safe and has a place to stay."

"It's probably a flophouse." I wipe Julie's mouth with a napkin.

"Flophouse!" she says with excitement.

"No, now don't go around repeating that," I scold. I turn to Leo. "Melinda should spend the remainder of her senior year in a boarding school."

"Ma, even if I had any control over her whereabouts—do I look like I can afford that? I can barely afford private school, let alone boarding school. My bank account is bleeding trying to keep up with Woodward's bills right now. And they're the most affordable place around."

"Maybe if your wife hadn't gone off on her hysterical holiday—"

He bangs his fist on the table. "Don't you dare say that. You don't know what it's like in there."

Agape, I press my hand to my chest. Leo never yells at me like that.

"I'm—I'm sorry, Leo," I say. "You're right. I don't. I never had the time and space for a nervous breakdown. I raised you on my own, with no help from anyone—"

Leo scoots his chair up. "I'm heading to the office."

After he leaves, there's a stink of dissatisfaction in the air. I pray at the altar I set up next to the television, but Julie keeps squawking and yanking my apron strings. Lord, I have no space of my own, no time to myself. I've begun to miss my own apartment, lonesome as it was. This house is haunted by Rose.

I take the baby for a walk in her buggy, looping around the block twice before returning home and parking the baby buggy out front again.

"Stay here," I tell her. "I'm going round back through the kitchen door."

I walk through the side yard to the back gate. Leo refuses to give me a key—he still won't forgive me for the time I made a copy of his apartment key without telling him. And with a possible prowler in the neighborhood, I'm not about to leave the front door unlocked. So I'm forced to come and go through the back door like a shameful mistress. Honor thy mother indeed!

I cross the backyard overgrown with dandelions and crabgrass and turn up the back porch stairs.

That's when I see a man there with the door open, as if he's about to step inside. He turns to me, and my knees threaten to give.

"Heavens to Betsy!" I yell.

"I'm so sorry, ma'am," he says, closing the door. "I'm—I was—"

"I know who you are," I exclaim, backing down and holding onto the railing. "You're a prowler. And be warned, I am armed and will be calling the police."

"No, you've got it wrong," he says, stepping out of the doorway.

He's smartly dressed—crisp ironed pants, shined shoes. Not exactly like the shadowy, masked cartoon thugs in the crime prevention pamphlet, but sinners are a motley crew.

"I'm looking for Leo Crawford," he says, his hands up.

I narrow my eyes at him. "My foot you are. Leo's friends don't come snooping around our back door."

"I'm not a friend, I ..." He stands up straighter. "Ma'am, I'm so sorry to scare you like this. I'm just a salesman. From Valley Builders. We spoke about replacing doors and windows a few weeks back. I stopped by to take measurements, give him a proper estimate."

I study him, my heartbeat steadying. I'm not afraid of this man, no matter who he is—I'm the one with a pistol in my purse. He does look well bred. He's quite handsome, actually. Tan and strong, straight-teethed. Lucid eyes. His suit jacket looks expensive. I can't imagine this man pilfering candlesticks and porcelain poodles.

"A salesman, you said?" I repeat. "From Valley Builders?" I know the store; I've passed it on the freeway and seen its many billboards.

"That's right, ma'am." He closes the door he had opened. "Again, I'm so sorry. I'll be on my way. I can come back another time, when your husband is home."

"Leo's not my husband," I say with a laugh. "He's my son."

"You don't say." His eyes widen. "Gee, you look so young."

I haven't felt a blush like this come on in years. Mistaking me for a woman half my age! Imagine. This man is either near-sighted or Rose's cold cream I've been borrowing must be doing wonders. Or he's just buttering me up—and I'll gladly take the compliment.

"Well, I *am* the woman of the house now." I'm unable to help a small smile. "Would you like to come inside and have a glass of lemonade? I'd be happy to take a message for Leo."

The man smiles. "Thank you so much, ma'am. Don't mind if I do."

harriet

I show the man to the kitchen and pour him a glass of lemonade. My recipe is extra tart—slimming and stimulating. He compliments it right away.

"Why, this is delicious." His eyes twinkle with approval. "Really puts a bullet in your gullet."

I laugh at his phrasing. "You know, I used to be a saleswoman myself. I sold ties and scarves and stockings, door to door."

His eyebrows raise. "Really?"

"During the Depression. I was widowed, raising Leo on my own. It was how I made ends meet."

"Now I know why you're so charming," he says wryly.

"Stop," I say, batting a hand.

But it's true. I was charming. And beautiful, and strong, and young—and hungry. I know the need you walk around with in this job, the sharp eye for opportunity. And I recognize it in this young man.

"These windows—where'd you all get them from?" He

points to the window over the sink with its paisley curtains. "They come with the house when it was built?"

"You would have to ask my son."

"How many bedrooms, again?"

"Three."

"Mind showing me around so I can get a tally?"

I swallow as he puts the empty glass on the counter. I'm a trusting woman, but I'm not a fool. I've lived on my own long enough to be vigilant about my safety. He must see the doubt flicker on my face, because he puts his hands together and bows.

"I'm sorry." He nods. "I'll come back another time when the man of the house is back. Thank you for the refreshments."

He begins to turn, but I stop him. "Go on ahead. You can check the windows. He's hardly home these days—"

Both of us stop talking at once, hushed by the muffled sounds of screaming.

"Oh my word, it's my granddaughter," I say, gasping and running for the front door. "I forgot about her."

I open the front door and there she is, red-faced and wailing in the seat of her buggy, shaking the sides like a baby earthquake. I rush over and pick her up.

"Let's not be dramatic, now, we've got company," I tell her. "Shhh. Manners." I kiss her cheek as she sniffles and calms down. "You think Grandma would forget about you? Never, ever, ever."

Raising children is crisis after crisis. I recover my breath and come back inside.

"Sorry about that," I tell the salesman.

But he's not in the living room behind me. I peek into the kitchen—he's not there, either. My heart sinks like a failed soufflé. He snuck out the back without a proper goodbye. I had so been enjoying our chat and he skedaddled as soon as he had a chance, buttering me up for nothing but a glass of lemonade.

I put Julie on the floor, letting her run to the altar. She's a pious child, transfixed by the holy cross and the tissue-thin Bible pages. Despite the hardship, I've been a much-needed good influence on this family.

When I turn, I'm shocked to spot the salesman now standing in Leo's bedroom in front of the window, near the vanity table.

"My goodness, I thought you'd left!" I exclaim, stepping into their doorway.

"You told me to take a look around, so I started my tally. Hope you don't mind?"

"Not at all."

It's odd to see this stranger next to Rose's vanity. He takes a notepad out of his front pocket, along with a tiny pencil, and takes notes.

"This your table?" he asks, touching the drawer's knob. "The pearl color is gorgeous."

"That belongs to Leo's wife, Rose."

"Ah. I see."

"She's away right now." I swallow. "In a *psychiatric* hospital."

"Oh my. Nerves?"

"Yes. Shall I show you the other rooms?"

"Please."

He follows me out, stopping near Rose's bedside table and touching the torn-up copy of *Valley of the Dolls*.

"Dog ate her bedtime reading?" he jokes.

I offer a pursed smile.

"If you don't mind me asking ... how is Rose doing?" he

asks as we step back out into the living room. "I ask because the same thing happened recently to someone I know."

"She's simply acting out. I'm sure she'll be home soon."

"Right." He offers a bright smile. "Next bedroom?"

I show him Julie's room, and Melinda's, although I warn him that it's an unholy mess in there.

"She ran away from home," I say somberly, letting him into the squalor she calls a bedroom. I *tsk-tsk*, ashamed he has to see this. "Probably strung out on drugs."

He steps over piles of clothing and records to view the window, making a note in his pad. "Kids these days."

"Don't I know it."

We head downstairs. I let him go first, admiring his haircut, so straight it looks like his barber uses a ruler.

"Your doors seem solid," he says, knocking on the doorway of Leo's room and peeking in again.

"Yes."

"The windows—have you considered double-paned?"

"No, but I can speak with Leo about it."

Julie must have rifled through my suitcase again, because she toddles out with one of my brassieres.

"You naughty girl!" I gasp, grabbing it from her.

The salesman hides a laugh with his hand.

"I'm mortified," I tell him, hiding the brassiere under the blanket on the couch. "I am so sorry."

"It's fine, Mrs. Crawford." He grins. "I won't tell anyone."

I let out a laugh, too, even though it's entirely inappropriate. The flames that scalded my cheeks just now cool down. His blue eyes linger on mine, deeply, in a way a man hasn't looked at me in a long time. My heart beats like a hummingbird.

"It's been a hard few weeks," I say without thinking, my

throat raw. I force a smile, but it doesn't stick. "Anyhow, I'll let Leo know you came by."

"And ... no chance of talking with Rose anytime soon?"

"Rose?" I ask, confused.

"Well, she was who I initially spoke with."

"Oh." I raise my eyebrows. "You know Rose?"

"I met her. We discussed new windows." He leans in. "To be honest, she seemed a little ..." He taps his temple twice.

"She's desperate for attention," I say, imagining Rose performing a one-woman show for this man in her living room. "She should have been an actress instead of a mother."

"She talked about the *strangest* things."

"She's always been off, I'm sorry to say," I say, quietly, so Julie won't hear.

"Off how?"

I shouldn't tell this man, but I can't help it. Leo never lets me speak freely about Rose, and no one else will listen. "She can't keep a house; her cooking is inedible; she daydreams; she's melancholic and sarcastic; she doesn't like bridge, and reads tawdry novels, and stays up hours into the evening writing nonsense."

"What kind of nonsense?"

"I've only glanced at it, and it reeked of sin. Stream of consciousness gibberish that wouldn't even make sense to Kerouac himself."

Julie tugs on my skirt. "Lunch!"

"Just a minute, angel." I swallow. I've flapped my mouth. Gossip is one of my worst traits—one I thought I'd given up long ago. "I've said too much. Forgive me."

"Mrs. Crawford, you're the most refreshingly honest person I've met in a long time." He puts out his hand. "Thank you for your hospitality today. I'll be back soon with an estimate for your husband. We have quite a few options we could go with."

"Wonderful," I say, reaching out and shaking his hand. The warmth of it is electric. I can't help but imagine how it would feel if he lay it upon my cheek.

Forgive me for such thoughts, Lord.

I see him out the front door, waving and watching him walk up the sidewalk. He passes Ida, who's walking her poodle toward me.

"Well, who was that?" she asks, stopping in our driveway.

"Just a friend," I say, unable to help my smile.

I didn't mean to say it, but he felt that way—polite as a priest, warm as a biscuit.

"I thought it was Errol Flynn," she jokes.

Back inside the house, Julie entertains herself by taking everything out of the refrigerator, and I don't have the energy to stop her. Hands on hips, I survey the house, trying to envision it through the salesman's eyes. Did we seem pitiful to him? Did he think we lack taste? I grimace, remembering the way he saw Rose's battered copy of that horrid drugstore novel.

I step inside her bedroom and move to the place where he was standing when he examined the window. A few perfume bottles have been knocked on their side, but I doubt that was him. I slide open the drawer, frowning at Rose's ledger. As if she ever balanced a checkbook in her life. She's probably writing love letters to that Dale man. I pull it out and open it. I start reading. And I freeze.

This isn't a ledger.

This is the diary of a stark-raving madwoman.

excerpt from rose's ledger

3:17 a.m. Another Dream Box dream. Couldn't move legs, arms. Paralyzed. Clicking sounds, endless faint tapping, mechanical rain. The sweet sound of children singing. Dolls' faces flickering. So many of them. Multiplying. Like a kaleidoscope. Then they melted into demons. I tried to scream. Something stopped me. Something stuck between my teeth. The taste of copper. Then everything hurt and went white.

leo

I walk through the front door repeating a line that struck me soon as I turned onto Winnetka. A clean line that fits Night Ease perfectly. Can't let myself forget it.

"*We'll take care of the rest, we'll take care of the rest.*" I pass Ma and Julie at the table, both eyeing me like I've lost it.

"Leo, it's been *quite* a day over here—"

"Shhh, I'll forget it, don't push it out of my mind." The words loop through my head as I rush into my study and pen it down as fast as I can. Then I catch my breath. Inspiration, you sneaky bastard. Always hitting me in the shower or in traffic—never when I'm conveniently at my desk.

I head back out to the kitchen, pausing in the bedroom doorway. I loosen my tie, swallowing hard as I glance at our bed. My side is always unmade these days, and Rose's is always made. Her ghost is clean. I shed my suit jacket and toss it on top. Then I duck out of the room and into the kitchen, rolling up my sleeves.

Julie shoots her arms up in the air. "Daddy!"

"Come here, honeydew." I pick her up and kiss her on the

cheek. She squeals. I spin her around and make her giggle—
the bubbly, infectious way only toddlers do.

"Leo, you're going to whirl-a-twirl her right into
Pukesville," Ma scolds.

"Pukesville, huh?" I stop. "Now I know where my poetic
skills came from."

She smiles. The sight of it is almost unfamiliar. She's a
miser when it comes to displays of joy.

"Want a plate?" my mother asks, tying her apron on.
"Casserole's still warm."

"Sure." I sit. Julie crawls onto my lap. "What are you so
happy about, Ma?"

"Well, this *gentleman* came over today," my mother says as
she lumps food on my plate. "This lovely salesman from
Valley Builders. It was a pleasant surprise."

"You and salesmen. It's like other women with fire-
fighters."

"He said he was there to take measurements for new
windows?"

"New windows? Not exactly on the top of my mind these
days."

"I hear the double-paned ones are very nice."

Double the pane, double the pleasure, my mind instinctively
whispers, as if I'm writing a catchphrase for them.

"Well, the gentleman said he'd be back to speak with you,"
she goes on.

"I don't want to speak with him."

"Rose already set the plan in motion. I thought you knew?"

The word *Rose* is an arrow to my chest.

"I think we can postpone Rose's plans for now," I say,
putting Julie on the floor.

"Daddy, up!" Julie cries.

"Daddy tired. Daddy hungry. Go play with your lawnmower."

Her favorite toy: a plastic lawnmower she pushes around the carpet saying *vroom vroom*. Wonder if she'll grow up to be a high school dropout who runs away from home, too. Melinda was cute as a button. Now I've got an APB out on her with the SFPD.

"Speaking of Rose," Ma says as she serves my plate. "I made a *shocking* discovery." She retrieves something from the kitchen counter and brings it to the table. "This so-called 'ledger.' Have you seen this?"

"Where did you get that?" I'd like to snatch it away from her. "I've told you time and time again—"

"The good Lord gave me eyes and I'm going to use them. Leo, this is no ledger."

I point to the word LEDGER in gold on the front. "Title begs to differ."

"Rose is one disturbed creature." Ma eyes the ledger as if she'd like to douse it in holy water. "It's full of incoherent ramblings."

"It's her little book of nightmares." My chest tightens when I realize what I'm looking at. "That's what she called it. She had nightmares sometimes and her psychotherapist told her to write them down."

"Have you read them?" Ma demands.

"No, and I don't care to. There's nothing less interesting than other people's dreams."

"She has a disturbed mind."

I shake my head, seething. The bounce I had walking through the front door has turned to dead weight again.

"You're in denial about her." Ma opens the ledger, licks a finger, and turns a page. "*The Dream Box has eyes and ears. It's music and whispers and screaming and out of tune pianos. Time and space cease to exist, my body made of bricks—"*

"Enough. Put it back where you found it."

"Don't you—"

"I said *enough*," I snap. "Stay out of my marriage."

If only it was the first time I've said those last five words. I doubt it will be the last. Ma slinks out of the room.

I shake my head and eat the tepid noodle confusion in silence. The room seems to stare back at me: the color TV gathering dust, the silver in the cabinet no one uses, the forgettable furniture. For a second, it's unfamiliar, like I'm a guest. I don't live here.

This home, without Rose, is just a house.

leo

The bosses are wooing a toilet paper company in Commerce, the secretaries are at lunch celebrating a birthday, and the rest of Creative left early. It's not usual to be left alone at Century. The stillness screams. My door is wide open, and the ticking of the sunburst clock in reception is deafening.

My gaze keeps flicking to Victor's office, also wide open. Usually he locks it. Usually the door's shut because he's on the phone. Then my gaze flicks back to my notepad, where the words *Pacific Institute of Human Research* stare back at me. A random note I jotted when I spoke with Rose's psychoanalyst. I looked them up after writing it down, but the company isn't listed in the phone book. But you know where they would be listed?

Victor's files. They're Victor's clients, after all.

He wouldn't be too keen on me going through his paperwork without asking, but what Victor doesn't know can't irk him. I tuck my pen behind my ear and walk quickly into his office. My heart is pounding like a jackhammer as I open the drawer. The files are organized alphabetically by company name. *Flick, flick, flick.* There it is: The Pacific Institute of Human Research. I pull it out.

It's empty.

I wrinkle my brow and open another drawer. Pull out the folder for Woodward. It's a fat file, years of campaigns dating back to 1962, which was right around when Victor started. I remember because he started the year before I did. There's nothing interesting in there—just paperwork about ad spends, blueprints for creative, payment records. *Flick, flick.* It's how most of the files are, as far as I can tell.

There's only one empty folder in the cabinet, and it's The Pacific Institute of Human Research.

Empty folders don't exist here. We only make files when there's something to put in them.

An invisible spider crawls up my neck.

I jump at the sound of the front doors opening. Footsteps. As quietly as possible, I slide the file cabinet shut and turn around to sneak back to my office—but to my horror, Victor nearly runs into me as I'm leaving his doorway.

"What the hell are you doing in here?" he asks.

The look on his face says he'd like to punch my lights out. I might deserve it. I scramble to think of a reason, any reason, why I would be in here.

"Just looking for a pen," I say.

Victor steps in closer and his hand moves to the side of my face. I flinch as if he's going to hit me. Instead, he pulls the pen from behind my ear.

"You're going senile, old man," he says with a smile.

"Jeez, I guess I am." I eke out a laugh. "Sorry. Guess I've been working too much."

Back in my office, I shut the door. I pace. I steady my breath. That invisible spider creeps across my scalp. The empty file now makes me more curious than ever about The

Pacific Institute of Human Research—but I can't ask Victor now. It would make him suspect me of snooping around his office, and I'm skating on razor-thin ice as it is. I've got to ask someone else about it.

The light bulb in my head blinks on. I stop in my tracks. Of course. Why didn't I think of him before?

leo

Traffic throbs like a migraine, stop and start. I roll down a window. The toxic perfume of diesel makes me roll it back up again.

"...US casualties rising in the new offensive," drones the radio. *"Meanwhile, Johnson defended the war, saying—"*

I flip the station.

"Dr. King criticized the Vietnam War in his new address—"

Flip it again.

"Civil rights protests—"

Finally, a dumb song. The Turtles' "So Happy Together." Numbing as a salve—which I sorely need as I pass the exit for Woodward. I hold my breath like a superstitious child. It's been over two weeks since I visited her. My eyes sting, and I tell myself it's the smog.

I make it to Hollywood, land of the flashy hillside sign and endless broken dreams. The last place I want to be on a Friday night is crawling Sunset Boulevard. Every time I see some straggler with a backpack and their thumb jammed out on the side of the road, the thought of Melinda makes my belly ache. I keep comforting myself with the thought that she'll be eighteen in four months, she's practically an adult anyway, but it doesn't do much. I park on a side street and hurry past longhairs and hustlers until I get to The Starline Room, Dale's home away from home.

There he sits: royal blue turtleneck, plaid pants, thin mustache, and curly hair slicked back. Besides the gray at his temples, he could pass for twenty-five.

"I was about to give up on you," he says, lighting a cigarette as he sits at the bar. "I'm on my second martini already."

"Traffic."

"The nerve of those people to come home all at once."

I sit and flag the bartender—the saddest-looking man in a bow tie you've ever seen—and order a beer. This whole place reeks of despair. The woman in a crooked wig and fake fur crying into a pay phone about her agent, a pissed-off greaser glaring into his whiskey glass, the neon sign above the bar that says LIQUOR with the middle two letters dark. Even the beer is flat.

"How is she?" Dale asks.

"I'm waiting to see her again."

"Waiting for what?"

I swallow another uninspired gulp of beer. "It was awful in there."

"I'll bet it was."

"She was hiding her medication, completely out of her mind. I'm waiting for her to improve, because my being there only seemed to make her worse."

"When's she coming home?"

"They don't think she's nearly well enough for that discussion yet." There's a tickle in my throat. I clear it until it subsides. "Excuse me."

Dale is a cheerful, smarmy guy, ever the joker, but right now, he's got the gravest expression. And there's something haunting about it—when even the clown can't fake a smile.

I light a cigarette and Dale nudges the ashtray closer. "I remember you were telling me about the study, how Rose wanted you to look into it."

"So you've finally come around." He eats his martini olive. "Maybe there's hope for you yet."

"Here's the thing, Dale. I'm not a fan of conspiracies."

"Of course not. Uncle Sam's never done us wrong, right? JFK was offed by Lee Harvey Oswald and Lyndon Johnson has our boys' best interests in mind," he says bitterly.

"This is why I didn't want to talk to you, see? Why does everything have to become a political discussion?"

"Then what do you want to know?" Dale asks, sounding annoyed with me.

"About The Pacific Institute for Human Research."

"Never heard of it."

"It was connected to the study Rose was in."

Dale stubs out his cigarette and trades it for a pen in his pocket, along with a palm-sized notepad. He scribbles the name down.

"I looked it up in the phone book," I go on. "Wasn't listed."

"I don't know, but I can dig." He taps his pen on the counter. "Harold Lumer is the name Rose gave me. Rose remembers hearing it. He led the study."

"Harold Lumer," I repeat, memorizing the sound of it.

"Director of psychiatry at Pacific Crest University in West LA. Formerly at Oklahoma City, Cornell, et cetera. He has ties to so many organizations it's *dizzying*."

"How do you know Rose was ... remembering correctly?"

"How do you know she wasn't?" Dale taps his glass at the

bartender. "Another please. Thank you, love." He turns to me. "Anyhow, what do you want to bet Lumer's connected to this —" He rereads his pad. "Pacific Institute?"

"I'm not a gambler."

"You're truly no fun at all."

"So I've been told." I glance at my watch. Ma's probably waiting at home to serve me tepid hamburger casserole. "Century—my agency—we worked with the Pacific Institute. But when I went to look for the file today, it was gone."

"It probably grew legs and walked off on its own, didn't it?" Dale shakes his head at me. "Like my mother used to say: *time to put on your listenin' ears and crank 'em up.*"

leo

The next morning I'm walking across the Woodward parking lot, birds *cheep-cheep*ing in the trees, when a spell of vertigo comes out of nowhere and nearly knocks me to the asphalt. It's been there since this morning, when Dr. Monroe called to tell me they'd like me to check in on Rose and discuss her treatment—a nauseating tipping that almost reminds me of seasickness. I sit on the steps, catching my breath. It's quite a bomb to be this afraid of seeing your own wife. I get up again and walk toward the building. The grounds are so peaceful. So serene.

So inhuman.

The questions knot my gut, whispering frantically. *Is she better? Worse? Cooperating? Will she be released?* And of course, the doozy—does she still fancy she's married to a demon? I step inside, my shoes clicking across the waiting room floor. I sign my name on the clipboard.

"Here you go," I say, handing the receptionist my tie. I'm learning.

I plop in a chair, lounge music oozing from invisible

speakers. Wipe my brow with a handkerchief. It's not long before the doors open and Dr. Monroe appears. I stand and meet him, shaking his hand.

"Mr. Crawford."

"How is she?"

"Improved."

He leads the way down the hall. I can't believe my ears—his words were delivered with such surgical precision I feel no relief.

"She's better?" I verify.

"She's been enjoying her rest. No more fits. We're quite pleased."

I take the deepest breath I've had in weeks. "So she can come home?"

He stops in front of her room, the same room as last time. "Let's not jump the gun. Her condition is quite serious, but her improvement is encouraging." He walks into Rose's room, seemingly surprised to find a nurse there changing soiled bedsheets. The room stinks of ammonia. My stomach turns. "Where's Rose?"

"She's in the Recreation Room," the nurse says.

"Ah. Yes." Dr. Monroe smiles at me encouragingly. "She's been spending a lot of time out there—also a good sign."

The hallway stretches forward, a tunnel threatening to tip at any moment. I walk beside him. All this talk of improvement, but why was that nurse changing her bedding?

"Is she taking her medication?" I ask.

"Indeed. It's made a remarkable difference. Around this corner over here." He gestures to the right as we reach the end of the hallway, but my attention is pulled by the sound of screaming behind closed steel doors to the left.

"Don't put me in there!" a wretched voice yells, scraped raw as if she's been at it for hours. The pitch of it goes beyond

desperation—it's a howling, primal wound in stereo. *"Don't touch me! Don't take my baby away! Don't put me in there! Don't! Not the Dream Box! They took my baby!"*

The Dream Box. For one terrible, eternal second, I am sure that it's Rose wailing in there. But then Dr. Monroe snaps his fingers to get my attention, already heading the other way, to the right. "She's this way, Mr. Crawford."

"Doctor, wait a minute," I say.

We stop in the middle of the hallway, lined with plaques, awards, and other accolades of Woodward's esteemed history. All gold frames and symmetry.

"That woman was ... she was yelling."

"There's a lot of yelling around here." He smiles politely, but not happily. "One gets used to it."

"What is the Dream Box?"

Dr. Monroe adjusts his glasses, peering at me with the curiosity of a scientist studying a microbe on a slide. "Come again?"

"That woman was screaming about it. Just now. The Dream Box."

His eyes fall to the floor, and he works his way from my shoes up to my receding hairline. Maybe he's fitting me with an imaginary straitjacket. "If you start entertaining these patients' delusions, you're halfway to sharing them."

He shows me to the Recreation Room. He glances at his wristwatch. "I'll let you two visit, and then we'll discuss her treatment in about, say, ten minutes?"

My head's whirling. It's all too much. "Sure."

He opens the door for me, and I step into the Recreation Room, which might be the most audacious spin I've heard in all my life. He shuts the door behind me and locks it. There's no recreation happening in here. Nearly every patient is in a wheelchair. There are tables with puzzles, but no one is looking at them. No music, just the quiet murmuring of voices as the patients talk to themselves. No television, just a woman dancing alone in a corner. There's a desolate ping pong table, no paddles in sight.

And there, in a wheelchair by the window, is the shell of my beautiful wife.

leo

"Rosie." I sink into a chair near her, scooting it closer, reaching for her hands. She wears a crooked slash of red lipstick. Her hair appears to have been brushed. But it's her posture that disturbs me—shoulders hunched forward, slumped. She tilts her head and takes me in with dark, drowsy eyes.

"Leo," she says with a smile.

"I've missed you so much." I kiss her cheek. "They say you're doing better."

"Mmm."

"That's great." I squeeze her hand, waiting for her to elaborate, but her eyes flutter closed instead. "Hey. My little thorn. I drove all the way out from the Valley, don't sleep on my visit."

"Sorry," she says, opening her eyes again. "I'm gooey."

"You sure are. What do they have you on?"

She contemplates the bars on the window deeply. From here, from our angle, you can't see anything but clouds.

Behind her, a nurse breaks up an argument between an old woman and her imaginary friend. Someone else is weeping and chain-smoking. A girl who can't be much older than Melinda is singing a Bob Dylan song with an invisible guitar. And all at once, I know, the same way I knew she belonged with me the second I saw her: My wife does not belong here.

"I don't like seeing you like this." I tap her jaw lightly to keep her here with me. "They said you were better."

"I am better." But the words ooze out like molasses.

I scrounge for something to say, something that will keep her tethered here and not floating away like a balloon full of Thorazine. "Melinda ran away from home."

"Sure, you bet."

"Your daughter," I clarify, sharper. "Your teenage daughter. She's in San Francisco, chasing Jim."

"Okay."

"Jim," I say, even louder. "The bad news kid from down the block."

"I remember."

But she doesn't. Because the Rose I know—the Rose I've loved since she was in roller skates—she would have a conniption if she knew her daughter had done such a thing. My chest tightens.

"I saw Dale," I say, louder, as if I'm talking to a senior citizen.

That doesn't do the trick, either. So I pull her wheelchair closer, and even though I don't like it, I grab her arm. Hard. I want her to wake up. I want her to yell at me, or cry, or *something*. I didn't think anything could be worse than her hysterics last time I was here, but I was wrong.

"What happened to you, Rose?" I whisper urgently. "I'm sorry I didn't listen before. I was—I wasn't ready to, but I'm ready now." My voice shakes. "What's the Dream Box? Even if it's crazy, even if it's not true, I want to hear about it." Tears escape, and I wipe them as fast as I can—but I guess the looney bin is an apt place to lose my marbles. "Whatever you need to tell me. I want to know."

I look down. My grip is so tight around her arm, it's left a red mark. Shocked, I pull my hand away.

"I'm sorry," I say, but what's sorry anyway? Five lousy letters and a puff of air. So I just sit with her hand in mine, letting her fall asleep.

Dr. Monroe returns a few minutes later with a cheerful smile, escorting me from the room and down the hall. He's intercepted by a nurse with an urgent question, and they side-step for a conversation. I'm left staring at the wall of Woodward's many accomplishments, stunned and reliving that awful, one-sided conversation I just had with my own wife.

My eyes fall on a gold plaque on the wall and spot something that freezes me. Under BOARD OF DIRECTORS, a familiar name: Harold Lumer.

"You're kidding me," I whisper.

It's a small world—but not *that* small. What in hell is going on?

"Mr. Crawford, so sorry. We had a situation that needed input. Let's go to my office."

Dr. Monroe leads me down the hall. I'm still wrapping my head around Lumer's name up there in gold. And I get this itch, deep down, almost like when I was in the Navy and the General Quarters Alarm would sound, scrambling everyone to action in a matter of seconds.

"She did seem improved," I say. "I think she's ready to come home."

"Oh, she's far from that," he says gravely. "Her condition is quite severe."

"Maybe another facility." I'm desperate suddenly to get her out of here, to try something else. "Closer to home."

Dr. Monroe stops in front of his office door. He turns to me and heaves a great sigh.

"Mr. Crawford, I know how it feels seeing her like this. But she's calm, rested, and healing. And moving her now—changing any course of her treatment—could backfire tremendously and leave her much worse off than she currently is." He pats my back a little too hard. "We wouldn't want that, would we?"

I shake my head, unable to find the words for a response.

"There's a reason we discourage visits before a patient makes their recovery. It's difficult to witness. But give us two weeks before making a drastic decision. We've just started her course of electroconvulsive therapy, which takes time."

"What is that?"

"ECT is a humane and routine treatment involving tiny electrical currents. It has an incredible response rate. We use it with over forty percent of our cases."

I swallow. I've vaguely heard of it, but know nothing about it. "I'm not sure—"

"You already signed the paperwork, Mr. Crawford. Last time you were here, you gave us permission to continue with our recommended course of treatment. This is it."

"I didn't realize—"

"Let me tell you a story. Just last week a woman left our hospital early after refusing our prescribed course of treatment. You know what happened?" He raises his eyebrows. "The following week, she hanged herself in her laundry room. It's a shame, because it was entirely preventable."

"Jesus," I can't help but say, imagining the gruesome sight of a housewife hanging from a homemade noose.

He smiles. "You're a good husband. I know you'll do

what's right for her." He steps into his office. "We'll be moving forward with two weeks of electroconvulsive therapy, and after that, she *may* be ready for release ..."

And with a sick and prickly knowing, I don't just feel that invisible spider crawling along my skin—I feel the first threads of its web.

excerpt from rose's 1964 composition book

March 6

See? Already, my second entry, and I've dropped the ball. It's just so busy every day with the kids, and you'll never guess what: I'm expecting again. What a shock. I'm nearing forty! I'll be elderly by the time this poor thing graduates from high school.

The baby blues are bad. Sometimes I remember back to the days in my Hollywood apartment and life seemed wide and open. Now I sew buttons, iron slacks, make meat loaf, vacuum ... and grow big as a hippo. I'm both busy and bored. But if I bring it up to Leo, he takes it personally.

I yearn for a world of my own. I considered going to school, but that was before I found out I was expecting. That VitaSmile ad made me realize I wasn't built for the commercial business, either. Repeating the same thing into a microphone in a fake-happy voice—just shoot me!

I jokingly asked Leo the other day if there are jobs for ice cream taste testers, because boy, I'd make a great one. Apparently, there are third-party research firms that run such tests and he asked around at work for me. Alas, no ice cream taste tester positions available, but there is a scientific study on dream and memory through a university-affiliated group they're working with. I thought, why not?

So here I am, packing my suitcase for a weekend away at a lab building in Culver City. I don't know what to expect. The study is top secret, which makes it exciting. I hope it distracts me from the blues. Regardless, it gives me an excuse to just be on my own for a weekend, which I will savor.

March 10

Where to begin? I'm in hell.

The study started off fine, in an office: interview and paper-work, snack and a drink with diazepam to put me to sleep. Then I was escorted to a room where I was tucked into a hospital bed. But once I went to sleep, it was as if I was still awake. Everything became nightmarish. Then my memory goes black. I vaguely remember getting out of my hospital bed and fighting off demons. The next thing I knew I woke up in my bed at home and Leo was telling me I had a psychotic break.

It's like a night of heavy drinking. I've blacked a lot of it out. I remember fragments—a rainbow TV screen, palm trees screaming the word UGLY. A woman mopping a floor, her face melting. Am I making these things up? It makes no sense. I no longer know what is real and I haven't left my bed since.

melinda

Every time I open the composition book, I'm halted again by the sad sight of my mom's neat handwriting. And yet I can't bear to rip them out: just three pages, three short entries. When I have something to write down—which I do constantly, because so very much is happening around me now—I skip past Mom's ink with an ache. I've penned dozens of pages of my own now.

I've lived a decade in ten days.

Lazy mornings making jewelry with Deb, Sue, and Jan, laughing over jars of instant coffee. Long, dreamy afternoons peddling bracelets on the sidewalks or riding cable cars through Chinatown, stalking steep hills to catch the sunset over the Bay. Late nights cruising Haight for impromptu rock shows, house parties, and adventures. So many joints smoked, friendships made, stories spun.

A *decade*, and no sign of Jim.

I bumped into Boone yesterday in the park. He was shirtless and blowing bubbles while the band's warbling guitar riffs droned on. I hadn't seen him since he disappeared with Jim the weekend before, and I nearly tripped over my own two feet sprinting to him.

"Lindy," he said, hugging me. He smelled like cigars and feet and was drenched in sweat. I wrinkled my nose, not loving the way Jim's special nickname for me sounded on Boone's lips. Then he drew back and blew a big bubble in my face.

"What happened?" I asked as it popped, a soapy kiss on my cheek.

"What happened?" he said, sidestepping back and forth, that crooked grin spreading. "Exactly. *What happened?*"

I studied him: erratic energy, black hole pupils, gnawing jaw. He was far more jittery than when I'd seen him the week before. I'd had an education about drugs from the Freaky Fam (Jan, Deb, and Sue's nickname for their crew I'd been adopted into). What he was on, I couldn't say, but I could tell he was on something.

"Where's Jim?" I asked, a cloud blowing over me.

The question didn't change his expression.

"Jim?" I reminded him. "My boyfriend with the maroon jacket—"

"Oh, he ran into some crazy chicks. Hippie types, real cute, short 'n sweet. They were in a bus and he hopped in. They were going to head to Berkeley and go in on a pound of grass."

I couldn't say I was surprised.

"Where's Berkeley?" I asked.

"Across a bridge or somethin'. Hey, you got a crash pad? I know a place."

I blinked at the surrounding crowd. There were familiar faces. This pocket of San Francisco was like I'd gone to summer camp and made instant friends, but it broke my heart to think that Jim wasn't a part of it—that maybe he ditched me for some "crazy chicks" in Berkeley.

"You're cute, you know that?" Boone said, slithering an arm around my back and pulling me into him.

I shoved him away. "I'm with Jim."

He was still dancing, as if he couldn't stop. He almost reminded me of a kid who needed to use the toilet. Mom used to call it the Bathroom Jitterbug.

"How can you be with him if he's not here?" he asked.

He offered me some bennies, but I declined and we parted ways. His beady stare bore a hole in my back as I headed back to the apartment.

At the kitchen table, over a shared tub of ice cream, I talk it all over with Jan. I ask her sisterly advice. It's not like my heart is broken—simply confused. It's my *compass* that is broken.

"You think Jim would just leave me like that?"

"You know him." She hands me the spoon. "We used to call him Tumbleweed when he was a kid—you never knew where he'd end up. But he always came home in the end."

"What if he doesn't love me anymore?"

"His love never bends, Lindy. I know my brother. Even if he hooks up with someone else, I know he'll always come back to you."

I nearly drop the spoon. "You think he's hooking up with someone else?"

"I don't know what my brother's doing." She pulls the spoon from my fingers and digs back into the rocky road. "But maybe love should be free, you know?"

I've never thought of love that way—as having any cost at all.

I sit with the worm of that discomfort in my belly awhile, letting it squirm. Writhing a little at the thought of Jim's lips on someone else's, or his hands discovering another girl's skin. But then I let him go. Let him tumble and ride the wind. Why not? I don't want to lock him up in a suburban cage like our parents: factory-farmed marriage, babies, rinse and repeat. I love him, and my own freedom, that much.

I wake up the next morning feeling just the same: Joyful. Grateful. Fine on my own. I stretch in the early morning light and reach for my notebook, wanting to jot down my revelations. Then the phone rings, and I can hardly believe the voice that answers when I chirp hello.

"Lindy?" Jim says in disbelief, his voice staticky and far away. "That you?"

melinda

"How did you—" Jim starts to say.

"Where are you—" I start to say.

Then we both laugh. I sink down into the couch, heart pounding like the first time he called me, a lifetime ago, back on the other planet called High School. I can hardly catch my breath. I close my eyes and narrow the world to two things, just two things: his voice and mine.

"What a relief, Lindy, I've been worried about you. I'm up in Oregon, if you can believe it."

"*Oregon?*"

"I came through the Haight again before I left, trying to find you, or Jan—I couldn't."

"You just wandered off," I say, playing with the phone cord's tight spiral.

"I know, I got swept up."

"Boone said you got in a bus with some crazy chicks to buy a pound of grass."

"Remember those girls that were there when I burned my draft card? On Sunset? Remember them?"

"Yeah ..."

"I ran into 'em. What a world, right? We ended up crashing out in Berkeley for a night, then they said there was this bitchin' commune up in Oregon, so I figured, why not, you know?"

I'm why not, I don't say. But jealousy is nothing but an ugly reflex. I let my chest burn for a second, then move on.

"You planning on coming back down here or what?" I ask.

"Yeah, of course. What's my sister's address?"

I tell him. He says he's writing it down on a napkin. He's calling me from a diner outside of Eugene. Then we lean into the conversation, let it stretch its wings. I update him about Jan, and he asks about my family. I tell him about how I've fallen for the Haight, I've learned to do macrame, and I saw my own face on an SFPD flier for runaways—a real trip.

"Speaking of trips ..."

Jim proceeds to tell me about the wild nights he's had tripping on mushrooms and LSD at "The Farm" since he got to Oregon.

"It sounds freaky out there," I say.

"These people are so far out, man," he laughs. "One guy I talked to saw UFOs over Joshua Tree. He swears up and down. Another guy was in the Army, honorable discharge, and he says he was used in experiments where they popped him full of pills and gave him acid, and he's with this chick Maude who says she can read minds when she's high—"

The line beeps. His pay phone's running out.

"Shoot. I only brought a buck," he says.

My disappointment aches. "That *does* sound far out. Don't fall off the deep end."

"I won't, Lindy, it's just wild. Wish you were here."

"I feel the same." I swallow. "Is this really goodbye?"

"I'll hitch down there soon as I can."

The relief swallows the hurt. I can hear in his voice that his heart still belongs to me. "We're still good, right?"

"Lindy," he says, almost scoldingly. "We're *solid gold*."

melinda

It's been a week since that call, and Jim's silence lives on.

"Don't be so glum," Jan says as she braids my hair.

"I'm not glum at all."

"Tell that to your pouting mouth," Deb says. She's painting Sue's portrait in the corner of the living room.

"I just feel restless," I tell them. "I wish he'd either be here or not be here."

"He loves me, he loves me not," chides Deb.

"How about we get some buttons?" Sue asks.

At first, I think she's talking about the kind you sew on a jacket.

"She's a *kid*," Jan says protectively.

Then I realize what she's really talking about.

"No, I'm not," I say, offended. "I'll be eighteen in August."

"What?" Sue says. "She can smoke a joint, she can handle acid."

Jan braids tighter, faster, then heaves a sigh. "And if you freak out, what then, Lindy?"

"Then you can call my dad."

They all laugh.

"What?" I say. "I mean it. They can cart me to the looney bin. I'll share a padded room with my mother."

They laugh again, because they don't know anything about my mother. They think it's a joke. And all at once, the thought of her aches like a phantom wound. I've betrayed her by kidding around. But we get up, dressed, and hit the street in search of buttons before I can fall down the black hole of worrying about my mom.

On the street, we hit up the Free Store for a soup pot, the smoke shop for some papers, and then knock on the door of a guy named Benedict who wears a bathrobe everywhere he goes. After buying the buttons, we head toward home. A block away from the apartment, at the intersection waiting for the light to change, I spot Boone. He's pushing an empty shopping cart and ranting to no one as if he's lost his mind.

"They're taking over our consciousness through the radio waves!" he screams in a blown-out voice, as if he's been at it for hours.

"Poor guy," Jan says softly.

The light changes and we keep moving. I only look behind me once, stunned when Boone meets my eyes and stares right through me.

"I know him," I say to Jan, Deb, and Sue. "I saw him just a week ago. He seemed okay."

"A week's a long time," Sue says.

"Yeah. I had three boyfriends this past week," Deb agrees.

They laugh in unison. I pinch my lips into a smile.

Inside the apartment, we decorate to set the mood: pillows on the floor, dim lamps, plug in the strings of Christmas lights. When Jan brings out bubbles, I push the thought of Boone from my mind. Deb doles out paper and colored pencils. Sue shows off her clarinet. We pick out the perfect albums—*Between the Buttons* (of course), *Pet Sounds, Revolver,* etc. Let the records spin, the music warm against the static LP pop. Cross-legged in a circle on the floor, we dutifully roll out our tongues and eat two tabs each.

Nothing scares me.

I am *perfect* in my own skin.

Then, slow as the ticking of the clock, an oozy warmth trickles in.

My smile spills out like honey.

I melt into a joyful puddle, resting my head on a pillow. A *Surrealistic Pillow*—which makes so much sense to me, because that's the album playing right now, the one the other three girls are dancing to. From here, in the dark sparkling light, they're flower girls frolicking around a maypole. The air pulses, alive—every note a color, the color at full volume, each item in the room a character, a creature with purpose. I love this womb—this room.

"How is she?" they're asking each other in whispery voices.

"She is perfect," I say back.

And I can see the letters spelling out the words in the air, quivering like butterflies:

S-H-E

I-S

P-E-R-F-E-C-T!

Fireworks pop from the Christmas lights. The maypole dancers—my friends—shrink, as if through a telescope, or maybe a wee television screen. I lie here for a stretch of time so long, lifetimes go by. But according to the clock, it's only been an hour now. How?

I close my eyes, and a secret cinema of fractals keeps shifting.

"Kaleidoscopic," I say, the word light as a puff of smoke. I like it so much—that word—like tapping a tiny xylophone. *Ding-ding-ding-ding.* "Kaleidoscopic."

The word echoes. When I open my eyes, I see it spelled out again, alphabet soup floating in the air.

"Kaleidoscopic color," I say, and something unsaid clicks into place.

I sit up. The entire room seems to be quivering with breath the way lungs would.

"The walls are seething."

My maypole dancing friends are gone. I hear them laughing in the bathroom, the *ahh* of the shower running, their voices overlapping.

"English that doesn't sound like English."

I'm out here alone. It doesn't feel like I'm alone, though. More like I'm inside another living being. In fact, if I listen— if I really do—I hear whispering through the static on the stereo. The record's over, needle stuck and repeating, but it sounds like a voice.

It says, *"Do you remember?"*

And like someone cracked the egg of my heart, I gasp.

It's my mom's voice.

The realization arrives with a spell of rain—actual rain, spilling from the ceiling, sparkling in the air, silver confetti.

"Mom!" I say, in awe.

And I let the rain come—it pelts me, hard, the missing. She is me. I am her. We're connected by invisible strings, and I know, wherever she is, she is loving me. She's my mirror and it all makes sense.

"It's raining!" I tell Jan, Deb, and Sue when they emerge from the bathroom. They're dripping, fully clothed, wide-eyed confusion painted on their faces as they eye me down here in my pillow-pile on the floor.

"Why are you crying?" Jan asks, face falling.

The three of them kneel around me, tending to me, touching my face. The rain stops. And suddenly I understand it wasn't raining, though it seemed it was, it really did. *I* was raining.

My inner siren swirls.

"I miss my mom," is all I can think to say.

They exchange shocked expressions. Secret-language eyes.

"I can feel her," I explain. "Inside. Like something on the tip of my tongue."

The girls engulf me in a hug, as if this is ordinary homesickness. But it's more profound than that. My mom's handwriting is swirling around my brain.

This all means something, even if I don't have the words yet for what it is.

harriet

I'm pushing Julie up the sidewalk in her buggy. Sunshine, daffodils, and blossoming trees—spring is my favorite season.

"Soon it will be Easter," I tell her. "You know about Easter?"

"I want a park," she whines.

"The park is filthy and full of miscreants. I found a cigarette butt in the sandbox."

"Park," she says again.

"You're as muleheaded as your sister," I tell her, glancing across the street at the Carrolls' house with its peeling paint and horrid jungle of a front lawn. That devil boy. Melinda's likely strung out on drugs now, living on the streets. I'll be attending her funeral soon, sure enough.

I smile and wave at the milkman when he passes, even though my friend suspects him of breaking and entering. Same with the mailman and the afternoon paper delivery boy. Who knows what the truth is, you can't trust anyone these days. But right now, I'm delighted to bump into Ida again, and even more delighted that her oaf of a husband is nowhere in sight. I pause in her driveway and wave.

"Hello, Harriet," she says, taking a brown bag of groceries out of her car. "Looking forward to tonight's neighbors' meeting?"

I nod.

"Sal refuses to go with me anymore." She closes the trunk. "He says my obsession with the prowler embarrasses him."

"Well, *I'm* on your side."

"You're a treasure, Harriet."

We say goodbye and I cross the street. I don't tell her that it wouldn't surprise me if the alleged thief was her own husband. I have impeccable intuition.

Back inside, I put the baby down for a nap, even though she tells me, "I not tired."

"Well, *I* am," I say.

She wails and clutches the bars of her crib, shaking them. She's a tiny ape, that's what she is.

"You don't know what's good for you," I say.

I leave her to whimper herself to sleep. At the top of the stairs, I pause, shaking my head at Melinda's shut door. *Pigsty* is too kind a word for what's in there. And Leo keeps it that way, like a shrine, while I'm toiling all night long on that couch with buttons in my back.

I open her door, whispering, "Demons, I rebuke you, in Jesus' name, Amen." Stepping inside, I shield my eyes from the wreckage on the floor. I use my hand to block out the unholy image of a shirtless man. Makes me sick to my stomach, imagining that naked man in front of me, his hairy chest and inviting lips. *The Doors*, the poster says.

"Doors indeed," I murmur. "Doors that lead straight to Hell."

But after the shock subsides, I begin mentally rearranging

the furniture. I imagine stripping the walls bare, replacing this sin with tasteful wallpaper and my Christian paintings. The floors would be swept, and I'd bring my braided rug. In the corner, where the sun comes in, I'd set up my altar.

I knock on the oak of her dresser. This will stay. I can use this. I put my hand on her top drawer, pausing to whisper "The Lord is my fortress" in case there are drugs inside. But when I slide it open, shock overwhelms my senses.

This is so much worse than drugs.

My word. My *words*. I can't even speak.

The room carousels and I clutch the wall for balance, staring in horror at what is inside her drawer among her underthings. I touch each one, just to prove myself they're real.

A silver candlestick.

An ivory comb.

Ida was right, there is a prowler after all. And it's my own granddaughter.

harriet

I nearly hyperventilate as I go downstairs, clutching the stolen goods. I place them on the kitchen table and weep at the sight of them, as if they're evidence on display at a sordid trial. What a fool she's made me! What a laughingstock I'll be when the Concerned Neighbors find out! The fireplace winks at me, and forgive me, Lord, because for a good minute I imagine throwing this all in there and lighting it ablaze. But that's my pride talking.

No, I must tell Ida. As soon as I stop sobbing, that's what I'll do.

The doorbell rings, and I nearly yelp at the sound.

I'm in no state for company. I open the door just a crack. "May I help you?"

As soon as the words leave my lips, though, I recognize this handsome stranger. My posture straightens and I wish I'd pinched my cheeks. It's my salesman friend from a week or two ago. He's smiling on my doorstep, holding up a roll of measuring tape.

"Mrs. Crawford, Lady of the House. Just who I was hoping to see."

"Me?" I can hardly believe it. I'm on a roller coaster with all these highs and lows I've experienced over the past few minutes. "What for?"

"Well, I feel like a bit of a fool. When I went to make the estimate, I realized I hadn't taken measurements. I think I was distracted by the excellent conversation."

"Of course," I say with a smile. "Please come in."

His smell is intoxicating—cedar, masculine, and expensive. He holds a measuring tape in his hands. "I'll start in the kitchen?"

"I have to tell you, Leo seemed uncertain about whether he wants to move ahead with new windows. He's been under a lot of stress."

"Because of Rose?"

I'd forgotten I'd run my mouth last time he was here. Now my cheeks prickle with embarrassment. "Yes. It's been such a trying time for us all."

"I had an aunt with a psychotic condition, so I understand."

"You?" I ask, taken aback. He's so proper. Who knew rot ran in his family tree?

"Yes. She prattled all sorts of nonsense. She wrote a lot of it down." He pulls out the tape and measures the kitchen window above the sink. "You said Rose did the same, right? Scribbled nonsense? Wrote her madness down?"

"Yes." I shake my head. "Drivel."

He jots some notations down in a tiny notebook. "What kinds of things did she write about, if you don't mind me asking?"

"Some made-up world she called the Dream Box."

"And did she describe what it was?"

He's a bit nosy, isn't he? My mouth hangs open as I try to pivot the conversation to something more interesting, but Julie's wailing from upstairs interrupts me.

"The baby," I say, getting up. "Let me settle her; I'll be right back."

I head up the stairs, skin prickling at her cries. It's as if she knows when I need peace and quiet and chooses that exact moment to scream. I open the door, not turning on the light, and step into the dim room. The slanted blinds cast lines all over her teary, pink face.

"Can't you just sleep like a normal child?" I whisper.

"No sleep."

"I see that. But if you don't nap and give me a break, guess what? I'll really give you something to cry about."

She cries. "Mama."

"I told you, Mama is gone. Bye bye, Mama."

"Mama!"

"I know you miss her, angel. She'll be back just as soon as she can."

She howls, and I can't help the sting. I crouch to speak to her through the bars.

"Honey, you think I want it this way? Do you know how my ankles swell and my head aches at the end of the day? I should be playing bingo at the senior center, and instead I'm raising a baby again."

I turn away from her in exasperation and something silver glints in my eye. It's the pistol poking out of my purse on the diaper table. I left it there, within arm's reach of Julie. I stand up and grab it, shuddering at my mistake.

"You are running me so ragged you're going to get us all killed," I tell her. "Sleep. Now. No ifs, ands, or buts. I've got a friend I'm entertaining downstairs."

There's a creaking sound behind the door—footsteps at

the top of the landing. The noise of them, nearly silent, like someone creeping, not wanting to be heard. I open my mouth to say his name but ... I don't know it.

"Sir?" I try, softly.

The footsteps continue across the landing, getting further away. Why would he be upstairs? Measuring windows? Looking for me? I hear the pop of Melinda's door opening.

I open Julie's door and poke my head into the hall. A happy family photo, covered in dust, is the only thing on the wall. Melinda's door is ajar, and I hear drawers opening and closing, shuffling sounds.

What on earth is he doing?

I take a few steps into her room. "Sir, I—"

He turns to me, her dresser drawers open. He's clearly rifling through them with one hand. And in his other, he holds Rose's ledger and address book. My jaw drops.

And, like the first glimpse of moonrise, I spy the devil dancing in his expression.

"You're no salesman," I say.

I pull the pistol from my purse and point it straight between his tricky blue eyes.

harriet

"Mrs. Crawford," he says in a soothing voice. "Don't do something you'll regret."

"Regret is not a word in my vocabulary."

"I can explain," he says, still charming, still smiling.

"You'd better start."

Behind his frozen expression, I sense him spinning a story.

"Why do you have Rose's ledger?" I ask. "Whatever would you want with that? And her address book?"

He can't answer. He's an actor who forgot his line.

"Are you having an affair with her?" I ask. "Is that why you've been poking around about her?"

"Yes," he says, visibly relieved at the explanation.

But now that I've spied the snake in him, I don't believe a word he says.

"No you're not. Rose likes them tall, dark, and handsome."

He opens his mouth, but I interrupt him before he gets a word in.

"I've already been played for a fool today, young man. If

you don't tell me what you're doing here I'm going to shoot now and beg God for forgiveness later."

"I'm not a bad man," he says, sweat beading on his brow.

"Your actions beg to differ. Sit on the bed."

He widens his eyes and I point to Melinda's bed with the nose of the gun.

"You heard me," I say. "Sit. Now."

He stumbles over a pile of dirty clothes and takes a seat on the bed with a stunned expression. He thought I was some pitiful old biddy. He didn't know he was messing with someone who can shoot a can across a football field. My daddy used to shake his head, saying my impeccable aim was wasted on a young lady.

"You sit here and you don't move and maybe, just maybe, I'll let you keep your head," I say.

I back out of the room, gun pointed, keeping my eye on the doorway for any sign of movement. When a reasonable spell of silence has passed, I pick up the phone on the stool behind me. I use the rotary to pull a zero.

"Operator," a voice chirps in my ear.

"Mama!" yells Julie from her open doorway.

I'd forgotten all about her.

I cover the receiver and turn to whisper-yell, "You just lay down and hush up, now." I pull my hand off the phone and say, "Hello, I need the number for the local—"

But then lightning strikes my skull.

Everything goes black around the edges.

I'm tumbling, bones cracking, the walls twirling like I'm inside a washing machine. The pain screams from my scalp to my soles, my shoes knocked off me, and then finally, it all goes still.

The last thing I taste is blood.

The last thing I smell is cedar cologne.

The last thing I feel is the pistol loosening in my heavy hand.

The last thing I see is a man's shadowy figure at the top of the stairs.

The last thing I hear is the baby crying for her mama.

a clipping from the los angeles times

OBITUARY
Wednesday, April 19

CRAWFORD, Harriet, beloved wife of the late
Sidney Crawford, loving mother of Leo Craw-
ford: also survived by two grandchildren.
Service 1 p.m. Saturday, Bethlehem Church,
Burbank. Forest Lawn Mortuary.

leo

Every time I spy an airplane sailing through the sky, I wish I were on it. I shield my eyes with my hand and watch one until it disappears behind the clouds. If Ma were here, she'd lecture me about staring too close to the sun.

"You'll be wrinkled as a raisin and blind as a mole if you keep squinting like that."

I let her voice echo, then disappear. My watch says it's 12:15. I'm baking in my black suit on this bench in front of Bethlehem Church. Why Pastor Whitaker told me to get here this early when even he isn't here yet is beyond me.

A car pulls into the lot. An orange VW bug, which isn't what I'd expect a pastor to drive. I stand up as a man emerges from the car. He has a telltale burst of curly hair and wears John Lennon sunglasses—this isn't Pastor Whitaker after all.

"Dale?" I call, crossing the lawn to meet him. "What are you doing here?"

Dale shakes my hand. His suit is tailored and tasteful, but his shoes are blue suede. He scans the empty parking lot, the locked brick building in front of us. Aside from the gold cross up on the roof, it could be a community center.

"Am I late?" Dale asks, confused.

"No. You're early. You're here before the reverend. Congratulations."

"I thought it was at noon?"

"One."

He heaves a sigh and takes off his glasses. "I'm so sorry, Leo."

"So am I." I reiterate the spin I've given her death since it happened, saying, "But she had a good life. And I guess slipping and falling down the stairs is a quick way to go."

"How are the kids?"

"Julie's back at home with our neighbor. And Melinda said she would be here by now, but I guess she's too busy getting high in San Francisco to live up to her word." My throat tightens. After she called yesterday, I told her what happened to her grandmother and asked her to come to the funeral. Foolish, I know, but I really had expected her to come. She's responsibly irresponsible—the kind of teenager who runs away from home and still calls to check in twice a week. But what do I know? "We're surviving."

"Sometimes that's enough." Dale flicks open a silver cigarette case. "Smoke?"

I nod, taking one, and let him light my cigarette even though it makes me uncomfortable. I can't help it. Dale's a decent person, but men who prefer the company of other men make me antsy if they get too close.

"I'm sweating like a sinner in church, as my mother would say." I laugh uncomfortably and point to another bench beneath an oak tree near us. "Sit?"

We take a seat, the cool shade a relief. I glance at my watch and wonder what's taking the pastor so long.

"Your mother was a character," Dale says.

"That she was."

"I'm sure you miss her."

I take a drag. I consider agreeing with him, but instead, I tell him the truth. "Something must be broken in me, because I don't feel a thing." I twist my wedding ring, almost not recognizing my own hands. I've had these moments lately where I'm so confounded, so adrift, I'm a movie, not a man. "Want to know something rotten?"

"Always," he says, almost playfully, though he doesn't smile.

"My first thought when I walked into the house and found my mother dead on the floor was, *Damn it. Who's going to watch the baby now?*" I laugh, but it hurts. Shrapnel in my throat.

Dale doesn't laugh with me. He taps his cigarette, ashes falling next to his blue suede shoe. "How's Rose? I hoped maybe she'd be here."

"She's in no state. The doctors advised me against telling her. She's hanging on by a thread."

"Have you considered it might be time for a second opinion?"

I swallow. "I've been a little busy, if you haven't noticed, what with my mother dying and my daughter running away."

"I wasn't planning on bringing it up today, but ..." Dale stops and shakes his head. "Never mind. You have enough on your plate. We'll talk next week."

"Spit it out, why don't you?"

"Well..." He blows out a sigh. "Since we spoke a couple weeks ago, I dug into that Pacific Institute place. They're mysterious. Not a lot of information readily available, even for a guy like me who knows how to dig. With a little legwork, I was able to track down some Secretary of State records showing they've changed their name several times.

The Institute of Behavioral Research. American Consumer Research."

"What does that mean?"

"Nothing on its own. But last week, I searched the *LA Times* archives at the public library and found a few business section blurbs about their funding over the years. And it's almost all Defense contracts."

I'm truly lost, trying to understand what this possibly means. Dale appears to read my confusion, because he presses on.

"Department of Defense research contracts, Leo. That isn't normal."

"Why not?"

"The military funding random psychiatric research?" he asks incredulously. "It's usually universities. Public health organizations, private foundations."

This conversation has me so stumped, it's like we're speaking two different languages. His eyes are wide with worry, he's jiggling his leg, but I don't understand what the big deal is.

"Spell it out for me," I say, irritated. "I'm not in the mood for guessing games."

"I can't spell it out for you because I can't see a damn thing beyond what I've told you. There's hardly any information about this study and the people who ran it. And everything I *could* find was classified."

The thought of the file missing from Victor's cabinet makes me dizzy. "It makes no sense."

"Who said it was supposed to?"

I drop my cigarette on the sidewalk, crushing it with my shoe. Blood hums in my ears, a circle repeating, repeating, repeating. I'm suffocating in fresh air.

"Do you know about my mother, Leo?" Dale asks.

I straighten my posture, glancing at the church beside us. "No, Rose never mentioned her."

"I don't talk much about her. She died when I was ten."

I soften at the turn in conversation. My own dad died before my memory starts. "Sorry to hear that."

"She was a teenage suffragette. Fiery. A little wacky. You know when girls started shearing their hair into bobs and wearing flapper dresses and listening to jazz? That was my mother."

"Sounds like a gas."

"She was. She was my favorite. And I was hers." Dale's lips turn up, but it's more grimace than smile. "But she was, as my dad called it, 'trouble.' She drank a lot. She was part of a group that protested regularly for labor rights. She got arrested for 'disturbing the peace.'"

Dale's sitting in a new light. I had no idea he had such a spitfire of a mother. Maybe that's why he turned out the way he did—a flamboyant gossip columnist.

"After that arrest, she was taken into an inpatient program at the local hospital. They gave her a hysterectomy under a program that was supposed to 'protect society' and 'safeguard against hereditary illness.'"

I can't believe what I'm hearing. "They *what*?"

"They sterilized her." He tosses his cigarette on the sidewalk, letting it burn. "Something broke in her after that. She spiraled and drank herself to death just a year or two later."

My mind grasps to find where this fits into the puzzle of my life right now. Is Dale telling me this because we both lost our mothers? Or is he telling me this because of Rose?

"Who would do something like that?" I ask. "That's obscene."

"Doctors, that's who. Under orders. Perfectly legal. Perfectly acceptable."

It's sickening.

"It's a different world now," I say, glancing at my watch. 12:31 p.m. and still no sign of the pastor. "I'm sorry to hear about all that, Dale. What about your old man?"

"He loved her fire ... before they got married. Then he did everything he could to extinguish it." He shakes his head. "He was a head down, do your work, say your prayers type of guy. Plus, he was a Russian immigrant. Terrified of authority. His English wasn't great. So when they suggested sterilizing her, he just signed on the dotted line."

My neck prickles. Is he insinuating I'm like his clueless father? I don't like the turn this conversation has taken. "So what are you trying to say?"

"I think that if the institute, or the institution, or the military did something wrong, someone like you might not want to see it."

"Because I *am* the military," I say between gritted teeth. "You know how naïve that sounds? Just lumping everyone together into one gleaming, conspiratorial nugget? I served for two years. I dropped out of college to join when I was nineteen years old—"

"So did I, but they wouldn't take me." Dale taps his head. "Hereditary instability, they said. Because of my mother's record. And 'suspected sexual deviancy.'"

I'm sweating, balling my fists. Out of nowhere, I'm so enraged, I could punch Dale in the nose. I could break him right now if I wanted. Where is this coming from? Dale's conspiracy theory nature and off-color opinions never bothered me before, not like this. But as I breathe through it, the anger becomes unrecognizable. It transforms. Maybe it isn't anger at all. Maybe it's something bigger—a disorientation so vast, so swallowing, gravity is off kilter.

It's as if we're living in two different Americas, both imagined.

"Harold Lumer was on the board of directors at Woodward," I murmur, remembering as I say it.

"See? And he's the guy that Rose kept remembering. The one behind the Dream Box."

I never took Rose seriously when she talked about the Dream Box because it sounded like, well, a dream. Nothing she said made any sense, and I told her to go to a psychoanalyst. They're the dream experts. But that woman was yelling about the Dream Box at the institution. That woman who wasn't Rose.

The Dream Box.

The sound of an engine sputtering snaps me back to the present. A rusted truck in the parking lot idles. I'm expecting a pastor to hop out, apologizing for his tardiness. Instead, Melinda jumps out the passenger side.

"Have fun in San Diego!" she calls to the driver, and the car turns around and drives away.

Melinda's bright smile for the driver settles into a sad scowl as she walks toward me. She's in a pair of velvet bell bottoms and a fringe-covered black tank top. Awful, I know, but my first thought is that I'm glad my mother's not alive to see the outfit Melinda's wearing to her funeral.

"Excuse me," I tell Dale.

Each step might as well be a mile. My head is an emotional battlefield. I'm livid that Melinda ran away from home, put herself in unthinkable danger, and abandoned us when we needed her most. I'm disappointed that I can't trust her anymore, that something between us is broken. And I'm overwhelmed with relief to see her in one piece: golden and glowing, a flower pinned in her hair. When I pull her in for a hug, I wish I could stop time. Stop it right here. The grief, the monumental grief I've been drowning in, finally sucks me under.

Good thing she embraces me for a solid minute so she can't see me cry.

leo

Ma would die all over again if she knew her beloved Pastor Whitaker shows up late to her funeral, arriving with shaving cream on his upper lip and bourbon on his breath. Twelve people attend. Psalms are read. The woman from across the street delivers a eulogy about Ma's brief but selfless work with the Concerned Neighbors Committee. The funeral parade ends at Forest Lawn Cemetery. I don't know what ties the knot in me tighter—the sight of my mother under a fresh pile of dirt, or the sight of my full-grown daughter alive and breathing beside me. It's a special kind of loneliness, to stand between the dirt and the future incarnate.

On the horizon, the cityscape winks at me from beneath a smear of smog. I try, again, not to think of Rose.

Now, it's evening. I can still smell Ma's rosewater on the sofa as we eat frozen dinners on TV trays—just me and my daughters and *The Jetsons*.

"I need one of those robot maids," I say, chewing rubbery Salisbury steak.

"You have one," Melinda says under her breath. "Her name is Mom."

I stop chewing, shocked by her comment. "What's that supposed to mean?"

Melinda blinks at me, raising one eyebrow. "It was a joke."

"Don't joke about her."

"Geez." Melinda pushes some peas around in some wayward gravy. "You talk about her like she's dead."

I'm about to snap back at her—Melinda knows exactly where my tenderest points are, and exactly how to poke them—when she asks, "When can I visit her?"

"Mama," Julie says, joining the conversation.

"Soon. She's improving." I turn to the cartoon again, but Melinda's gaze is as searing as a magnifying glass in a ray of sunshine. "What?"

"Do you ever wonder if there's a reason Mom lost it that night we were on vacation a few years ago?"

"Of course I wonder," I say quietly.

"Or why that night last month, you know?"

"Sometimes there are no reasons."

I heave myself off the couch. The knitted blanket and pillow Ma slept with are still there. Her altar, too. It should elicit some kind of despair, the sight of these things, but instead, I just can't wait to throw it all away. Terrible of me. Every time I thought of her today during her funeral, each memory that came up about her, brought nothing but resentment.

"I need to do some work," I say.

"Wait, Dad." Melinda pulls my sleeve to grab my attention. "Let me put Julie to bed and we can talk, okay? I want to catch up."

I'm taken aback by this. I'd assumed she was bitter at having to cut her adventure short and come home again.

"Okay," I finally say. "Thanks, Mel."

She helps Julie get ready for bed and I plop back on the sofa with a generous lowball glass of Scotch. In the corner of the room, there's a cardboard box that just says MA on the side. I'm still not sure what I'm supposed to do with her purse, her shawls, her toiletry bag, her Bible she left here at the house, not to mention her entire untouched apartment.

Upstairs, Melinda is singing "Yellow Submarine" to her sister. With a twinge, I realize how long it's been since I heard anyone singing in this house. Maybe since Rose left.

I can't believe my mother's dead and buried in the ground and Rose doesn't even know. Somehow, that's the sharpest arrow yet. Dale was there today, and Rose wasn't. I hang my head, paralyzed by her absence.

Melinda shakes me and says, "Dad?"

I must have dozed off with my drink in my hand. Melinda's seated beside me, still in her funeral dress. The light is dimmer and she reaches, switching on a lamp. She shows me a composition book.

"Do you recognize this?" she asks.

It looks like the kind you'd pick up at the dime store. Rose used to buy them by the dozen before the school year started. "It's a notebook?"

"Yes, but Mom wrote in it." She traces her delicate fingernail over the front. "In 1964. I guess she was trying to journal?"

"She did that a lot. She's got a short attention span. I'll bet she abandoned ten journals since I knew her."

"Like the ledger," she says. "I peeked inside that one once."

"It's not nice to peek at other people's private journals."

"I didn't know what it was."

"She called it her little book of nightmares. She wrote her bad dreams down in there."

"The Dream Box?"

I snap to attention, the phrase tickling my mind. "Where did you hear about that?"

"In the ledger." Melinda leans in and whispers, "What does it mean?"

"I—I don't know what it means." My heart thumps loudly in my ears. "I wish I did."

"Does it have something to do with the study?"

I stare at Melinda, at a loss for words. "How do you know about that?"

She holds up the composition book. "She wrote about it in here."

"Let me see it."

"Wait." She opens the book, rips some pages out, and hands them to me. "The rest of the notebook is my stuff. No offense, Dad, but I don't want you reading about what I was doing up in San Francisco."

It's just three pages she's given me. I skim them, holding my breath. It's not an easy read. It's Rose right before and after the study, at her most hopeful, then at her worst. Then nothing.

I hold them up. "This is it?"

"As far as I know. You should have them, not me." She gets up and yawns. "I'm going to take a bath."

She goes upstairs and I sit still, reading the pages and draining my glass. The conversation echoes in my mind. I can't believe Melinda mentioned the Dream Box. It keeps coming up, circling round, casting its shadow like a vulture. What is the damn Dream Box?

"The ledger," I mutter.

Her little book of nightmares. The one I ignored. I'm sick with myself suddenly for being too much of a coward to read it. Because cowardice is exactly what it was—I've been afraid to peek inside my wife, to scrutinize her thoughts too closely, for fear I might discover that she really is insane.

It never occurred to me that I might discover she really *isn't*.

I head to her vanity, annoyed but unsurprised to find the ledger is missing. Ma's invasion of our privacy reaches beyond her time on this earth. Diaries, letters, prescriptions, shopping lists—nothing was safe with her around. She took the ledger, hid it somewhere, and now I'm forced to play a game of hide and seek.

It's not in the living room, nor the kitchen drawers. I search Julie's closet as she tosses and turns, and even peek under her crib. Melinda's room is like foraging through a psychedelic city dump and reeks of incense so badly I cough. Then, like a madman walking in circles, I search the whole house again.

It's a small house. My mother hardly left it these past few weeks. She kept the other items she stole, the cold cream and the costume jewelry swiped from Rose's vanity.

Why would she not keep the ledger?

And if she didn't have it ... who does?

leo

I'm on a tightrope at Century: accounts stacked a mile high, NightEase breathing down my neck every waking moment, my personal life shadowing my professional. My favorite part of the workday has always been when the door is shut, the office nothing but a background hum. I was an only child, and my mother had a loud voice. I do well when it's just me and my imagination.

But these days, I'm stuck. Poring over the legal pad, etching out line after line. I used to be an atheist when it comes to writer's block. This week might make a believer out of me, because every time I scribble something down on my notepad, I read it back and don't know what to think about it. I'm staring at Greek. Is it good copy? Is it garbage? I can't tell anymore.

There's a knock on my door. I look up and see, through the picture window that peers into the open office, my neighbor Ida Giordano. Cat-eyed glasses, a cardigan sweater, waving. The one who came to Ma's funeral and sang her praises. She's holding a file folder and all at once I remember how she told me about some plan involving a plaque to go on a bench at the park, some memorial on behalf of the Concerned Neighbors Committee. The day of the funeral was a blur; I'd forgotten all about it.

I let out a groan, then slap a smile on and open the door.

She dresses like it's 1945, shoulder pads and all, and her shiny cross necklace catches in the light. Very much my mother's type. "Leo, I hope I'm not bothering you."

"Of course not, but why'd you come all the way out here?"

"Remember, I told you, the engraver is a block away, so it's no inconvenience at all. I just wanted your approval before I give it to them."

"Come on in."

She steps inside. I close the door behind us and gesture toward the mountain of yellow paper balls on my desk. "You'll get a glamorous behind-the-scenes peek at copywriting life. Have a seat?"

"No, thank you," she says.

Down to business, this one. She opens the folder and flashes me the single page inside. A white page with big block letters.

IN MEMORY OF HARRIET CRAWFORD
Devoted member of the Concerned Neighbors Committee

I peer at it for half a second, then snap the folder shut. "Quite the tribute." *Especially considering Ma went to what— three, four meetings?*

Mrs. Giordano dabs her eyes with a handkerchief. This woman has shed more tears over the death of my mother than I have.

"I still can't believe she's gone," she whispers.

"It's touching. I'm sure Ma would appreciate it."

"I'm sure she does." She tucks her handkerchief into her purse, then twists the cross around her neck with white-gloved fingertips. "She's probably looking down on us right now."

I nearly shiver at the thought. "Indeed."

"Oh! I ran into her friend out there," she says, taking the folder back from me. "I had no idea he worked here."

"Pardon?"

My mother and "friend" are not often words I hear strung together.

"Her friend?" she says again.

I blink. "What?"

"In the office across from yours." She turns and points through the picture window. "Him. That one right there. I saw him leaving your house and Harriet said he was a friend."

Victor's in his office on the phone behind his desk. It's a stretch to see him from here, and Mrs. Giordano's statement is so bizarre I'm stuck for a response.

"I don't think so," I say.

"I never forget a face. He looks like Errol Flynn."

Maybe if Errol Flynn were five foot five and built like a Christmas ham. This woman's got to be senile.

"I'd tell him you said that, but I think his head's big enough as it is."

"Well, it's awful nice of him, befriending an elderly woman like that." She taps the file folder in her hands. "You approve?"

"I do. Typo free and ready to ship."

"I'll bring over a lasagna later."

"You don't have to. But thanks."

I close the door behind her. Will that be me in twenty years? Senile, weeping over people I hardly knew? Maybe I'm broken; I'm dry as a desert. But I can't mourn what I don't understand.

And I don't understand a damn thing.

I sit at my desk, hang my head. Why is my first impulse to pick up the phone and call Rose and tell her an old lady compared Victor to Errol Flynn? I can just imagine her throaty laugh, followed by some sarcastic comment that would send me next.

But then, a bug of a thought. I rewind the tape in my mind and go over the conversation again. What sticks out this time is the idea that Ma had any friend at all, whether he was a Victor lookalike or an Errol Flynn lookalike or anything in between. A male friend? She would never. The only men I ever saw my mother let into the house were door-to-door salesmen.

I don't realize I've been twirling my chair, lost in thought, until I stop. The room tilts.

Ma said something about a salesman stopping by weeks ago. What did she say he was peddling again? Windows?

Yes, that's it. Double-paned.

Valley Builders. *This lovely salesman from Valley Builders.* But ... her friend?

The bug is still buzzing in my skull, though I'm not sure why. It was one offhanded comment made by a near-sighted neighbor. But I can't shake it.

I open my bottom drawer, pull out the phone book, and find the number for Valley Builders. I dial.

"Hello, I wanted to ask if I could get one of your salesmen out to my house," I say. "He stopped by recently. I was hoping to talk with him again."

"I'm sorry, sir, but we don't have salesmen. We're in-store only."

I pause and try again. "He came through my neighborhood a few weeks ago."

"It wasn't one of ours. Must have been another company."

I hang up. Now the bug's buzzing even louder, back and forth between my ears. Because I know she said Valley Builders. I'm positive that was where the salesman was from; they're an account we've worked on before. I know the same way Ida Giordano was sure that Victor was Ma's friend.

A wave of nausea makes me close my eyes.

If there was a man in my house saying he was from Valley Builders, he lied. And if Mrs. Giordano isn't senile—if she really can remember a face the way I can remember a name—

When I open my eyes, my forehead is dripping with sweat. My heart pounds. Across the open office, across desks, secretaries, and typewriters, Victor sits in his corner office. Still on the phone. In his own world. I stare behind him, at the file cabinet. The one with the empty folder.

I breathe deeply. I'm turning inside out right now. I'm having thoughts so outlandish I'm ashamed. Because it's psychosis, imagining Victor would be in my house for some reason, without me knowing. It's utterly insane. For what? More files? Info on the Pacific Institute he apparently doesn't want people finding? The ledger?

Oh cripes. That's it, isn't it?

I grab the phone book again with shaky hands. Maybe schizophrenia is contagious and I'm catching what my wife has. Paranoia sweeps over me heavy as the flu.

I need to know what was in that ledger.

Flipping through the phone book, there it is: *Allan Wells, psychoanalyst, 1492 Bell Street,* and the phone number. I dial.

"We're sorry," a robotic female voice chirps. "The number you have dialed is no longer in service."

I hang up and try again.

"We're sorry ..."

My ears are ringing now. I'm trapped in my own private earthquake and the walls are crumbling, threatening to bury me. Victor is smiling on his phone call. Natalie is delivering memos to the office floor. But the light has changed. Either I'm not well, or something here—something at Century—is rotten at the core.

I hop up, grab my hat, and hurry out of my office. I don't look back.

leo

"1492 Bell Street. Christopher Columbus Bell Street," I mutter to myself, to not forget.

I drive side streets in a daze until I hit it, just off Ventura Boulevard. I pull to the curb and take it in: a two-story building with palm trees out front. It's beige brick—or was. Now it's blackened from the ground up, a loop of caution tape around the building.

"You are *kidding* me," I say.

I've had an easier time catching my breath with the wind knocked out of me. I grip the steering wheel as tight as I can, studying the wreckage. After a stunned minute, I emerge from the car. To hell with the caution tape blowing in the wind. I step over it, crossing the parking lot. The closer I get, the more damage I see: embers smeared everywhere, palm trees scorched, front steps barbequed. I study a blackened directory for the building in a glass sign and can just barely make out which office belonged to Allan Wells—2C. The map tells me it's around the corner.

I step on the walkway, holding my nose. The smell is atrocious. Burned rubber, melted plastic, and smoke. The ground is littered with shattered glass. Around the corner, it's even worse. I stop in front of the enormous hole where a door once led into 2C, and it confirms exactly what I'd feared. This is the most damaged unit in the building. It's gutted inside, wiring exposed, ashes everywhere, cement piles.

This seems to be where the fire started.

I back away from it, nearly tripping over a fallen palm branch. I still can't quite believe the thought that keeps looping through my mind.

Someone burned his office down.

As I go back to my car, I scan the street, making sure I'm not being watched. It's the first time that thought has ever occurred to me—though who would be watching me, or why, I don't know.

I start the engine. On the radio, Vin Scully is yapping about spring training, but I shut him up. I steep in the silence as I drive. All I can think is, if someone is willing to burn a building down—if someone's willing to steal Rose's little book of nightmares—what else are they willing to do?

"Rose," I say, her name a barb in my throat.

I break the speed limit driving to Woodward.

leo

There are no open visiting hours, I have no appointment, and I don't care. I pull into a parking spot. I undo my tie, toss it in the back seat. Deep breath. Can't have a heart attack, not yet.

I head across the trimmed lawn toward the gray building and head inside. The polka coming out of the radio behind the desk is so absurd, so the opposite of my hammering paranoia, that it almost sounds like circus music.

On the clipboard, I sign my name. "I'm here to check my wife out."

"Have a seat," the woman says without looking me in the eyes.

I do as she says, sinking into a maroon vinyl chair, my hands clasped and shaking.

Woodward Neuropsychiatric Center, the sign on the wall says. *You're In Good Hands.*

But she's not. And it's just hitting me now. Sure, she had a breakdown. She was moody. She hallucinated demons on the TV. But she was also a mother, a wife, a person. She still cracked jokes and drove to the grocery store and sang Julie lullabies at night. And now, what is she? A vegetable. A ghost.

Rose needs help, but not like this.

How has it taken me this long to wake up?

"Mr. Crawford," a voice says.

It's Dr. Monroe in the doorway that leads to the clinic, eyes open wide behind his glasses.

"I didn't realize you were coming today," he says.

I stand up. "It was an impulsive decision."

"I'm sorry, but Rose can't see you today. We don't allow visits, except by appointment."

"I'd like to take her home."

Dr. Monroe doesn't move, doesn't flinch. He blinks, then smiles, as if I'm a silly kid.

"I see. I have a few minutes. Can we discuss this in my office?"

I nod. He holds the door open for me, and I join him on the other side. The door clicks shut behind us. The lights change from sunny to fluorescent. The windows disappear. Our footsteps echo as we pass doctor's offices, doors shut tight. He pushes open the door with his name on it and I take a seat across from him at his desk. The thought of taking Rose home—of leading her away from this mess, of starting over again—is all I can think about.

I glance at his dog's portrait. It's still the only personal touch to the room. Dr. Monroe eyes me with a new curiosity.

"Are you okay, Mr. Crawford?" he asks. "You seem nervous."

"I'm not." I wipe my brow with a handkerchief again. "I just—I've been doing some thinking. I'd like to get a second opinion."

Dr. Monroe scratches his balding head.

"I—I think she's come as far as she can here with her

treatment," I say. "I understand she's got paranoia, schizophrenia. I'm not disagreeing with that. But maybe it's time for another look."

"We have some of the best recovery rates in the state."

"Right. But I want to take her home today."

"I'm sorry. We can't allow that. Sending a patient home before they're ready can lead to disastrous results."

"I'm willing to take that risk."

"Are you?" He folds his hands on the desk. "What about your daughters?"

"I—" The word catches in my throat. "How do you mean?"

Dr. Monroe's expression goes faraway and dark, as if considering whether to tell me whatever's on his mind. "I'm sorry to be the bearer of bad news, but Mrs. Crawford has expressed homicidal urges toward her children."

He might as well have told me Rose has turned into a cockroach. "*What?*"

"She has," he says gravely. "Several times, during her episodes."

I sit with this for a moment. I close my eyes, center myself, and really ask myself—can I see Rose doing that? Can I hear her voice saying something that bleak? I can hear her crying that she's overwhelmed. I can hear her complaining about her aching back from picking up too many toys. I can see her sitting on a couch, not paying attention to them, daydreaming as she faces the window. But violence? She catches spiders and puts them outside, that's how softhearted she is.

"She has never *once* hurt our children. Not even so much as spanked them."

"Regardless of her history, she's made threats. And we take the safety of our patients, and their families, very seriously."

He glances at his watch, like he can't wait to be rid of me.

"Let me see her," I say. "Let me talk to her."

"I told you, appointments are necessary for visits."

"Fine. I want to bring her home, then."

He steeples his fingers, examining me. Then he smiles. It's a sorrowful smile, the smile of someone with all the power who's unwilling to give you what you want.

"Mr. Crawford, it's quite ... bold of you to propose. But Rose can't go home until we deem her safe. She's here on an involuntary commitment."

I balk. "'Involuntary?' She willingly came here."

"Yes, but she's since been involuntarily committed."

"I'm her husband, and I want her home. How is this legal?"

"It's how the law works, Mr. Crawford. The administrators of this hospital are who get to decide what is best for our patients, not family members."

"Well, I object."

A joyless, cruel bark of a laugh escapes his lips. "This isn't a courtroom drama. It's an order signed by two physicians."

"Who?"

"Myself, and Dr. Harold Lumer."

I feel the blood as it drains from my face. If I weren't sitting down, my knees would buckle.

"You know what?" I say. "I see right through you."

Dr. Monroe shakes his head. "Dare I ask—do *you* need to see someone here, Mr. Crawford? Because you're not making a lot of sense."

I'm backed into a corner, forced into silence, jaw tight.

"You can't both go off the deep end now," he says, with concern. "Your children need you."

"What do I need to do to get her out of here?" I ask, my voice breaking.

"Just keep doing what you've been doing—up until today, that is. Leave it to us. We're helping her improve. We know what we're doing."

I sit still. It's a minefield, this conversation. The more I dig in, the crazier I seem. This isn't how I rescue Rose. This is how I get myself committed—and it's horrifying to imagine that if this man wanted, he could slap a hospital bracelet on my wrist and call me an involuntary commitment. It's apparently that easy.

So I sigh and say, "You're right. You're the experts."

And he says, "You're a good husband, Mr. Crawford. You know that?"

I don't anymore. I used to. But I smile and nod and say, "Yes, doc, I do."

melinda

The same way the whole world's color changes after a spell of rain—lawns greener, sidewalks darker, blue sky stark against the clouds—my childhood home here in Canoga Park seems intangibly altered. Mom gone, Grandma dead, and Dad a zombie. Even Julie—a ray of sunshine, babbling nonsense, following me from room to room since I came home—is a walking heartbreak. Because she doesn't seem to have any idea that our family is nothing but dust.

I haven't told her that as soon as I can, I'm leaving again.

Haven't told Dad, either.

"Lin-Lin stay," Julie keeps saying as we build block towers on the rug.

"Lin-Lin here," I agree.

But I swallow a lump, because what's to become of her? Grandma was a pest, but at least she took care of Julie and the house. Somehow, I've been stuck watching my sister every day since I've been back. The only way dinner gets made is if I cook it, and the only way dishes get done is if I do them, and on and on it goes. Sometimes, I glance down at the apron I'm wearing and wonder—how did I get here?

I think of Mom a lot.

I feel her absence now in a way I never felt her presence when she was here.

I dust her picture on the mantel and marvel at how radiant she is in a youthful portrait, one taken as a headshot when she did some modeling years ago. The soft, curly hair and slightly crooked smile and the twinkle of mischief in her eye. My own reflection gazes back from the glass, superimposed.

"Who that?" Julie asks, pointing at the picture.

"You don't know who that is?" I crouch and show her. "That's Mama."

She places a tiny sticky hand on it. "Mama."

"Isn't she pretty?" I say, standing up and placing the photograph back on the mantel. "Her name is Rose."

After I put Julie down for a "rest" (don't call it a nap, she won't fall for it) I come downstairs. The phone rings and I grab it in the kitchen.

"Crawford insane asylum, Melinda speaking," I say.

I shouldn't have made a joke like that. Dad would kill me.

"Lindy," Jim's soft voice says.

On one hand, I'd like to yell at him for taking so long to find me. On another, I just want to smooch his face. I close my eyes. I lean against the counter. "I'd started wondering if you had disappeared forever. Where *are* you?"

"I'm at Jan's! I told you I was coming."

"Yeah, like, a year ago."

"Weeks. Sorry, I got caught up. There were these bikers— it's a long story."

I press my tongue to the roof of my mouth, not knowing what to say.

"Jan told me your grandma passed away," he says. "Man, I'm sorry. I wish I had known."

"I do too." I swallow a little shard of feeling. "But how could you?"

"I would have hitched down there."

"No need." I twirl the phone cord on a fingernail. "I'm fine on my own without you, Jim."

It hits me as I say it that not once since I returned to this bummer scene in Canoga Park have I wished Jim were here to prop me up. I didn't need his shoulder to cry on, his advice, or his help. And that lights me up in new places.

"I love you, Lindy," he says softly. "You're coming back to the Haight, right?"

"Probably. I'm not sure when though."

"I came back here to be with you," he says with disappointment.

"Well, I went to San Francisco to be with you, and then you ran off."

"So you're ... punishing me?"

His voice is gentle, pleading, like he's really trying to understand. But he can't. Because I can't.

"Just do your thing and I'll do my thing and maybe we'll meet up again one day," I say, voice tight.

"That sounds like some kind of goodbye."

He sniffs. The static on the line pops.

My eyes burn and I don't know what else to say.

"Goodbye, Jim," I finally answer.

I hang up the phone.

My eyes burn but don't leak. I go into my mom's bedroom and view myself in her vanity mirror. Turn this way and that, tilt my head, study my eyes. I can see similarities between my reflection and Mom's headshot on the mantel.

In her closet is a disaster of dresses, a peek inside her loud mind. I had no idea there was such chaos—a bright pile of pumps mixed with slips and skirts, pantyhose hanging from the doorknob. I lean down and pick up her favorite polka-dotted dress. Sniff the collar and inhale her. She's still here. She's still alive, and she could come home, and for some reason that is what pinches the most—the hope.

I take off my clothes and slip into the polka dotted dress, struggling to reach behind and zip the back up. How on earth did she do that without help? I settle for halfway zipped and buckle the belt. Mom's favorite string of pearls hangs on a hook, and I grab it and clasp it around my own neck. I step out of the closet and in front of the vanity mirror, tilting back and forth, holding my hair up in a pretend French twist. The dress is loose, but it fits. Slap some red lipstick on me and call me Mom.

A chill rolls up my spine. I let my hair fall on my shoulders. When I was a little girl, I might have told you this was what I wanted to become one day—a mother, a wife, lady of my own house. But I was a different Melinda then. And if that much has changed for me in just a few years, imagine what could change between the woman on the mantel and the woman in the hospital right now.

I'm haunted by the Mom I read in those journal pages—struggling, full of hope, wanting to be more than she was. I had no idea. I thought she wanted to be a homemaker. And then there are the eerie details of that study—

The front door slams, and I jump. That's odd. It's the middle of the day.

"Dad?" I call.

No answer. The hairs on my arms stand on end. I stay perfectly still, listening to footsteps. My pulse goes from a walk to a sprint.

And then a man appears in the doorway.

melinda

It's Dad, but it doesn't look like Dad. He's Shadow Dad—unshaven, shirt wrinkled, dark circles under his eyes.

He left this morning before Julie and I got up, scribbled a note about working early. But he resembles someone who crawled out of hell still wearing his Fedora hat and carrying his briefcase.

"You look just like her," he says, voice hoarse.

"Are you okay?"

He keeps staring with glassy eyes.

"Did something happen at work?" I try.

"No. Nothing."

Dad's sleepwalking expression gives me the creeps. Reminds me of Mom during her trances.

"Have you had lunch?" I ask, intercepting him in the doorway and placing a palm to his forehead. Lukewarm. Human. "Let me make you a sandwich."

I lead him to the kitchen table, sit him down, bring him a glass of milk and a peanut butter sandwich. We're in Bizarro World now, where the roles are flipped, children are adults and adults are children, and I'm wearing Mom's favorite dress.

"Why aren't you at work?" I ask.

"Called in sick."

"You don't have a fever."

"Not that kind of sick."

"Playing hooky, eh? Just like you told me never to do?"

"Well, you're a high school dropout now, so looks like you won that war." He glances up, elbows propped on the table, sandwich in both hands. "I don't suppose you'd think about going back to school?"

He suggests it so gently.

Seventeen, and I'm the one with the hammer.

"Dad, I have no interest in returning to school. Frankly, I can't wait to get back to San Francisco."

He flinches. "I was afraid you'd say that."

"I love it up there."

"What about your sister?"

I cross my arms. "Why is Julie my problem?"

"Because we're a family," he says, his voice quavering just once. "And we help each other."

"But why is it always Mom, or Grandma, or me? What about you?"

His eye twitches, his gaze fixed, as if he's really trying to understand what I'm saying.

"When I read Grandma's obituary, you know what struck me as the saddest thing?" I ask, leaning on the kitchen counter. "Her whole life was just boiled down to her connections to the people around her. Wife to Sidney. Mother to you. Grandmother to us."

"That's what obituaries do," Dad says, straightening his posture.

"No. The ones on either side of hers in the section that

day weren't like that. One was a retired general who fought in the cavalry in World War I. The other was a longshoreman who loved football."

"Well, I guess I'm lousy at writing obituaries," Dad says, draining his glass of milk.

"It wasn't just you. That's how *all* the women's obituaries read."

"Am I about to get some feminist lecture, because—"

"All I'm saying," I say, louder than him, cutting him off. "Is that I want my obituary to say more than that."

"Well, god help me, I hope I'm never here to read your obituary," he says. "But if you go back up there and get strung out ..."

I fight the urge to roll my eyes. Adults are such fools. I almost pity them.

"Well, Mom did everything right and she's in an institution. So I don't know what to believe anymore," I tell him.

Dad purses his lips and says nothing, because I'm right. His hair needs combing. The lightning-struck glaze in his eyes scares me.

"Something very wrong is going on with your mom," he finally says.

"I'm aware—"

"No. Not with her. With her treatment, with the doctors, it's—it's bigger than that."

I wrinkle my brow, waiting for him to make sense. I sink into a chair next to him and fold my hands on the table. "Does it have anything to do with the study she talked about in those pages I gave you?"

"It might. But it's impossible to find out details to prove it."

"What *was* that study? What happened in there?"

Dad shakes his head. "I wish I knew, but there's no public information."

I swallow. There's something that has been niggling my thoughts ever since my acid trip—that spooky déjà vu I felt, that connection with Mom that I can't quite put into words. "Do you think they drugged her?"

"They gave her a sleeping pill, that much we know."

"I mean something more than that. Something ... psychedelic."

Dad snorts. "I don't think so."

"Why not?"

"I don't see the purpose."

"But some of the stuff she jotted down in the ledger talked about the walls breathing and kaleidoscopic color and ... I don't know. It kind of sounds like an LSD trip."

"How would you know, Melinda?" he asks sharply.

I just raise an eyebrow at him and shrug.

He shakes his head. "I'm trying to figure out how to get her out of that hospital and back home, but I need your help. I can't do it alone." He swallows, his Adam's apple bouncing. "Please don't go running away to San Francisco again. I can't face this without you."

Without me, or without my free babysitting? But I spare him the lip service because he's trembling. He's on the edge of something that I don't want to see him plummet over.

"Don't worry," I tell him. "We're going to get through this."

Eventually, I am going back to San Francisco. I fell in love with the bustle and unpredictability and the friends I made.

But until my broken family is repaired, I'm here.

a letter from woodward

Woodward Neuropsychiatric Center
Los Angeles County, California

Monday, May 1, 1967

Dear Mr. Leo Crawford,

Your recent request to visit Mrs. Rose Crawford has been received by this office. At the present time, Mrs. Crawford remains under active medical observation and is not considered well enough to receive visitors.

In accordance with the recommendation of her attending physician, Dr. Wallace Monroe, visitation privileges must remain suspended until further notice.

We appreciate your patience and cooperation while Mrs. Crawford continues her course of treatment.

Sincerely,
The Administrative Team
Woodward Neuropsychiatric Center

leo

In the past week, I've consulted a lawyer who informed me I have no case against Rose's involuntary commitment at Woodward.

"You're talking about you versus one of the most prestigious hospitals in the state," he said in a weary voice. "Good luck with that."

I've left countless messages at the hospital.

I've called Victor, even though I'm supposedly sick with the flu. I begged him to help use his ties to get Rose out of there, and he just feigned ignorance.

"Old man," he said sadly. "You know they have one of the best recovery rates in the state?" And then, the gall of it: "Have you thought about checking *yourself* in there?"

His icy tone had a sprinkle of amusement in it—that's what really lit my fire.

"What was in that ledger that made you so desperate you broke into my house to get it?" I asked. "Just tell me."

"Ledger?"

The silence stretched so long I could hear the distant

drone of office life behind him: typewriters chattering, voices overlapping, telephones ringing. It was like listening to the bustle of a distant planet.

"Leo, I … really worry about your whole family, at this point," he said sadly.

Was that a threat? I couldn't tell anymore. Lately, life seemed to say one thing and do another.

"Do get some help," he said quietly.

And then: *Click.*

When all that failed, I tried to track down Harold Lumer. Dale and I drove around, scoping out the listed addresses for the Pacific Institute of Human Research and its previous iterations. The Institute of Behavioral Research, American Consumer Research. All we found were mailboxes—not actual businesses.

That's what all this investigating has been: circles, circles, and circles that lead back to other circles.

I update Melinda about this right now, trying to catch her up to speed. She's become my partner in figuring out how to get Rose out of Woodward, and I've been shocked by how adult and sharp her ideas are.

"I don't understand," Melinda says, braiding her hair as she sits across from me at the kitchen table. It's dark out and Julie's in bed and it's just the two of us trying to hatch some kind of plan. "So the institutes are a part of Woodward?"

"No. The institutes are some kind of funnel for money coming from the Department of Defense. Woodward and the institutes share people, though."

"And Century …?"

"…. worked with the institutes, though they swept it under the rug."

"Confusing."

"Yes. By design."

"What do they want with Mom, then? I don't understand."

"This is what I think: Something happened to her in that study. Whatever they did, they went too far. And the more she tried to remember what it was they did, and the more she tried to talk about it—the more they wanted to shut her up. They wanted her notes from her private psychoanalyst and when he didn't hand them over, they burned his office down."

"Who is 'they?'" Melinda asks.

I close my eyes. I see a million blank faces. I see no one.

"I don't know how it all works, exactly," I admit.

We steep in contemplation a minute before a light bulb pops behind Melinda's eyes. "You said the Department of Defense?"

"Yes. No idea how that fits in."

"Jim met an Army vet at a commune who said the government had experimented on him and made him pop pills and drop acid."

"Sounds like a very reliable source," I say sarcastically.

"You have to admit, though, it sounds similar."

"It sounds insane."

"It *is* insane. And don't you think if anything like that was going on, they would want to shut people up about it?"

She's got a point, but I just can't come up with a why for all this. What would motivate the military to do such a thing, let alone under the guise of consumer research?

"I've got to get her out of there," I say. "Even if it means breaking her out."

Melinda's watching me as if I'm a grenade that lost its pin. But she reaches and puts her hand on mine. "I'll help."

"No. I don't want you sucked into it all."

"I'm her daughter. I'm already sucked in."

I shake my head.

"A giant hospital isn't going to let you just walk in there and escort Mom out," Melinda says, jumping up and grabbing a pen and notepad from the kitchen drawer. She sits back down, turns to a fresh page. "We need a plan. What's their security like? How do you get in?"

"Melinda, absolutely not."

"Don't try to stop me."

"It's dangerous. I don't want anything happening to you—"

"Haven't I proven I can keep myself out of danger?"

"I can't, in good conscience—"

"Dad," she says firmly. "We're doing this together. End of story."

She's the most stubborn girl I've ever known. When Melinda gets set on something, you're just wasting air and energy trying to persuade her to change her mind.

I blow out a sigh and roll up my sleeves. "Well," I begin reluctantly. "The front doors lead into a reception area ..."

leo

The next morning, I knock on Mrs. Giordano's door and ask if she can watch Julie. She seems shocked and flattered at the request, despite the fact she's still in her robe and curlers.

"Sorry, Melinda and I need to go to the hospital to visit her mother," I say. "I didn't know who else to ask, with my mother gone."

"Of course," Mrs. Giordano says, taking Julie's hand. "Why hello, little one. You like oatmeal? I was just making some ..."

Melinda and I drive to Woodward, going over the plan one more time before falling into a nervous silence. God, I hope it's Rose riding shotgun on our way home. And if they come back for her at our house, I'll tell them they need a warrant. And if they come back with a warrant, I'll sneak her out the back door and drive away.

I won't let this damn hospital hold my wife hostage any longer.

We park in the far corner of a lot under an oak tree. I glance at Melinda, who has a book of matches in her hand.

"Again," I say, "do not tell *anyone* your name. Understand?"

"I understood the first fifty times you told me."

"I don't want anyone linking you with me or your mother."

"I'm just a random walk-on part, Dad, not the star of the show."

"As soon as the plan is in motion, I want you to go wait in the car."

"I *know*. How many times are we going to go through this?"

"Please be careful," I say. "The last thing I need is you getting arrested for arson."

With glassy eyes, Melinda surveys the grounds. It's late morning, and hardly anyone is around. Sprinklers rain on the lawn with little hissing noises.

"They're not going to know who started it," Melinda says.

"Where are you going to do it?"

"I think that one right there," she says, pointing to a trash can along the walkway near the entrance. "It's far enough away that it'll give you some time but close enough that they can really see it from the front doors." She shakes her head as she stares at the hospital. "God, this place gives me the creeps."

"I won't be able to forgive myself if something happens to you," I say, throat tightening.

"It's not me you have to worry about. It's Mom."

My hands remain on the wheel. Am I really about to do this?

"She needs us," Melinda reminds me. "Now go."

That ancient wound in my abdomen burns with worry. But I nod and get out of the car, striding through the sunshine toward the towering building that holds my Rose.

I smile politely at the receptionist.

"Good morning. I'm looking to have a quick check-in with Dr. Monroe about my wife."

"I'm not sure he's in yet. Do you have an appointment?"

"It's urgent. I'll speak with whoever's on duty."

"Regarding?"

"Personal."

With a sigh, she puts down her nail file and picks up the telephone. After a murmuring conversation, she hangs up. "Dr. Monroe isn't here yet, but Dr. Townsend is on duty and he'll be down soon."

I exhale with relief. Dr. Monroe not being here is the best-case scenario. I head to the same seat I took last time and the time before that, the one right next to the door that leads to the offices and patient rooms.

From here, my view of the glass doors at the front entrance is perfect. I see the front steps leading down to the walkway, the green grass, the shivering trees.

And after a minute or two, I see the first sign of smoke drifting through the air.

Melinda comes up the steps, giving me the thumbs up—an actress waiting in the wings. It occurs to me how strange it is that this waiting room is always so empty. A typical hospital is a party compared to this place.

Pushing the glass doors open, Melinda hurries inside, straight to the front desk.

"Excuse me, ma'am?" she asks. "There appears to be a fire outside."

The bored look on the receptionist's face turns to suspicion. "Where?"

"In a trash can. Someone probably threw a cigarette butt in there." Melinda beckons her. "I'll show you."

The receptionist stands and follows her to the glass doors,

where she stops to look. She puts a hand over her mouth and gasps. Then she runs out, the glass doors swinging shut behind her, leaving Melinda and me here alone in the waiting room.

"Go," I tell her, shooing her. "Get in the car and wait."

"I will as soon as you get in there."

I stand up and push the doors that lead to the rest of the hospital. But they're locked. I should have expected as much, but my heart chokes my throat. "Dammit."

Without a word, Melinda races behind the front desk and I follow.

"Go, *please,* I'll figure it out," I tell her.

Her voice shakes. "There have to be keys." She opens drawers frantically.

"No, I think there's some kind of button ... there!" I whisper, pointing to a switch on the wall.

Melinda flips it. The doors make a clicking sound, and I hurry across the room to push one open. Melinda steps over to the entrance and peers out the glass doors.

"Dad, she's heading back inside," Melinda says.

"Melinda, just go back out to the car, I don't want them connecting you to—"

But she doesn't listen. She bursts out the glass doors, saying, "I have an idea, do you have a hose? Let's find a hose to put it out..."

I release the longest breath and step through the doorway, into to the rest of the hospital.

It's astonishing, lighter than air, to be on this side. I sprint up the hallway with an energy I haven't felt in years. I pass Monroe's office, the fool, and use the back stairwell to the second floor. I find my wife's room like a rat in a maze. The sight of her stops me short in the doorway.

She's asleep.

I step inside, beholding her. She's the most comforting sight. Sane, insane, she looks the same when she's asleep.

"Hey Rosie," I say, moving toward her.

I come and squeeze her arm. It's cold and covered in goosebumps.

She doesn't respond.

I snap my fingers in front of her face. "Pssst. My little thorn. I've come to take you home."

"Mmm," she says with a drunk smile, eyes still closed.

It's the first hint that she's in there somewhere.

I pet her hair. "That's right. Can you get up?"

"I'm tired."

"Of course you are, they have you all doped up. You need a chair?"

"I'm not in the mood for ... furniture." Her words are gluey.

Baffled, I laugh. "Okay. Hold on. I'll be right back."

I poke my head into the hall. At the end, two nurses with arms full of bedding are engaged in hushed conversation. I wait for them to move on, then steal into the hallway. The previous times I came here, I was disturbed by the distant screaming. But right now, it's the other way around—I'm disturbed by how dead silent it is. Sure, there's a wail now and then, but that's one person. The entire ward, meanwhile, is nothing but quiet. And now I see why. In room after room, the patients are the same. They're lying in their beds in the middle of the day. They're standing at windows. They're sitting in corners, heads hung.

"Sorry," I say to an elderly woman whispering at a wall, as I step inside her room. "Just borrowing this."

I bring the wheelchair back to Rose's room. She's fallen asleep again, and it takes some shaking to wake her back up.

"Come on." I scoop her up with my arms. Her eyes flutter open, but she's dead weight.

"I hate pudding," she says.

"Put your arms around me."

She opens her eyes and gives me a sly smile. "What would my husband think?"

I laugh, thinking she's cracked a joke, but her eyes flutter shut again and her face goes slack.

"Rose, I *am* your husband. Come on." I slap her face softly, *tap-tap-tap*. "This is serious. We've got to get you out of here."

"Chocolate, vanilla, tapioca," she says. "Doesn't matter."

I try pulling her up from behind, lifting under her arms, transferring her to the chair. She slouches over, nearly falling off. I scoop her back up and try to readjust her. She won't sit up straight. She's goo.

I could scream. I've been here too long already. I'm running out of time.

"Are you tired, ladies? Suffering from mood swings?" she murmurs in a radio-friendly voice as I adjust her on the chair, leaning her back.

I hold onto one of Rose's shoulders because I'm scared she'll tip right over. I wheel her out of the room and wonder how the hell I'm going to get her down a flight of stairs, until I see what awaits me at the end of the hall.

A doctor I don't recognize stands with two men in blue security uniforms.

"What do you think you're doing?" the doctor asks me.

In a frenzy, I turn around, as if I might run the other way, but there's a trio of nurses blocking the other end of the hall.

I wheel back around the other way and face the doctor and the guards.

"I just want to take my wife home," I say, my voice breaking. "Is that so much to ask?"

In less than five seconds, the guards have me tackled to the ground.

✺

I've been locked alone in an empty hospital room for what feels like hours. No matter how hard I bang on the door, no one will acknowledge me. Besides the hospital bed, it's like an interrogation room. No windows. No frills. No evidence of humanity. Eventually I just sit and wait and pray that Melinda's all right.

We were so close, and that's what guts me most. We were almost out of here. Another three minutes and I could have been home with Rose. But I mucked the whole thing up.

Finally, the door unlocks and swings open. I stand up and face Dr. Monroe but freeze when I see the policemen behind him, hands on their batons.

"Give us a few minutes, please," Dr. Monroe tells the cops, and pulls the door shut.

Dr. Monroe is freshly shaven, hair gelled back, smelling of cologne as if he just arrived at work. He stands inches shorter than me, but I sure feel like the smaller man.

"Why are the police here?" I ask.

"Why do you think? You just attempted to kidnap one of our patients."

The accusation gives me vertigo. "She's my wife."

"She's involuntarily committed to this hospital and can't be removed from the premises without administrative approval. You know this."

I sink to a seated position on the hospital bed. I can't speak, trying to imagine what will happen to my children if I go to prison.

"Now," he says. "If you can be civil, we can go to my office and discuss all this before I decide whether to press charges against you." He smiles. "What do you say?"

leo

I sit in the chair across from Dr. Monroe. A clock on the wall ticks like a metronome. That photo of his dog mocks me. I want to ask him if he drugs his dog up and locks him in a cage all day long.

"What do I have to do to make this stop?" I ask. "Whatever it is, I'll give it to you."

The doctor creaks back and forth in his chair, observing me.

"You already have the ledger," I go on. "Burned her therapy records to smithereens."

He wrinkles his face. His confusion looks genuine. "Mr. Crawford, I have absolutely no idea what you're referring to."

"Well, maybe not you. The *collective* you." As soon as I say it, I realize how paranoid it sounds. I also recognize where I'm sitting—on the other side of a psychiatrist's desk, one who could have me arrested by the end of this conversation. But I have only one card left in my hand, and I've got to play it. "I know something fishy is going on here. I've been poking around. And I might have to call my friend down at the *Times*, see what he thinks."

I don't mention that I'm talking about the *Sunset Times*, and that my friend's a gossip columnist.

Dr. Monroe makes a funny noise, kind of like a balloon letting out air, and sinks deeper into his chair. He twirls a pencil around in his fingers, contemplating. I can tell he's angry by the way he's grinding his teeth—but everything else about him is unreadable, clinical, blank.

"I'm afraid Rose's condition has taken a steep dive in the past few days," he says, sitting back. "When a paranoid patient is stubbornly resistant to treatment, and suffers from debilitating delusions such as your wife, and *especially* considering the homicidal comments she's made—"

"Is there a record of that, by the way?" I ask, leaning in, but he cuts me off.

"—unfortunately, our only course of treatment left is psychosurgery."

The word is a brick lobbed into the middle of a window.

"Surgery?" I repeat.

"A therapeutic brain procedure." He opens a file in front of him, making a note. "A very small surgical intervention on the frontal lobes. I'm confident it would alleviate the excessive emotional strain she's been experiencing."

I swallow. "You're talking about ..." What's the word? I can't remember. "The thing with the icepick ..." My stomach drops. I've somehow transcended panic. I'm in a desert of feeling, waving goodbye to the life I thought I knew before. "A lobotomy."

He continues writing, the pencil whispering on the page.

"But ... that turns people into vegetables."

"Just a minor procedure to relieve emotional distress," he says, in an almost singsong voice.

"No."

I ball up my fist and hit the table to get his attention. Finally, he stops writing and meets my eyes. The most chilling part of his gaze is how human he appears—like a man who's sure he knows the answers. Who's convinced he's doing the right thing.

"I can't allow that," I say.

"We will require your signature in order to move forward with her new treatment plan."

"Well, you won't get it."

"Then the alternative is, in her incapacitated state, Rose will remain here. We will restrict visitors. She'll remain the way she is now, and she'll stay here for good. She'll be one of our 'lifers' as we call them. We provide them with the most excellent of care. Meanwhile, you'll go to jail for attempted kidnapping."

My mouth goes dry. The air seems to thin.

"But the choice is up to you, of course." He smiles, closing the folder. "Consent to the surgery, and she'll be home in a matter of days. As for the policemen waiting upstairs? I could tell them we've dropped charges and send them home."

My heart pounds like a bass drum. I shake my head.

"That's a shame," Dr. Monroe says, crossing his arms. "Are you aware your daughter Melinda is currently being booked for intake?"

I feel myself blanch. I stand up, wanting to wring his neck. "For what?"

"It didn't take long after security took her upstairs before she spilled everything. She's hysterical." He tut-tuts. "The apple doesn't fall far from the tree."

I'm shaking, staying as still as I can because otherwise, I'll explode. Imagining Melinda scared and restrained here—it makes me want to cry. What if they do to her what they've done to Rose?

I could strangle him. I could.

Feel his vertebrae crack between my hands.

Watch the life drain out of him. And I wouldn't be sorry.

But I'd only be pulling one screw out of a giant machine that'll keep running.

It's hopeless; I put my elbows on the table, head in my hands, and I can't help it. I sob. Here comes the flood.

"There, there," Dr. Monroe says, pulling out a box of tissues. "I know what a hard decision it is. You're a good husband, Mr. Crawford, and a good father, too. You're doing the best you can."

Next, he pushes me the paper and a pen. CONSENT FOR SURGERY, the title says.

Consent.

When I sign my wife's life away, it barely makes a sound.

leo

I drive home in silence, an automaton. The ordeal of getting Melinda out of there ended up taking the entire afternoon. Melinda sits beside me, blank-faced, puffy-eyed, and hollow as a prisoner of war. We hit traffic right at rush hour. Twilight turns the sky violet, then blue, then midnight. Not a star to be seen—just the glitter of the city waking up to the night.

"Are you okay, Dad?" Melinda asks tentatively when I pull into the driveway and leave the car idling.

"Are *you*?"

It takes her a moment to respond. "I think so."

"Your mother's coming home soon."

"Really?" Melinda watches me doubtfully.

"As early as late next week, they said. Isn't that great?" My voice catches in my throat.

"Well ... that's good, right?" Melinda says, trying to read my face. She's so shrewd. So hard to fool. "That's what we came there for?"

"Yep." The smile hurts, so I turn to face forward again,

dropping it. "Now you go grab Julie from Mrs. Giordano's, all right? I'll be home in an hour or two."

"Where are you going?" Melinda asks softly.

"Errand to run. I'll bring home a pizza."

"Are you sure you're okay?"

"I won't be if you keep repeating the same questions."

She puts her hand on her door hesitantly.

"Melinda, I'm sorry."

"It's okay," she says, popping the door open. Her voice is hoarse and she flashes me a tired smile. "If we're getting Mom home, it was all worth it, right?"

I nod. "See you soon."

I watch her cross the street to the Giordanos'. I watch the house wake up as she rings the doorbells, the living room windows lighting up like yellow eyes.

And I drive toward the Hollywood Hills.

The quiet of the valley bleeds into a freeway crawl, and soon I'm cutting through Hollywood. Every stoplight's a new movie to watch: hippies shoving each other on the sidewalk, a Chevy Impala crashed into a fire hydrant, the cherry-twirl of police lights. Clubs with girls lined up in go-go boots, stunned-sad veterans with cardboard signs. At an A&W, cute waitresses in roller skates glide across the parking lot, delivering hot dogs to car windows. Déjà vu weighs heavy, and at the same time, it's an alien planet.

This isn't my world.

Rose used to say that. Bring her to a church picnic at Bethlehem and she'd whisper, "This isn't my world." Tell her to join the PTA if she had so many opinions. "That isn't my world." Ask her why she's a housewife but the house isn't clean: "This isn't my world." College, jobs, modeling, radio voicework ... nothing was her world, nothing. It was a running joke between us. But right now, I understand more than ever that she was serious.

This isn't our world.

I pass a billboard for Valley Builders and inhale sharply. It's a sign, it's an actual *sign*. I choke on my own unexpected laughter. And as I make my way up into the darkening streets, winding up into the hills, I know just what I'm going to say when I get to where I'm going.

I park two streets away, at the end of a cul-de-sac, under a squat palm tree. Crickets croon and the city twinkles. I start up the street but think the better of it and double back to my car. Grab a tire iron from my trunk, tucking it in the back of my pants.

I walk uphill, with my head down, to Victor's house.

The thing about those giant picture windows is, at night, you can see everything. You can stand and watch someone's living room like a television screen, and that's just what I do. I watch Victor coming in and out of the room—first fully clothed, then in his bathing suit. Then the light is on, the overhead fan is whirring, but he's gone. Next, I hear the splash of him in his pool. I creep into his side yard, so dark I nearly stumble into a cactus. It's the same escape route I took when Rose and I left that godawful potluck, which feels like a lifetime ago. I hide here a while, listening, making sure he's alone. After a few minutes, I hear him get out of the pool and head up the back stairs, whistling.

I circle up front, walk up his driveway, and ring his doorbell.

He opens the door in his swim trunks, hair wet, towel around his neck.

"By Jove, it's Leo!" he says when he opens the door, and chuckles. "You're kidding me. The King of Spin lives and breathes!"

I stare at him.

He gives me a look. "Leo? We've all wondered what happened. Natalie thought it was a family emergency. The creative team has bets going about whether you'll be back. Some of us assumed you went off the deep end."

I don't say anything. I just let him wriggle.

"You're making me uncomfortable," he says with a hard-edged laugh. "What are you doing on my doorstep, old man?" He snaps his fingers. "You stoned or something?"

"I'm from Valley Builders," I say. "Wanted to know if you were interested in some double-paned windows."

His eyes widen. His skin pales right in front of me. He puts his hands up, as if I'm about to take a swing at him. And who knows, I might.

I don't wait for him to answer.

I snap my fist back and punch him in the face. Pain explodes through my knuckles.

"Jesus, Leo!" He stumbles backward, falling on his back on the carpeted floor.

I step across the threshold.

I kick the door shut behind me. Flip the lights off. Pull the tire iron out of the waist of my pants.

"Thanks so much for inviting me inside."

leo

In the dark, my eyes try to adjust. I can barely see anything.

But no matter.

"Tell me about the study Rose was in. Tell me everything you know."

"Study? Gee, I'm not sure—"

I bring the tire iron down once, twice, metal thudding flesh. He shrieks.

"What are you doing?" he yells. "What is this?"

"Don't pretend you don't know." I bring it down again, this time hearing a crack of bone. "That only makes me madder."

"Stop!" he screams. "Stop. Okay."

I almost hit him again, the tire iron raised above my head. He starts to sit up.

"Don't move," I tell him.

"Okay." I can see his hands raised up. My focus is returning and I can better see the shape of him—and the glint of his frightened eyes. "I'll—I'll tell you whatever you want, okay? Just ... don't hurt me." He groans, clutching his side. "Christ."

I may not be mistaken for Errol Flynn, but I do have a good six inches on this guy and a tire iron in my hand. He's not going to fight me. He knows better.

I kick him, hard, in the stomach. "Tell me about the Pacific Institute of Human Research. You got rid of the files. Why?"

He catches his breath, clutching his stomach with one hand and using his other to protect himself from the next blow. "We worked with them on a study, you know the one that ... Rose never finished." He pants. "Gimme a second. Please." He blows out a long, steady breath. "That study ... didn't go so well. It wasn't just Rose. It backfired. A few people ended up ... having breakdowns."

"What kind of breakdowns?"

"You know. Losing touch with reality. When things went wrong at the study, I heard they gave them electro-shock to wipe their memories—that made things worse. I don't know for sure, Leo, these are just things I heard."

"'You heard, you heard.' Where are you hearing this?"

"Staff at the institute. They pulled the plug on the study because it went so wrong."

"What was the purpose of the study?" I press.

"Not sure. Something to do with subliminal messaging, dreams ... that's Lumer's specialty."

"And why is the military funding it?"

"That I don't know, and please don't hit me. I really don't."

"What role did you play in all this?" I ask, gripping the tire iron harder.

"None! Honest, I wasn't there. I heard all this second-hand. I'm just—I'm just someone who works with places like the Institute on the agency side to benefit from the research they do. And sometimes they use casting, other resources on our end to ... to recruit patients. That's how Rose got signed up, remember? They were looking for pregnant women."

The more he explains, the less it makes sense.

"What else?" I ask.

"That's it. That's my involvement. That's everything."

I consider if I believe him. I whack his shin with a tire iron, just to see if anything comes out—a human piñata of information.

"Fuck! Okay! The only other thing I heard was a rumor, just a *rumor*. I heard Lumer's run studies before where he doses subjects with hallucinogenic drugs. Drugs that come *from* the military. But I don't know why, and I don't know what they did in there."

My knees nearly buckle. Melinda's comment about it sounding like an LSD trip—I never in my wildest dreams thought she'd be right. What Kafkaesque hell are we living in?

"Who told you this?" I ask.

"A drunk nurse. So take it with a grain of salt."

I let these details swim together in my mind. They're so dizzying, so impossible, my anger recedes.

"I'm not with the Institute, Leo," Victor says pleadingly. "I'm your *colleague*."

He catches his breath, his chest heaving in the light. I almost believe him.

"What about my mother?" I ask.

There's a pause. "How do you mean?"

"Did you hurt my mother?"

He doesn't respond, which only pours gasoline on the blaze of my suspicion.

"I know you took the ledger. Did you kill her, too?" I ask, raising the tire iron above my head.

"Leo, no. No. Of course not. She was a sweet old lady."

"But you took the ledger."

"I got paranoid. I wanted to make sure all the evidence was gone. That's all."

"What about the fire at Dr. Wells' office?"

"I don't even know a Dr. Wells. Honest."

A horrible wave of nausea hits. All at once, the tire iron weighs heavy in my hand.

Am I overreacting? Yes, Victor was involved. But he seems like a patsy in this vast conspiracy.

"I got rid of the ledger," he insists, groaning and pushing himself to his feet again. "I got rid of the files at Century. But the other stuff? No."

"You're telling the truth."

"Of course. You just beat it out of me."

My hand with the tire iron drops to the side. All this information swims around my dizzy head. I consider my next move.

Takes a single second for Victor to swipe the tire iron, pull back, and hit me across the forehead with it.

leo

I stagger backward, blocking my head with my arms. He lashes out the tire iron and hits my forearm. I'm stunned with pain.

"Son of a bitch," he says.

I manage to kick his legs out. He stumbles backward to the floor. I lean over him, grasping the tire iron, trying to wrench it away. It's a game of tug of war.

"And I mean it," he says, pulling with all his might, panting. "I've met your mother."

Those words pulsate with my forehead. *I've met your mother.*

He yanks the tire iron in the one distracted second when my grip on it slips. Now my hand is empty and he lets out a laugh. He's got it now. As he pushes up to his feet, I run past him, nearly tripping on a step into the dining room—damn split-level house—and bang into the dining room table.

Insulting my mother on top of everything else. I'd like to bury him alive.

I hear his footsteps scuffling behind me. I duck under the

table, because it's the closest place to hide. His hairy legs walk past me, his ugly bare feet stopping and then turning into the kitchen. A light flickers on, then off. I think maybe he's spotted me but then I hear footsteps across linoleum.

He's in the kitchen.

All I can see from here is a credenza with a crystal decanter gleaming on it, catching the moonlight. I wait a second to make sure he's not in the room and emerge from under the table. I grab the decanter of whiskey.

I'm in the dining room, he in the kitchen. A few feet separate us.

He flicks the kitchen light on and we spot each other at the same time. He lunges toward me and I bring the decanter down on the crown of his head as hard as I can. The impact stops him, crystal shattering, and he falls to his knees, dropping the tire iron and immediately covering his head. He's drenched in blood and Scotch and shards. He's moaning. I've got him this time.

"Please," he says. "Enough."

"Damn you to hell." I kick him, not too hard, just enough for him to topple on his side. I pick up the tire iron and squat next to him, catching my breath, ready for whatever dirty trick comes next. But his skull's bleeding into his sharp haircut. I don't know if he has much fight left in him.

Am I really going to kill a man? There seems no other way out at this point.

"What did you do with the ledger after you stole it from my house?" I ask.

"I ... disposed ... of it." His breath is ragged. "Burned it ... no paper trail."

My memory blows smoke. I blink and see ashes under my shoes. "Like you burned down Wells' office?"

"Rose became ... my liability. She was talking to media. If

Lumer found out ... if details of the study were leaked ... I worried ..."

He's shivering, bloody and battered in his bathing suit.

"What was he trying to learn?"

"Lumer studies mind control," he murmurs, "and Century would love to benefit from his findings. Both the military and the advertising industry are invested in psychological manipulation. Can you imagine? If we were able to use images on the television to unlock certain brains?"

"You're all sick."

"I didn't mean to kill her, Leo." The gash on his head glistens in the light as he contemplates the mess around him. "That wasn't my plan at all." His face twitches with pain, one eye. "But she pulled a gun on me."

"Excuse me?" I hear myself say, but I know what I heard, and what he meant.

I let it sink in.

I give the thought *he killed my mother* room to air out.

Something in me turns to ice.

"She snuck up on me and pulled a gun ..." He winces, touching his side delicately. It's purpled and bruising. "Then she wanted to call the cops. So I panicked. I hit her on the head with the cradle of the phone. She fell down the stairs. It was one blow. It was over fast. No pain."

He must detect the wild animal I'm restraining within my bones, because he shrinks back and blocks his head with his hands.

"I'm not a bad man," he says.

"Neither am I," I say.

I take a step, grab his hair, and drag him across the threshold, into the kitchen. He yells, thrashes, kicks. He's a heavy load—short, but stocky. His hair is slick with blood, my palms slipping. He starts screaming so I get him in a chokehold.

Now he's quiet, gasping for air. I drag him through the kitchen. A smear of blood follows us. The back door is wide open, city lights winking back at us under the moon and the black expanse of sky. I pull him out there, to the patio, high up above his yard.

As I drag him into the fresh air, I get a flashback to the party here that day—the kitchen filled with potluck dinners. The sunshine, the records playing, the laughter.

Victor coughs, choking. "I'm not the enemy, Leo. This is bigger than that."

"Then who is?"

Victor is sniveling now, one eye swollen shut, bumps on his face.

"If the man who killed my mother, stole personal property from me, burned down a building out of paranoia, and referred my wife to the study that broke her brain isn't the enemy—then who is?"

"Her brain was already broken before she got there," he says. "Come on."

And that's the comment that sends me over the edge. And him too. I wrench his head in another chokehold, this one with everything I've got, and with a roar, I pull him up against the balcony railing. He resists, trying to turn to dead weight and drag me to the floor. But apparently when it comes to adrenaline, rage is one hell of an accelerant, because I lift him up all the way off his tiptoes and turn him around. He faces the canyon, the Hollywood sign, the circuit board of Los Angeles. He's thirty feet up, teetering over the wicked blue glow of his swimming pool. Just two wooden beams between him and his end. And then—

I push him over.

He screams for just a split second, because a split second is all it takes. He plunges facedown into the water from all the way up here, falling, falling, smacking his skull against the lip of the pool on his way in. Around his head, blood explodes like a mushroom cloud. He's bleeding into the water, turning the blue crimson, then violet—arms out, legs splayed, spinning like a wheel, then slowing, and then stilling. Next to him, a neon pink flamingo inflatable bobs in the water.

Catching my breath, the air shifts. It's so quiet up here. Crickets play violins and an owl hoots. The view—delicate grasses in the breeze, shadows of palms—it undoes something in me. I sob, eyeing my trembling hands. My bloody knuckles.

It's some kind of irreconcilable difference, isn't it?

To have a world so beautiful and so horrible all at once.

I wipe my eyes and nose, then head back into the house. Track down the tire iron. Tuck it back in my pants. The house is a wreck. Looks like a break-in gone wrong. I glimpse it for just a second before turning off the kitchen light and heading outside, down the back stairs. I take a moment, just one, to pause and watch Victor's body there in the shocking blue pool.

I wish I felt more satisfaction than I do, but he was right. The enemy has no face. No name. It's bigger than him, me, the hospital, the study, the agency, and the institution.

And that is the scariest enemy of all—one that is made up of a thousand blank faces, smiling and doing their jobs.

I sneak out the side yard and walk back to my car, two blocks away. Before leaving the neighborhood, I wipe off my hands and face and take off the blood-spattered button-up shirt. I shove it in someone's trash can out near the curb. I'm disheveled, a little bruised, wearing an undershirt—but you'd never guess looking at me that I just committed the ultimate sin.

I get in, drive to the pizza parlor, and wonder how I'm ever going to look my daughters in the eye again.

leo

Tonight is the longest, quietest, darkest night of my life.

Sleep isn't happening. I sit atop my unmade bed, catatonic. I can't even bring myself to change into my pajamas. I still smell like blood and Chivas Regal. Melinda asked if I'd gotten in a barfight when I got home, and I let her keep thinking it. Sure. A drunk loose cannon. Better than a murderer.

Murderer.

Ma's rolling over in her grave.

I went to war. I was in combat. I hit targets, human targets. I knew I'd snuffed lights out, but that was different. That was following orders for a just cause. Defending something.

This, tonight, was intimate in a way war was not—my hands on another man's throat, his teeth marks in my arm. And now, Victor is a part of me.

I blink and see blood billowing into the water.

The clock ticks and I hear his head hitting the cement, that wet *snap* that undid a man's life in a second.

And what was it all for?

Rose, that's who. And Ma. And my entire family.

I swallow a lump, staring at Rose's vanity. Imagining her coming back here in a few days and what she'll be like. I tear up, hands to my face. Will she need constant care? Will she be able to speak? Will she be the same Rose, just a little … simpler? Will she make sarcastic jokes? Will she remember when we met? Will she drool and say nothing at all? Will she be happier in her new state? Will she remember her daughters? Will she love late nights? Will she drink tea and jot down her thoughts into a notebook, just for her? Will she understand why I had to do what I did?

Will she ever forgive me?

I sob. Let it out, glad no one is here to see it. Just let it out. Vomit. Expel. Purge. I'd like to cut it right out of me. The emotions are so heavy, so painful, that I wish it were me going on the operating table tomorrow—

Wait. I check my watch. It's 3:36 a.m.

Today.

I close my eyes. I see Rose there in her bed, grayish walls, grayish sheets. Alone. Either she knows her fate or she doesn't, and each option is its own tragedy. I cycle through the options—but there are none. My brain is circling, a mouse trapped in a snake cage. One wrong move could wind me in jail, or Melinda in the hospital, or both.

An hour passes and the itch worsens. I'm pacing the floor of the house, trying to calculate. They said she was going in for surgery in *the morning*. What does that mean? Is she under the scalpel right now?

In a flash of desperation, I run to my office. I pull the phone book out with swollen, broken hands and find the number for Woodward.

"Woodward Neuropsychiatric Center, Night Nurse speaking."

"Hi, I'm calling about my wife. She's a patient—"

"Visiting hours are by appointment only."

"I know," I say, my voice breaking. "But she's set for surgery. It's an emergency—"

"Unfortunately, I can't discuss patient care," she says in a honeyed voice. "Who's her doctor?"

"Dr. Monroe. Can someone reach him for me?"

"He's not in, but I'll take a message for when he is—"

"This is urgent," I say, voice climbing. "It can't wait. Who's the physician on duty? Let me talk to him."

"He's busy right now, but I can leave a message and he can call you back—"

I slam the phone down and curse under my breath. I throw the phone book across the room, knocking a lamp over, and head into the kitchen.

The cat clock's eyes flick back and forth with every *tick*.

It's almost five a.m.

I grab a notepad and jot a note for Melinda. Then I take a quick shower to wash away the blood and the stink of Scotch, get dressed, comb my hair. Try to claw back some semblance of credibility, perform the part of a Sane Man. A Good Husband.

I grab my keys, head to the car, and drive.

leo

Woodward's visitor lot is completely empty when I arrive. Even the staff lot on the other side barely has any cars in it. The pitch black of the night sky is just beginning to soften with blue around the edges. Morning is on its way. The hospital is eerie, alone in the darkness, lit up with barred windows. A mausoleum. A prison.

Please Rose, don't be gone yet.

I try the double doors at the entrance. Locked. The waiting room is dark, no receptionist, no one inside. No doorbell. No knocker. It's the most seething fury, to have no one to direct it at. I bang on the glass with my raw fists and yell. I shake the doors. Finally, when I'm considering whether I should find a rock to bash the glass in, a security guard comes from the doors that lead to the doctor's offices with an irritated expression on his face.

"Hi!" I call, tapping on the glass.

The man approaches, cautiously, probably wondering if I need to be committed. He looks like he hasn't slept in a year, dark circles ringed around his eyes. I smile as wide as I can. Calm. Collected.

He speaks through the glass on the door, his voice sounding like he's underwater. "We're closed to visitors."

"I know," I enunciate. "But it's an emergency."

"If it's an emergency, go to the emergency room."

"Where's that?"

"At the hospital," he says slowly, as if I'm stupid.

"No. My wife. She is in there." I point behind him. "She's going into surgery."

He shakes his head. "Come back in the morning."

He starts to turn, but I smack the glass again.

"By then it'll be too late!" I say. "It's—I need to talk to the surgeon. I need to talk to him, okay? It's about—" An idea flashes to mind; I grab onto it like a life raft. "—an allergy. She has an allergy I forgot to disclose, and it could kill her."

The security guard looks mildly intrigued.

"Please! Her name is Rose Crawford."

"Just wait here," he says.

He turns and disappears behind the door he came from. I stare at the empty waiting room for what feels like an eternity. Then the security guard returns with a night nurse, who also looks annoyed. I explain the entire thing through the glass door again. She listens, her face softens, and she confers with the security guard.

"Rose Crawford, you said?" she asks me.

"Yes."

"I'm not letting you inside," she says. "You'll have to wait out there."

"Fine by me."

They leave again. I stand like a dog waiting for my owner to come home, hyperattentive to every little sound. I look up.

The sunrise has purpled the clouds and the birds are just starting to sing. It hurts the way beautiful things often do.

I check my watch. It's after 6 a.m. I sit on the stairs and wait.

The brighter the sun gets, the louder the birds sing, the more I wonder if I'm too late.

I hang my head in my hands. And then I hear a door open behind me.

"Mr. Crawford?" a man in surgical scrubs says.

I scramble to my feet and come to the door to meet him. "Yes, that's me. Thank you for coming, so much." I start to open the door to join him, but he holds it in place. It's just ajar enough for us to talk.

"I'm Dr. Taylor. I'm the surgeon here." I can't see his face behind his surgical mask. I can't see how old he is or anything beyond his brown eyes. "I understand you had something urgent to relay regarding your wife's procedure?"

"Am I too late?"

"What was it you needed to relay?"

"Can I come inside?"

"You can't. We're not open."

"I wanted to talk to her."

"She's already under anesthesia."

My eyes sting. "Has it already happened? You already performed it?"

He doesn't answer. "Mr. Crawford, I came down here under the impression you had something urgent you had to tell me, something that could endanger your wife. I don't appreciate being tricked."

He starts to pull the door shut, but I stick my foot in to stop him.

"It's not a trick," I say.

His grip on the door reveals the glint of a gold ring on his finger.

"You're married," I say, pitch rising. "You have a wife."

Our eyes meet. His brow wrinkles.

"Maybe you have a daughter too, or a sister, or a cousin," I say. "You have a mother, I know that much."

"I'm going to call security if you don't get your foot out of the door here."

"And I'm sure you love her, your wife." I lock my eyes to his. "I'm sure there's no one quite like her. Maybe you love the crooked way she smiles, or the letters she writes, or the way her laugh sounds across a room. The way she reads books to your children. The—" I swallow the emotion, feeling the sand in the hourglass. "—the things she says, that aren't things anyone else in this world can possibly say."

I choke back a sob.

"Mr. Crawford, please," the surgeon says.

"They're forcing her to do this. She doesn't *need* this surgery."

"That's for Woodward to decide."

"You just have to know. You have to know." I tear up, not even caring that there's pity screaming in his eyes. "She's different, and imperfect, and she's sensitive—and sometimes she's sadder than I thought she ought to be, or sassier, and she doesn't love vacuuming, or entertaining ... but she's ..." My cheeks are warm and wet. "She's her. She's just perfectly *her*."

The surgeon blinks at me, unreadable.

"Don't take her away from us," I finish.

Gently, the surgeon uses his shiny shoe to push mine out of the doorway. "Mr. Crawford, I've been instructed to call the police if you try to interfere with the surgery. Don't make me do it."

"Please do the right thing," I whisper. "What if it was someone you loved?"

He doesn't acknowledge what I've said. "We'll call you as soon as the surgery is over." He pulls the glass doors shut, locks them with a click, and disappears behind the door inside.

And it's over. Flatlined heartbeat. Bullet to the brain.

I've lost her.

melinda

Julie and I wait out on our front stoop like we're posing for a photograph. She's in a sundress printed with apples, wispy curls in pigtails. I wear a dress too, a long one that reaches my bare feet. We pick at clovers on the edge of the lawn and snap our gaze up every time a car passes. It's the strangest feeling, to be so nervous to meet my own mother.

The station wagon's familiar chug sends me to my feet. They pull into the driveway. I catch a glimpse of her there, in the front seat. A paisley scarf wrapped around her head. Cat-eye sunglasses.

"There she is," I say to Julie.

"Mama!" Julie yells.

"Remember, we talked about being quiet, being calm, not overwhelming her—"

"Mama! Mama! Mama!"

She doesn't hear a word I said, sprinting across the lawn to the passenger door.

I wait here on the porch. Dad told me she might be different. She might be a little slower and have memory issues from whatever treatments they did. I don't want to overwhelm her, but somewhere inside me, there's the ghost of a little girl who wants to run toward her shouting *Mama!* too. I clasp my shaky hands in front of me, watching as Dad gets out his side and circles round to Mom's.

"Give her room, Julie," he warns, opening the car door. "She's not too steady."

Mom's slippered feet come out first. Slippers—I'd expected heels. Dad helps her out. She's in a rainbow house-dress I've seen her wear a thousand times before, but she's startlingly thin and it hangs on her like it doesn't belong to her. He takes her arm and leads her across the lawn. She doesn't seem to notice me. She seems fixed on her own slip-pers shuffling, as if it's taking concentration to walk. Something in me dies and falls off, an autumn leaf on a tall tree.

She reminds me of an elderly woman.

"Mama!" Julie says, trailing behind her, oblivious and happy.

I hold my breath as my parents approach.

"Melinda and Julie are so excited to see you," Dad murmurs to Mom.

Mom looks up. I can't see her eyes behind her glasses. Her face is fixed, deadpan.

"Hello," she says, rolling the word out.

My throat tightens. She's not Mom. Mom never came back.

"We missed you," I say, choking on the words. "I'm glad you're okay."

"Thirsty," she says.

I'm relieved at the word. It gives me something to do. I turn toward the door.

"Sure, let me get you some water."

"Hi, Mama!" Julie yells behind her.

They walk into the living room, Dad leading Mom to the couch and helping her sit down. I grab a glass, fill it up, heart pounding. I'm shocked at her frailty. Why is she so weak?

"Here you go," I say, handing Mom the glass of water.

"Why, thank you," she says, and gulps it down. All of it. Then she hands me the glass and burps. "Well, that was unladylike."

We laugh uneasily. Except Julie, who thinks it's the funniest thing she's ever seen.

"Mama say scuse me," Julie says.

Mom tousles one of Julie's pigtails and smiles. "Scuse me."

She's still wearing her sunglasses, her scarf, and her coat, like she's visiting. She sits in the middle of the sofa, Julie on her left, Dad on her right. I grab a chair from the kitchen and pull it next to them.

"You're home for good now, right, Mom?" I ask.

How odd, to make small talk with the woman who made you.

"Very good," Mom answers.

I frown, bewildered. She reminds me of a drunk person, someone here but not. I glance at Dad, trying to read his face, but he won't meet my eyes.

"I missed ... this," Mom says, struggling to pronounce the words.

"Me too," I tell her.

"Mama home," Julie says proudly, touching Mom's knee.

"Mama home," she agrees.

A static silence spreads between us. I see our reflection in the gray television screen.

"I go potty," Julie says cheerfully.

I snort a laugh.

Dad clears his throat. "I'll take her upstairs," he tells me.

"Why don't you fill your mother in about your wild adventures up in San Francisco?"

They leave the room and it's just Mom and me. I come next to her on the couch, buzzing at her nearness. I grab her hand, fighting the urge to kiss it.

"I ran away from home, Mom."

"Oh no," she says, the words drawn out.

"I know. I hitchhiked there with Jim." The memory makes me smile. "And then we got separated the first day ..."

I fill her in on everything. Well, almost. Not the acid trip, the joints smoked, or the night I kissed a sailor. But I tell her about the Freak Fam, and fishing, and the Free Store. Dancing in the park and the concerts and selling jewelry up and down the sidewalks. I expect her to interrupt me, to lecture me on the dangers, but she just listens. Even when I get to the part about coming home for Grandma's funeral and breaking up with Jim.

"... I've changed, Mom," I tell her. "I feel like I've grown up since you've been gone."

I wait for her reaction, but there is none. Her mouth hangs open and a little snore escapes. My shoulder slump. How long has she been nodded off? I still can't see her eyes behind her glasses.

"Mom?"

No answer from her. Upstairs, Julie giggles.

Tentatively, gingerly, I pull Mom's sunglasses from her face. When I see what's underneath, I shrink back, covering my mouth with my hands.

She has small Band-Aids over each eyebrow. Her lids are closed, swollen with shocks of bruising, purple and yellow. She looks like someone beat her up. The novel *One Flew Over the Cuckoo's Nest* comes to mind, making me sick to my stomach. In horror, I put the sunglasses back on her face, wishing

I hadn't peeked beneath. I get up and sit back in my chair, pressing my fingers to my lips. I burn with an aimless rage. I can't believe it.

Mom is asleep, whether her eyes are shut or open.

Dad and Julie come back down, holding hands and taking the stairs one by one. I try to control myself, but I can't pretend. I shoot up from my seat.

"You let them do that to her?" I ask Dad as soon as he gets to the bottom of the stairs.

"Julie, go sit with Mama," he murmurs, nudging Julie toward the couch.

Dad and I stand face to face. His sorrow has aged him. I blink tears out of my eyes.

"I tried to stop it," he whispers. "They threatened to have me arrested, and to have you committed, and I didn't know what else to do."

I break down into tears. I can tell he's fighting them too. He reaches out and I shake my head. I know he didn't want this as much as me, but it hurts so badly.

"I need a minute," I say.

I run to my room and slam the door. I cry. I beat up my pillow. I start shoving my clothes into my backpack, planning my escape. I write a poem, then ball it up, then light it on fire and rub the ashes in my carpet. Once the tears have dried, I lie down on my bed. I listen to the nothingness. I put my hand on my chest and feel the wild, electric beat of my heart —still fighting, even as it breaks.

leo

Tonight, I sleep next to Rose, my arm slung over her all night long. I have the most vivid dreams—beaches, picnics, and some kind of carnival. I win Rose a goldfish and we ride the Ferris wheel. Young and careless, taste of her cherry lip gloss on my tongue, wind in our hair.

I open my eyes.

In the haze of early morning, I can hardly believe my luck. She's here. It wasn't just a dream, she's *here*—Rose's familiar warmth pressed into me, fitting together like we were carved from the same tree. The smell of her, sweet and salty.

But then I remember.

The shadows of the trees dance in the window. Those holiday dreams ebb and dissolve, and even though my arm is around her, my skin's on hers—I miss her.

I fear I'll spend the rest of my life that way.

I'm the first one up, so I make pancakes. Melinda spent half of yesterday crying on the phone to Jim, who I thought was old news. I'd bet she's planning her escape.

I eat breakfast and go through the classifieds, circling

copywriter positions. Magazine staff. Newspapers. Corporate communications. Anything but advertising.

Then I spot an article in the local news section: *Hollywood Hills Man Found Dead in Home Pool.* I nearly choke on my pancake.

Victor Ames, 38, an account executive at Century Advertising in Van Nuys, was found dead Sunday morning in the swimming pool of his Hollywood Hills residence. Los Angeles Police Department investigators noted signs of forced entry and a struggle inside the home, and are treating the death as a homicide. Ames, a bachelor, had been with Century Advertising since 1962, where he managed several prominent regional accounts. No suspects have been identified. Anyone with information is asked to contact the LAPD.

The phone rings so loudly I jump in my chair. I put the paper down and get up to answer it.

"Crawford residence, Leo speaking," I say.

"Mr. Crawford, this is Dr. Taylor from Woodward. How are you?"

The word *Woodward* is a knife in my back. I grit my teeth. I never want to speak with anyone in that hellhole again.

"Doing great, Doctor," I say, trying to hide my bitterness. "How about yourself?"

"Excellent. Just checking in to see how Rose is doing?"

Well, other than being part vegetable, she's great, thanks for asking.

"She's, uh ... she's been asleep for the most part," I say in as cheerful a voice as I can.

"It's very normal in the days after a procedure."

I close my eyes and imagine dousing the entire hospital with gasoline and throwing a match at it.

"How are the incisions healing?"

"I, uh, haven't looked at them yet."

Haven't been able to bring myself to. Her black eyes are bad enough.

"I see." He pauses. "Well, she's been quite heavily sedated for some time. It will probably take her some time to recover."

"Uh-huh."

There's another awkward pause. What is with this guy?

"Mr. Crawford, I want you to know I heard what you said," he says in a softer voice. "The morning of the surgery."

I take a sip of my coffee. "When I said ...?"

"And I performed the surgery because I was ordered to do so. It's my job. I'm not a psychiatrist."

"Right, just following orders, I get it."

"It's not that deep."

The fact this man has the gall to call me and try to defend himself makes me want to explode. "What do you—"

"I think you'll find it's not that deep at all," he says. "Please stay out of trouble."

He hangs up. I stare at the receiver, at a complete loss, and return it to the cradle.

Rose sleeps through the morning and Melinda refuses to leave her room. Julie and I go for a walk around the neighborhood. We point at daffodils and marvel at airplanes and when we get to the park on the corner, we stop and look at the shiny new plaque on the bench with my mother's name on it. She truly did aim for justice. There's something satisfying knowing that in her last moments, she pulled a gun on Victor because she was a tough old broad.

"You died a hero, Ma," I say. "You're certainly a better one than I."

"Where's Ma?" Julie asks, tugging my pant leg.

"Here, there," I say. "Everywhere."

When we get home, there's a beat-up green VW bus parked in our driveway. Somehow, I already know who it is before I even set foot through the front door.

"Hey Jim," I say as I step inside.

He and Melinda are in the living room. Her arms are crossed. I've clearly interrupted them. She eyes me defiantly, as if to say *what are you going to do?* Jim's got this goofy look about him, and now he's got a mustache on top of it. But he sure does watch Melinda like she didn't just hang the moon, she invented it.

"Uncle Jim!" Julie squeals.

"Hey, JuJuBean!"

"That your ride out there?" I ask Jim.

"I just, like, borrowed it."

"Far out," I say.

"Dad, don't say that," Melinda says with disgust. "Jim is here to pick me up."

They watch me, waiting for a reaction. I can feel them rigid and ready to defend their decision.

"I see. So you're back together, huh?"

"No," Melinda says. "We're just friends."

Jim says nothing, staring at the floor.

"Best friends," she says, more to him than me.

He nods, but doesn't smile.

"Well, where you off to?" I ask.

A moment passes, relaxes.

The two of them exchange a look.

"Um, well, Oregon maybe," Jim says.

"Just for a couple of weeks," Melinda says.

"What's up there?" I ask.

Melinda tilts her head, her expression softening a little. "This commune that Jim wants me to see."

"Sounds like an adventure."

"But then we're going back to San Francisco in June, right, Jim?" Melinda says.

"Sure, whatever you want."

Melinda stands up straighter. "Because we're going to the Monterey Pop Festival."

"Groovy," I say.

Melinda cringes. "Dad—don't."

I start clearing dishes off the table, stacking them in the sink. "When can I expect to see you again?"

"I'll visit soon," she says. "Promise. I don't want to be away too long, or I'm afraid Julie will forget about me."

"I hope so. It's not the same without you here."

She comes over to me and gives me a long hug. "I'm going to miss you all."

"Ditto." I kiss her temple, then swallow a lump. "Please make good decisions."

Melinda nods, her eyes watery, and takes a step back from me.

"So when are you taking off?" I ask.

Jim shuffles his feet. "Uh ... soon. Right, Lindy?"

"Yep," she says. "I'm packed and ready."

"Lin-Lin going bye-bye?" Julie asks.

Melinda picks up Julie and kisses her cheek. "I'll be back. Don't worry. And this summer, I'm going to get my own place in San Francisco, and you can come visit me." Melinda looks at me with glassy eyes. "You too, if you want."

I open my arms. "Come here. One more for the road."

Melinda puts Julie down and walks over to me. She's startlingly tall, but this time, she rests her head on my shoulder. For a single flash, like a photo in my brain, I remember the gentle weight of her soft head there on the first day she was born.

"I love you," I tell her, savoring each nanosecond. "Be safe."

She pulls away. "I am."

"And you," I say, pointing at Jim. "You take good care of her."

"Dad," Melinda says, annoyed. "I can take care of myself."

I can't argue with that.

Melinda pops upstairs, grabs her bags, and stops in my bedroom to kiss her sleeping mother goodbye.

"I'll call when I get to Bend," she whispers to her.

"Mmm," Rose answers.

Julie and I follow Jim and Melinda out front. The day is sweltering, sprinklers raining, and we wave at the sputtering VW bus until we can't see Melinda flashing the peace sign anymore. I'm heavy when I walk back inside—our quiet house that keeps getting quieter.

A while later, I find Rose sitting up in bed. Her hair is rumpled.

"I've been asleep a long time," she says with surprise.

She looks more lucid than I've seen her in months. I sit next to her.

"You sure have," I say, squeezing her hand. "God, I've missed you."

"You have no idea."

The way she says it unlocks something in me. It's her voice, the one I've missed—the one with a little bite to it, an edge. I take my hands and gently put them on her cheeks.

"Can I kiss you?" I ask.

"I don't know. *Can* you?"

I'm shocked that her tone sounds so sharp, a flash of the old Rose. I put my lips to hers and remember what hope tastes like. Warm. Promising. Tender. I pull back, my chest tight, focusing not on the bruises around her eyes but on her warm, brown gaze.

"May I?" I ask, touching one of the Band-Aids.

She nods. I pick at the edge of the fabric, peeling it from her brow. I brace myself, expecting stitches. A gash, at least. But there's just a pinprick. Like it was made with a needle—not an icepick, not a scalpel.

"How does it look?" she asks. "Am I *The Bride of Frankenstein?*"

I laugh. "You can hardly see anything. Hold still."

I peel the other one, ripping it off faster and making her say, "Ouch."

"Sorry. You know what they say about Band-Aids."

Here, too, there's nothing but the tiniest dot. Not an incision. I've had mosquito bites worse than this.

The surgeon's voice echoes: *I think you'll find it's not that deep at all.*

"My god, Rose," I say, stung with surprise. "You're still in there."

"Of course I am, you oaf," she says. "Where else would I be?"

"Mama wake up!" Julie says from the doorway.

Rose opens her arms. "Hi, baby girl!"

Julie climbs into her lap and they embrace, wiggling and laughing, Rose smooching Julie's plump cheeks. This is not the woman I brought home. She's alive. Bubbly. More present than I've seen her in longer than I can remember.

She's been quite heavily sedated for some time.

I reach for the right thing to say. Reach, but don't find. Right now, words aren't enough.

"I'm starving," Rose says to me. "What time is it? Feels like morning."

And she's right.

It does.

rose

Daddy used to say I was "born too much." I talked too much, ate too much, and asked for too much. That's not how a lady sits. That's not what polite girls say. I memorized the rules. Sit still. Curtsy, say please. Children should be seen and not heard.

One day, I thought, *I'll outgrow these silly rules.*

But then I grew older and noticed my mother hardly spoke at all. She was a background character serving drinks and cleaning floors. And yet Daddy was writer, director, and the starring role —a one-man show with an invisible cast.

For a few breathless years after leaving home, life was beach parties, raucous restaurant jobs, swing dancing in loud bars. I lived with a group of gals off Hollywood Boulevard, Dale in the same apartment building. I was ripe and wild and free. And yet, I've always had a dark streak—an echo of *too much, too much.*

"Rose darling," Dale slurred to me one night as he and I stumbled home from a bar, arm in arm. "Here's the problem with you: if you strut up Sunset Boulevard, you don't marvel at the neon lights; you fix your eyes on the drunk in the gutter."

"Someone needs to look at him," I said, passing the poor man who slept with his head in a puddle.

Right when my love affair with Hollywood was growing stale, I met an irresistible, wisecracking sailor named Leo. It didn't take long for me to be certain he was it. The first time he came over to my place, he studied my entire shelf and wanted to talk about every book.

"I've never met a man so interested in my opinions," I told him as he put *The Great Gatsby* back on the shelf.

"I've never met a woman with so many opinions to share," he said.

At that exact moment, the power in my apartment went out. He and I popped open a bottle of rum and drank in the dark and made each other laugh until tears spilled down our cheeks.

Then we cuddled on the couch and shared our dreams—the ones I never told anyone about. Maybe I'd be a movie actress, or a stewardess who travels the world. Maybe I'd open my own restaurant one day.

"I think that's great," he said, handing me the bottle for another swig. "You know, my mother worked nearly every day of my childhood. I don't think women have to be housewives."

I'd never had a man say something like that to me before.

In the dark, his lips found mine, and stars exploded.

"My favorite thing about you is your wild imagination," he whispered.

But time does funny things to people. Sometimes it makes liars out of us.

After we got married, Leo became an ad man, and Melinda was born. We bought our brand-new house in the valley—and year by year, the world narrowed. It became harder to be anything besides a mother and a wife. Melinda was a good kid, but my brain was starving. I felt myself retreating into the secret world inside me, the way I used to as a child. Daydreaming about foreign lands, other lives I might have led. Losing myself in a paperback book all afternoon. Scrawling lines of poetry on grocery receipts. Just sitting next to a window and disappearing into the deep space of my mind.

The second time I found out I was expecting, I burst into tears at the doctor's office. Melinda was a teenager, for heaven's sake. I was practically at the finish line and now I had to start all over again. Leo tried to convince me it was a blessing, that I could still have a life outside of the house.

And that's how I signed up for that overnight psychological study.

Leo dropped me off in a room with smiling women. The men in the lab coats took me to an interview room and asked questions like any old doctor's visit, along with some other strange ones.

"Do you believe in the Devil?"

"What is your favorite product to mop the floor with?"

"Who did you vote for in the 1964 election?"

"Do you associate the smell of lemon with a particular emotion?"

After that was done, I drank a glass of Tang with what they said was a sleep aid. And soon, the walls started melting and I couldn't find my tongue.

Then the nightmare started.

I went into a dim room called the Dream Box, lay down in a hospital bed. A rainbow was beeping on the wall and I jerked awake. Or was it still a nightmare? I was surrounded by mirrors, lights, and images with tracers projected every which way. Weird sounds like children laughing, a man chanting "you're not good enough," military parade music. I closed my eyes and tried to find the place inside me—the quiet, untouchable place, all for me—but I'd lost it. I began screaming and then there was intense pain all through me as demons in lab coats hooked me up to a machine and my mouth filled with the bloody taste of copper—

Leo was humiliated when he came to pick me up. I don't remember him coming, or how I left, or what the doctors said— those memories are dust. But for weeks and months Leo had this new faraway look in his eyes like I'd lost his respect. And the more I tried to explain what happened in that room, the less it made sense, and the further away his eyes got.

After the baby, there was a long weekend at Woodward, and they sent me home with pills. I took them as prescribed. I figured everyone was right. I was neurotic, I was hysterical, something was wrong with my brain. I'd been institutionalized twice in my life, which said everything about me, didn't it?

I'd never been anyplace colder and whiter than that institution. It was Antarctica. And I never wanted to go back there again.

I colored inside the lines after that. No more chasing silly dreams of being a career girl in my middle age. I played the model mother, the attentive wife. I got a ledger to try to become more organized, one of those women with neat shopping lists and balance sheets. But late at night, drinking chamomile tea and smoking cigarettes, whispers of poetry would tingle in my fingertips, and I'd chase down the daydreams and nightmares with my pen.

Something in that study warped my mind—the boundary between thoughts and reality broken. The curtains used to rustle, but now they whispered. A single drink could send me spinning. And every time I saw those rainbow bars on the TV screen and heard that beeping sound, it brought the horror-parade of memories back.

And then they checked me back into Woodward.

They tried to fry the truth out of me. As I chomped the bit and they electrocuted my temples, I remembered they'd done this to me before—back in the Dream Box, my brain buzzed and my mouth filled with pennies just the same. When I wouldn't shut up about it, they gave me injections that swept me away. I was a walking coma. Everything, for weeks, was happening just offscreen. I heard Leo's voice as if through plates of glass. I forgot why I was there—was I a prisoner of war? What had I done? The more I talked about the Dream Box, the louder they said *paranoid schizophrenia*. Soon I heard those words so often, I swallowed them.

Even now, jotting this down in the new journal Leo bought me, I'm scared of saying the wrong thing, or of it being seen by the wrong eyes. I get a chill, an arctic wind. I wish I could write my life story in invisible ink.

The sun shines through the window, promising another day. Julie pushes her plastic lawnmower along the carpet. Leo reads the paper at the table beside me, hand warm on my knee.

Meanwhile, somewhere, Melinda rides the highway with the wind in her hair.

Don't stop, something in me whispers. *Keep going.*

author's note

My favorite novels begin with a seed of truth. That was my aim here. *The Spin* is a work of fiction, but like so many stories, it started with something real.

I was named after my grandmother, who died before I was born. She was more myth than human—a stunning woman who existed only in photographs (sophisticated, in a fur coat and red lipstick) and a few scant, troubled memories my mother could recall. Faith had a breakdown when my mom was a baby, was repeatedly institutionalized, and unraveled permanently after that.

After tracking down her death certificate, I learned she died in her forties of alcohol-related illness—baffling because no one even remembered her drinking before she had her breakdown. She lied about her age at the hospital where she died and no one in her family was alerted about her death. No one mourned her. As far as my research can tell, her remains were likely buried in a mass grave in a cemetery in LA along with other people who had no one to claim them.

I've wondered about her my whole life. Who was she?

How did a vibrant woman who was described as gorgeous and smart as hell and funny and loved just ... spiral and disappear? And the more I learned about the "care" she received while institutionalized in the 1950s/1960s (cold baths, Thorazine, shock treatments) the more I wondered if the treatments were worse than the disease. She was diagnosed with paranoid schizophrenia. She hallucinated aliens on the television, but that happened *after* she was first institutionalized. What came first?

There's no way to know; her voice is lost. The only records of her are divorce documents and letters I found that my grandfather sent her during her courtship. I was shocked to learn, through these letters, she was working two jobs when they met. One was a government position in Richland, Washington, where the Manhattan Project was based, which raised so many more questions. In these letters, I also learned she didn't want to stop working and resisted the idea of being a housewife. I had no idea. I assumed she *wanted* to be one.

The divorce documents also painted a picture of how sexist and restrictive life was for women back then. Some reasons she was considered an unfit mother or wife included: not appreciating a new refrigerator enough; not being interested in carpooling other people's children; wanting to sit and do math problems for fun. I'm sure by mid-twentieth-century standards, I'd be considered unfit myself.

I thought of all these things when I was writing Rose. And it's also why I chose to write *around* her story by telling it from other points of view. Because that's how I know my grandmother. It's also how mentally ill women were treated. They were told who they were. They were locked in institutions they had no freedom to leave. And often all that is left of people like them are records through other people's eyes, ears, and words.

This was the heart of the book. But the brain of it—the plot, the conspiracy-riddled rabbit hole that Leo finds himself in—is all made up. This isn't a memoir. Rose isn't Faith. But I think they would understand each other. I sure understand them. And I love them both, even if I'll never meet them.

recommended reading

If you read the "study" in *The Spin* and thought, *Wow, that's insane, no one would ever do anything like that,* then I invite you to read these books:

Brainwash: The Secret History of Mind Control by Dominic Streatfeild. This fascinating book documents the US government's history with mind control from the Cold War to the twenty-first century.

The C.I.A. Doctors: Human Rights Violations by American Psychiatrists by Colin A. Ross, M.D. This outlines a lot of the horrific experiments done by psychiatrists funded by the US government.

If you'd like to learn more about the vibrant subculture that existed in Haight-Ashbury during the 1960s:

Season of the Witch: Enchantment, Terror, and Deliverance in the City of Love by David Talbot. I learned so much from this comprehensive history of San Francisco.

The Haight: Love, Rock, and Revolution by Joel Selvin has photos that really bring that era to life.

If you'd like a book that captures the essence of that time period in California, I highly recommend Joan Didion's spectacular book of essays *Slouching Towards Bethlehem*.

And everyone should read one of the best books about mental illness ever written, *The Bell Jar* by Sylvia Plath.

acknowledgments

Thank you to all these wonderful people:

My mom, for being the first reader, the first person I call for advice, and helping me navigate the real story of our family before I started writing this novel. You are just the most incredible, resilient person who has thrived despite the difficult hand your family was dealt. If your mom were here, I know she would be equally in awe of you.

My sister and favorite crazy cat lady, Micaela, for reading my final draft lightning fast. I appreciate your sharp eye for mistakes and supportive comments in the margins. You deserve a bouquet of kittens.

My extended family, of which there are too many of you to name. You know who you are. But a special mention to my aunt Paula, part of the family story that sparked the book idea.

The cult: Noelle Ihli, Steph Nelson, and Caleb Stephens. Your beta reads were crucial to how this book turned out and I truly appreciate it. I'm so lucky to know you all. This writing thing is a lonely business, but it doesn't feel that way with you all in my corner.

Audrey J. Cole, my kind, talented writing friend who read an early draft of this one. Your encouragement meant so much to me.

Jess Lourey and Erica Ruth Neubauer, for leading a

writing retreat where I finally started writing this book I had been mulling for years.

Pisces Patty, who sat down with me and shared her incredible stories about what it was like to be a teenage runaway living in Haight-Ashbury in the 1960s.

To Jamie, Roxie, and Zora, for being the best little family in the whole wide world.

To Harry Portman, who is no longer here, but whose archives helped me connect to a part of my history I never saw before. I'm so lucky to come from a family of writers and journalists who kept so many records. You encouraged me to be a writer back when I was a kid, and here we are. I think you'd be so happy to know how it all turned out.

And lastly, to Faith Pearson. I hope I did some tiny part of your story justice.

a note from the author

If you got this far, thank you for reading and supporting my work. As an indie author, I put a ton of effort into each book —not just writing, but editing, marketing, and everything else it takes to guide a book through the whole process from a glimmer in the brain to a real, actual thing you can hold in your hands.

If you enjoyed it, please consider leaving a review. Reviews truly make an author's world go round. If you're interested in keeping up with book news, please join my newsletter or follow me on social media. And I love to hear from readers anytime at faith@faithgardner.com.

As always, I tried my damndest to fix every typo, but alas, I am only human. If you spot an error, please let me know! I appreciate every reader who makes me look smarter.

also by faith gardner

psychological thrillers

Breakneck Bay

The Mirror House Girls

Like It Never Was

They Are the Hunters

The Second Life of Ava Rivers

the jolvix episodes

(standalone psychological thrillers set in the same world)

The Prediction

Violet Is Nowhere

What January Remembers

This Isn't Over

Eve in Overdrive

The Slaying Game

young adult novels

Perdita

If You Can Hear This

How We Ricochet

Girl on the Line

that one time i wrote a rom-com

Make Me a Double

about the author

Faith Gardner writes suspense novels. When her head isn't stuck in a book, she might be playing music, cooking, or playing with tarot cards. She's also a fan of documentaries and scary movies. She lives in the Bay Area with her family. Find her at faithgardner.com.